11/98

THE CHARLES DICKENS MURDERS

THE

CHARLES

DICKENS

MURDERS

EDITH SKOM

DELACORTE PRESS

Published by
Delacorte Press
Bantam Doubleday Dell
Publishing Group, Inc.
1540 Broadway
New York, New York 10036

This novel is a work of fiction. Names, characters, places, and incidents either are the product of the author's imagination or are used fictitiously. Any resemblance to actual persons, living or dead, events, or locales is entirely coincidental.

Library of Congress Cataloging in
Publication Data
Skom, Edith.
    The Charles Dickens murders / by Edith Skom.
        p.   cm.
    ISBN 0-385-31230-X
    I. Title.
PS3569.K65C48   1998
813'.54—dc21   98-21150

Book design by Jennifer Ann Daddio

Manufactured in the
United States of America
Published simultaneously in Canada

December 1998

10 9 8 7 6 5 4 3 2 1

BVG

For Elaine, Arthur, and Adele

ACKNOWLEDGMENTS

Special thanks to Jacquie Miller, my editor, and to Gail Hochman, my agent. You were terrific!

For technical help and for information on a variety of subjects, I would like to thank Andrea Baer, Judy Seeder Baskin, the Honorable William Bauer, Grace Collopy, George Cotsirilos, Geraldine Cunningham, Susan Finman, Dorothy Firestone, Elsa Leiter Gordon, Joan Hall, Christopher Herbert, Susan Pearlman Kagan, Mary Kasprzak, Kim Miller, Meezie Nierman Lazar, Marilyn Mendel Lichton, *Mademoiselle* magazine, Jerry Meinhardt, Fred Ott, Mae Svoboda Rhodes, David Roxe, Nicole Saharsky, Dante Scarpelli, Elaine Silets, Trudy Shoch, Kathy Skaar, Virginia Martin Solotaroff, Karla Stone, Neil Stone, and Anne Curry Wyant.

My thanks always to Roslyn Schwartz, who saw me off.

Always and forever, my without-you-I-couldn't-have thanks to Harriet Skom Meyer, Jean Smith, and Charles Yarnoff, for seeing me through—*everything!*

Most of all, my thanks to Joe Skom, for providing medical information, and for graciously accepting my rejections of all his plot suggestions. You are my favorite reader. You inspire me. I love you.

PROLOGUE

Manhattan Hospital
Intensive Care Unit
Early August—the present

At night the ICU dropped its daytime hustle for a quieter, more passive personality.

No distraught families waiting in the corridor to talk with the doctor. No clusters of attendings, residents, and medical students on rounds, making their slow march in and out of patients' rooms.

The very emptiness highlighted objects that usually receded into the background.

Now one's eyes were drawn to the mirrors, like huge silver bowls, that hung at intervals from the ceiling, there to prevent an around-the-corner collision between a linen cart and a trauma team.

Now one noticed the rough-lettered sign at the nursing station—REMEMBER! SIGN OUT YOUR PATIENT'S NARCOTICS *ASAP!!*—and above it the monitor, its continuous display of moving lines showing the electrical impulses of each patient's heart. The symmetrical red rows of peaks and valleys stood out boldly against the black of the monitor screen. At night, the watcher, drawn to the screen, was inclined to feel uneasy, almost breathless, fearful of peaks that suddenly inverted, of valleys that suddenly peaked, of a sudden conversion from a neat pattern to wild scribbling, or a sudden collapse into a futile straight line—changes that triggered triple beeps or Klaxon honks.

At night one could hear the sounds of silence—the compression and release of ventilators that breathed for some patients, the soft sighs of patients who could breathe on their own, the muted conversation from the lounge, where the staff had gathered to watch *Letterman*.

At night one looked more closely at the patients' rooms that lined the corridor. With their glass-windowed sliding doors, they resembled the compartments of a European train—a train that one could enter unobserved.

The head nurse, alone at the station, picked up the phone and called X-ray. "Hey! You were supposed to be here half an hour ago. . . . Well, speed it up!" Then, with an occasional glance at the monitor, she resumed writing progress notes and nibbled popcorn.

Unseen in the conference room, watching the nurse as she wrote her notes, was someone wearing a gray lab coat, a stethoscope protruding from a pocket. How much of life is based on trust, the person was thinking. Trust that the driver of the oncoming car would stop at the red light. Trust that the uniformed man really was there to read the meter. Trust that a lab coat, with stethoscope, automatically entitled its wearer entry to any hospital floor. Suddenly, from a far room came a high whine. Labcoat watched closely as the nurse went to replace a near-empty IV bottle. Once the nurse was out of sight, Labcoat rushed out of the conference room and entered a room at the near end of the corridor.

Quickly drawing the curtains over the windows, Labcoat turned to scan the room. Below the bed a network of hoses led to oxygen, suction, dialysis units, and other life-preserving devices. Above the bed the hanging metal apparatus for the intravenous looked like two hoses. Two IV's—that was convenient.

On the bed the patient lay sleeping, her hair, the pure white of a former blond, straggled over the pillow. The sheet clung to the long thin body.

Labcoat stood watching the patient.

Slowly, her eyes opened. She gave a sigh, looked up, saw Labcoat—and stared. "But I—you—" Mumbling something that sounded like "Can't talk," she gestured for water and was handed a glass with a straw. She drank eagerly. "But I know you—you're—"

"Shh"—lightly a finger was put over her mouth—"you don't want to wake anyone."

"Hell, I don't care. Then it's night?"

"Yes."

"I'm so upset—thought it was daytime." She lay there, looking up. "So many years. Where have you been?"

"You've kept busy, Dewey. Your book—"

Her hands clutched the sheet. "The collection?"

"I found it—enthralling."

Warily—"You read it?"

"There's something the matter with your IV. Let me fix it."

"Oh"—less wary now—"you work here?"

"Yes."

"Didn't know—so confused—so upset."

Out of a lab-coat pocket came a syringe. In one smooth movement, the syringe was injected into the IV plug. A split second later the color drained from the patient's face. Her eyes rolled upward, her head fell back.

Instantly the Unit was hit with an earsplitting blast of warning beeps.

Yelling "Code Blue," Labcoat raced out of the room and almost collided with an X-ray cart. The X-ray tech hardly noticed. The loudspeaker was announcing *Code Blue—7152,* and all hell had broken loose.

"How long has it been?" said the chief resident.

The nurse checked her notes. "Four and a half minutes."

"Let's shock her one more time."

The nurse put the defibrillator paddles against the chest. An electric shock went into the heart. Dewey's body arched, almost jolting off the bed.

There must have been twenty people in the room by this time—all staring glumly at the monitor.

Still a straight line.

"Oh shit," said the chief resident. "It's hopeless. Might as . well stop. Probably brain dead now."

At the nursing station, the chief resident was saying, "Know who she was?"

"Who?"

"Cob Conner's daughter."

"Who's Cob Conner?" said the medical student.

"Forget it. Someone has to notify the family. Get the chart."

In Dewey's room, the aides had removed the tubes, the catheter, the EKG leads. They had cleaned the body and wrapped it in a sheet. Now the crew came in to clean the room. They emptied the wastebaskets and were about to toss the EKG strips when the resident came back to the room.

"No," he said. "Save that."

He stood, threading the long EKG strips through his fingers.

Strange, he thought. Why were the T-waves so peaked just before she died? Well, maybe tissue necrosis. *But I want a post.*

Labcoat, in street clothes now, stood on Fifth Avenue and hailed a taxi.

PART
ONE

CHAPTER ONE

Midwestern University
Mid-August—the present

"Your turn," said her mother. "What are you working on, Beth?"

"Dickens—for next fall."

"The Mystery of Edwin Drood," said her mother, taking a book from the stack on the table. "Any good?"

"Some scholars think so. I prefer his other late novels. More coffee?"

Beth went to get refills, winding her way through the tables in the Student Center dining room. Late morning, so the place was fairly empty, only a few diehard students watching *The Young and the Restless* on the giant screen.

"What's *Drood* about?" her mother asked when she returned.

"A love triangle—among other things. Listen to this: '—for what could she know of the criminal intellect, which its own professed students perpetually misread, because they persist in trying to reconcile it with the average intellect of average men instead of identifying it as a horrible wonder apart . . .' Interesting, no?"

"Very—but it doesn't sound much like a love story."

"It's a murder mystery, really—with no murderer."

"Why no murderer?"

"Dickens died before he could finish the story—never even had time to produce a body. But there's no doubt there was a murder, though the critics still argue about who the murderer was. So"—Beth tapped the book—"we have here an unsolved murder. Oh, I have my ideas, but—you're not listening. Mother! Laurie!" Her mother, who had been gazing into the distance, turned her attention to Beth. "What were you thinking about?"

"A love triangle . . . An unsolved murder . . . My college days."

"Now why should a love triangle and an unsolved murder make you think of those halcyon days when fifteen-year-old Laurie Guthrie abandoned high school and found happiness at the University of Chicago? You've always said it was so marvelous, discovering that you were pretty, finding that there were people you could talk to. How in the world does murder fit in?"

"Because there *was* a murder, Beth."

"A murder?" A student turned, looking inquisitive. Beth lowered her voice. "Why didn't you ever tell me?"

"I'm not sure," said her mother, a curious expression on her face that Beth tried, and failed, to read. "But I can tell you this. The murder was never solved—and it never will be."

Beth asked why she was so certain, but her mother shrugged off the question. "Interesting," she said. "Dickens's idea that we try to reconcile the criminal intellect with the average intellect. I guess he means that's the only way we feel we can understand a crime like murder—I should leave."

"Wait, Mother! Your appointment isn't for hours. You can't just leave me hanging. You're as bad as Dickens."

"Hey—I'm still alive."

"Very much so—you don't look a day over forty." A comment that was almost true. "So you can tell me. Just look at what's happening out there"—and they both looked out at the dark clouds gathering over Lake Michigan. "Come on—tell! It's a perfect day for a murder."

"What do you want to know?"

"Well—where was it?"

"Where was what?"

"What have we been talking about? The murder, Mother!" They both giggled.

"Great alliteration," said her mother.

"You're stalling."

"Oh, all right, if you really want to know. But the question is, where to start?"

"How about with the murder?"

"Can't. That would be getting ahead of the story."

"All right, then. Start where you want to."

"I'd better start with the theft."

CHAPTER TWO

The University of Chicago
April—the past

It was morning on an unusually warm spring day in the late 1940's—so warm the lilacs were in bloom around either side of the entrance to Dall Hall. Up the broad steps past the elevator and to the left was Oyster Bay, the big lounge, where a maid stood looking out the window. She watched the students walking to their eleven o'clocks, smiled when a girl stepped off the walk to do a cartwheel in the grass—the same spot where just a week ago the Dall girls had built a snowwoman that looked like Daisy Mae. Heaving a sigh, the maid resumed dusting the grand piano, then, grumbling to herself, she stood on a chair and gave Letitia Dallworthy's portrait a flick with the feather duster.

Beyond the lounge and outside the dining room, the blue-uniformed Irish maids sat gossiping around a massive table piled with newspapers and magazines. From the kitchen came the aroma of lunch. "Giving them tuna casserole again. They'll have fits, they will." They—the Dall girls—were in class. "Save one—Miss Conner," the oldest maid remarked. "She's a strange one. Always up there of a morning." They pondered Miss Conner's strangeness, and then the conversation shifted to her father and speculation that he had numerous lady friends. The talk was just getting interesting when the campus phone rang.

A maid limped arthritically to the inner hall. "Miss Jansen? Don't think she's in. All roight, all roight." Mumbling she should know it by heart, the maid put on her glasses and looked at the sheet that gave names and corresponding signals. She pushed the button—two longs and a short.

In contrast to the activity below, the fourth floor was silent, the hallway empty. Then the door of one room opened, and a girl looked out. Hearing heavy footsteps, she hurriedly closed the door, keeping it slightly ajar. She watched as a man in overalls appeared. "It's only Herman, girls," he called, and looked around eagerly. No hope today, Herman, she thought, watching the handyman lumber by with his bucket of tools. He headed for the bathroom.

She waited until she heard noises that meant Herman was engrossed in his task. Then she slipped out of the room and moved carefully down the hall. She wore no shoes, only bobby socks. As she neared the stairs, the aroma of lunch wafted up and hit her in the face. She wrinkled her nose—then slipped and nearly fell on the polished floor. Damn that maid.

The buzzer sounded. She stood stock still and listened as it sounded again. Jill's. She moved on down the hall, went directly to the farthest room, and slipped inside.

As she glanced around the small room, her eyes lit on the dresser and a huge bottle of Tabu. She splashed some on, then opened a drawer filled with junk jewelry and tried on a charm bracelet. Outside, the bells chimed the three-quarter hour. *Hurry.* She opened all the drawers until she found what she was looking for: two stocking bags, one marked *Runs*, the other, *Okay.* She opened *Runs* and took out an envelope filled with dollar bills. She removed the bills and left the room, careful to close the door quietly. Her hand on the doorknob of the next room, she heard Herman coming out of the bathroom. She backed into the shadows, watching as he moved toward the stairway, whistling "Sentimental Journey." When he was out of sight, she rushed back to her room.

CHAPTER THREE

The University of Chicago
Later—the same day

Late afternoon and Dewey Conner and Carol Ross's room was beginning its day. Dewey's coterie—the Fawners, Carol called them—had arrived. Rebecca Simon sat on the floor, paging through a bridal magazine. Lana Goodman stood at the closet, eyeing Carol's shoes. As always, she had her Social Sciences I text in hand, perhaps as a talisman, since she never opened it. It was anyone's guess if Lana would ever graduate, since she had never been able to pass the course.

As the carillon started the pre-four-o'clock chimes, Dewey emerged from the curtain of blankets that draped her bunk against sunlight. She flung the blankets up on Carol's bunk, then removed her nightgown and let it drop to the floor.

"Thank God," said Carol, who had just returned from class. She made for the window, kicked Dewey's nightgown out of the way, and stubbed her toe. "Godammit, Dewey, when are you going to put your trunk in storage?" Savagely, she pulled up the shades.

"Never." Dewey was at the mirror, in bra and panties, pulling her long blond hair back in a ponytail. "I need it."

"For what?" said Carol. She looked at the trunk, covered with steamship stickers. "Are you keeping a body in there?"

Rebecca looked up from her magazine. "What are those initials all over it?"

"*LV*—Louis Vuitton," Dewey mumbled. She had finished applying pancake and was putting on lipstick so purple it looked like dried blood against her pale skin.

"Never heard of him," said Rebecca. "Listen, everybody, I've got news for you! You know that guy in my Bi. Sci. class? So cute. *And*—at least I'm almost sure—a premed. He walked me back to the dorm after class. I'm making progress. I just know it. Look at these—" She held up an ad for silver patterns. "What do you think? Strasbourg? Grand Baroque?"

Lana's long hair fell over her face as she leaned down to look. "I don't know. They're kind of ornate, Becky."

"Rebecca. Please!"

"Rebecca. Anyway, how about that one—Fairfax? It's more genteel," she said, then returned to her struggle to get into Carol's platforms.

"Genteel, hell," said Rebecca. "I want to wow 'em when I set the table."

"Wow who?" said Carol. "Lana! Get your big feet out of my shoes! You're wrecking them!"

"Oh, if you're going to be *upset*. Oh—look at that"—pointing to Carol's new red poncho—"It's hooded!" she said rapturously. "Can I try it on?"

"No, you cannot," said Carol.

"Ava Gardner has platforms exactly like those," said Dewey, "with an open toe."

"Ava Gardner! Wow!" Lana said. "Do you get to meet all the people your father writes about?"

"Some of them," Dewey said vaguely.

"Yeah," said Carol. "The ones whose reputations he doesn't destroy."

For a moment Dewey looked as if she were thinking about getting mad. Then she moved languidly to her closet. "Are you aware," she said, "that dinner is going to be icky?" They asked what it was. "Don't you smell it?"

"I smell Tabu," said Carol. "Is that what we're having?"

"Don't be so damn silly. It's mystery meat loaf and creepy cabbage."

"Ick and double ick." Lana clutched her stomach. "And me with the Curse. I'm so *upset*."

"Let's go to the T-Hut," said Dewey. She tucked a beige cashmere into a matching narrow skirt—an outfit, Carol thought, that made her look like a giraffe.

What would they use for money? the Fawners were asking. Rebecca was two weeks into her allowance, and Lana didn't have a dime.

"I'll take everyone," Dewey said grandly. She fastened a wide belt around her narrow waist, as Rebecca, short and squat, looked at her enviously. "Let's call a cab."

But could she do it? they asked.

Dewey opened her wallet. "Plenty of money. Ugh—pennies." She tipped them into the wastebasket, and immediately Rebecca and Lana dived for the change.

"Panhandling for pennies," said Carol. "Sometimes you creeps make me wonder if we're really living in the glorious postwar world. Now will you get out of here? I was actually thinking of doing some studying."

"Enjoy your dinner," the Fawners called, as the door slammed.

"The hell with them," Carol muttered. She went to her desk and opened Machiavelli.

CHAPTER FOUR

Midwestern University

"Carol hated rooming with Dewey," said Beth's mother. "She couldn't stand her or her Fawners. And she hated living in darkness. So she spent a lot of time in my room. I got lucky that year. I was assigned a double room, with bunks, but it was so small they used it as a single—I loved it. And I loved that everyone used to crowd into my room."

Around them the tables were filling with faculty and students having lunch. Someone had switched channels, and the news was on, a man talking about the threat of floods in the Midwest. Rain was coming down in sheets now, blending sky and lake into a mass of gray. The darkness outside made the large room feel intimate, Beth thought. "You were going to tell me more about the thefts?" she said.

Her mother ignored the question. "We had wonderful conversations," she said dreamily. "I missed them dreadfully after I married. I used to wish there was some place we could all get together. But everyone was scattered—busy with a different life. And there were other reasons—" She paused, looking at a table where a group of girls were talking and laughing. "The Fourth Floor Gang," she said. "That's what we called ourselves. We were a magic circle. We felt so easy with each other—so safe. We could be absolutely honest, whatever we talked about—and no subject was out of bounds. Parents. Boyfriends. Sex." She chuckled. "Always sex."

CHAPTER FIVE

The University of Chicago

"When you're dancing," said Jill Jansen, "and you're up really close, the guy starts breathing hard. That's when you can feel it."

"Feel what?" said Laurie.

It was a week or so after the scene in Dewey and Carol's room, and the Fourth Floor Gang had gathered in Laurie's room, dense now with the odor of Tabu—her birthday present from Abe. Someone had asked to try it, and then they all splashed some on.

"You know," said Jill. "A hard-on. Drives them wild. They want to do it!"

The buzzer went off and conversation halted. Two longs and a short. All eyes were drawn to Jill as she ran to take the call— her third of the evening. You couldn't help staring at her, Laurie thought, as she had thought so often. Oh, she was so cute. Everything about her—her name, her face—everything a cute girl's face should be. Half-moon eyes, perfect small nose, adorable little mouth, corn-silk blond hair that fell gracefully into a pageboy. But Jill's body wasn't cute. It was luscious. Full bosoms. Rounded sexy hips. No wonder guys instantly fell for Jill.

"But should we or shouldn't we?" Carol was saying. "That is the question."

"Should we or shouldn't we what?" said Jill, banging in again.

"You know—do it," said Carol.

"Of course we should," said Jill. "After all, it's—it's—"

"The sex drive," said Em Greenberg. "A natural function."

"With natural results," said Louise Hallman. "Remember Malthus?" She grinned. " 'An increase of population, if unchecked, will take place in geometrical progression—' "

" '—while the means of subsistence,' " they finished together, " 'will increase in only an arithmetical progression.' "

"So," said Louise, "take Malthus's advice—'moral restraint.' "

Hoots of laughter.

"But what if you did get pregnant?" asked Laurie.

"You could always get an abortion," said Jill.

"An abortion!" Louise leaned forward, her face stern, unsmiling. Sounding like a knowledgeable premed—which she was—she warned about back-alley butchers, dirty instruments—"and hemorrhaging! You could die!"

They were silent, thinking about what she had said. Everyone respected Louise—and liked her. You couldn't help liking her, Laurie thought. She was brilliant—always setting the curve on exams—but she was never obnoxious about it, even with Jill, when she might have been tempted. No match for Louise academically, Jill was way ahead in the boyfriend department. If they had tried, Laurie thought, they couldn't have paired roommates so different. Louise, cautious, steady—as sensible as her neatly cut brown hair. Jill, happy-go-lucky, impulsive, daring. But they got along. They complemented each other, Laurie decided.

"You could always get married," said Carol, humming a few bars from *Lohengrin*.

"Hideous," said Jill, using the Gang's latest adjective. "What about the guy? Who wants to force someone to marry you?" She shuddered. "In high school there was a girl who had to get married. She was just a year or two older than we are—seventeen. I saw her downtown once, pushing a baby carriage—like an old married lady. How would you like that?"

Wasn't she ever getting married? they asked.

"I suppose I'll have to. But not for years and years. I'm having too much fun."

"You know what Tocqueville says about married life," said Em. " 'In America a woman loses her independence forever in the bonds of matrimony.' "

"She's been studying!" said Carol.

"But Tocqueville was writing a hundred years ago," said Laurie.

"The wife's life still isn't any better," said Em. "I'm never getting married."

"If you don't get married," said Carol, "what will you do?"

"You mean what will I do without a man? I'll have a career."

Like Louise? they asked.

"No—I don't want to be a doctor. But I'll be something. Listen to me," she said, her freckled face serious, her frizzy hair standing on end. "You've been propagandized ever since they started tying sweet pink ribbons around your hair and gave you a doll to play with. And you're still being propagandized."

Just what you'd expect from Em, thought Laurie. Her mother had named her after Emmeline Pankhurst, who, Em had informed them, had founded the women's suffrage movement— and the name had taken. Em was always talking about rights—

the rights of the colored, the rights of the worker, and most of all, the rights of women.

"Take the movies," Em was saying. "Every time they show a woman with a career, she's unhappy. She could be a magazine editor, a lawyer, a reporter—but she's *miserable*. Hollywood makes it seem as if a woman's only happiness is running a home and doing whatever her husband wants. Cleaning for him, cooking for him—"

"Doing it with him," said Jill.

Em ignored their giggles. "Do you really think there's more happiness in darning some man's socks and ironing his shirts than in having a career? It's a crock. But everything—the magazines, the movies—is working to make you believe it. It's a hideous male plot. So that's why I study—" giving Carol a meaningful look.

"Foil the plot, and have some fun," said Carol. "College is your only chance."

"College," said Em, "is my chance to learn something so I don't have to depend on a man to support me—how much do diaphragms cost?"

And they rolled on the floor laughing, except for Laurie. "What's a diaphragm?" she said.

"Your diaphragm," said Carol, pointing, "is here—somewhere around your stomach."

"Oh, stop," said Jill. "It's a *BCD*—you know, Birth Control Device—for women. And you have to go to a doctor to get one. But I don't like them. They're icky."

"What do you mean, icky?" said Laurie.

Another buzz, and again the conversation halted. Probably Jill. But no. Short long—short long. Laurie got up. "Bet it's Abe," they called as she left.

"How the hell are you?" said Abe, and asked if she wanted to take in a movie on Saturday.

"Sure, but it has to be the right one," she said, looking at the other end of the side hall, where Rebecca was at the ironing board.

"What are you talking about?"

"Tell you later." She knew Rebecca was listening.

"I'm sending you a kiss over the phone," said Abe.

"That's very interesting," said Laurie.

"Not an ordinary kiss, but—" He went into considerable detail.

Laurie felt herself blushing. "That's very interesting," she repeated, and ended the call.

"What do you mean, icky?" she asked, as soon as she got back.

"Well, a diaphragm," said Jill—and she explained what it was and what you did with it. "See," she said. "Icky. It's much better if the guy just uses one of those things."

"What things?"

"Oh, God, Laurie. Where have you been? A rubber."

"You can't trust them," said Em. "They break—well, not exactly break, but . . . Diaphragms are better."

Carol asked if they had heard about the girls who went to Stineways to buy Kotex. "The first girl goes in and says very bashfully, 'A box of Kotex, please.' The second girl, more grown-up, says, 'A box of Kotex.' Then a U of C girl rushes in—'A box of Kotex, thank God!' "

They roared, and there were shouts of "Quiet Hours" from down the hall. They were about to close the door when Maggie Moynihan, the assistant head, walked by, her tall body clad only in a sanitary belt and Kotex. Again they roared—"At least we know she's not pregnant."

"*Quiet Hours! Quiet Hours!*"—coming from all sides now. They slammed the door.

"Wonder whose date Maggie has stolen tonight," someone said. Maggie took advantage of their hours—10:30 P.M. during the week, 1:00 A.M. on weekends—by taking over their dates after the girls came in. At one time or another, Maggie had stung all of them, except Louise.

Louise, who didn't date, still resented Maggie's ways. "She's so unethical."

"Well, she won't be going out with my dates anymore," said Jill.

They asked why not.

"I have my ways," she said, looking mysterious.

They looked to see if Louise could supply an answer, but she just said, "Gotta study," and left.

"Oh, she's so good," said Laurie. "I'm three hundred pages behind in Bi. Sci." Carol followed up with two hundred pages behind in Soc. and Jill with five hundred pages behind in Humanities—"but that's because I went home for a weekend."

"Well, I'm caught up," said Em. "Where are the cards?"

They cleared a space on the floor, lit cigarettes, and started to play bridge, Carol and Laurie against Em and Jill.

"You're not concentrating, Laurie," said Carol. She had missed a chance to trump.

She was thinking about what Em had said. A career. Laurie had never considered that possibility. As for her studies—don't worry, her parents had said, have fun, meet some boys—and she had followed their advice. Still, it had come as a shock that she couldn't get by at the U of C with her usual study methods: read it over quickly the night before, memorize, take the test, then forget it. Here the reading assignments were not only enormous, but also required thought—and your grade for each course depended on a single end-of-the-year exam, the dreaded comprehensives: *comps*.

She went to classes, but barely kept up with the reading, just enough to get by. And her quarterly grades—purely advisory, only comps counted—showed it. But sometimes her low grades bothered her. Before she left high school, she had been at the top of her class. Now the only course she was doing well in was English—where she had met Abe. She wondered if her parents' advice was part of the propaganda Em had talked about. Oh well. She was having a great time—"Whose deal?"

"God knows where Dewey is," Carol said once.

Meaning what? they asked.

"She wanders around at night."

"Seven no trump!" Laurie screamed. "Bid and made!"

After they left, Laurie remembered she needed some money tomorrow for stamps. She opened the drawer, took out her *Runs* bag, and opened the envelope. It was empty.

CHAPTER SIX

Midwestern University

"Your money was stolen!" said Beth. "How terrible!"

On the television, the Surgeon General was sternly declaring, "Teenagers should always carry condoms whenever they go out with someone they like. You never know what's going to happen."

"True," her mother murmured. "You never know." Someone had left a copy of *Prairie Gust*, the Midwestern newspaper, on the table. The headline screamed CONDOMS! Her mother was glancing at the article. "I see they're available in the dormitories."

"As well as in the Student Center," said Beth. "But the theft, Mother! What did you do about it?"

"Yes, that was too bad. There was Abe's birthday present. I'd been saving to buy him a new pen, a Schaeffer."

"Very Freudian," said Beth.

Her mother smiled. "Jill would have loved that comment."

"But what"—Beth was getting exasperated—"did you do about the theft? Didn't you report it?"

"Oh, I told Mrs. Primwell. She wasn't the least bit interested. Just said that girls were always misplacing their things, that I should keep looking and I'd find it. I might have had better luck if I'd told the Chancellor—Hutchins's house was just across the street from Dall." She sighed. "Hutchins was so handsome."

"What about this Mrs. Primwell? Who was she?"

"Mrs. P.? She was head of the dorm. You could say she traveled through life on the Sea of Gentility"—her mother giggled—"a passenger on the Ship of Social Aspirations."

CHAPTER SEVEN

The University of Chicago
A few days later

Mrs. Primwell, the dormitory headmistress, was having one of her cultural evenings, and much of the fourth floor had been roped in. When the Fourth Floor Gang arrived at her rooms on the second floor, Dewey, Rebecca, and Lana were already there, sitting in spindly chairs.

"Welcome," said Mrs. Primwell in her usual unwelcoming tones. Laurie knew exactly what Carol was thinking. Encased in a long black hostess gown, jet-black hair in a bun, Mrs. P. was at her most Danversish tonight. Recently Laurie and Carol had seen *Rebecca* at Documentary films. They had noticed a striking resemblance between Mrs. Danvers and Mrs. Primwell—the same creepy, thin-lipped look, the same ghastly gentility—and in private they had taken to calling her Danny. Just saying, "Oh, Danny's not so bad," was enough to throw them into fits of laughter.

"Dewey, my dear, will you help me? I know *you* can manage these things." Dewey made a face and went to help Mrs. P. serve coffee in demitasse cups. She passed a tray of shriveled cookies with some colored glop in their centers, terrible looking, but everyone ate them anyway. They were always hungry.

They sat stiffly in a circle, talking uncomfortably, careful not to bump the tables covered with tiny china ornaments. Everything was tiny, Laurie thought—the tiny gold clock on the mantel, the tiny glass inkstand on the tiny desk in the corner. Whenever she was here, she felt huge—as if, like Alice, she needed something that said, "Eat Me," so she could shrink to the appropriate size.

Mrs. Primwell cleared her throat and stretched her lips into a dreadful smile. "Apparently," she said, "we have all the young ladies we can expect for the evening. Shall we begin?" She opened the *New Yorker* and began to read.

She must have chosen the *New Yorker*, Laurie thought, because she wanted to be intellectually up to date. But her reading selection—a Hyman Kaplan story—clearly resisted her idea of culture. As she read Kaplan's criticisms of the ships provided for Columbus, her high Bostonian voice conveyed resentment of this forced association with Kaplan's vulgar accent: " 'Boats full likks! . . . vater commink in!' " Mrs. P. bit off the words as if she were picking them up with tongs. " 'An det's vy I'm saying, *Shame* on you, Foidinand! *Shame* on you, Isabel!' " Mrs. P. read Plonsky's response: " 'Maybe in 1492 they should manufacture already a S.S. Qvinn Lizabeth?' " She paused, frowning.

" 'Qvinn?' " she said. "I wonder what that means."

Rebecca finally broke the silence. "I believe he means 'queen.' "

"Of course," said Mrs. Primwell. "*You* would know that, Becky," and she returned to the reading, heedless of Rebecca's glare.

Suddenly she rose from her chair, saying she needed her other glasses. They watched her go to the tiny desk and lift the silver cover of the inkwell. She took out a key and unlocked a drawer. Inside—was it?—yes, it was!—a gun! Tiny, dainty, almost a toy, but definitely a gun. Laurie and Carol nudged each other. Jill winked at them. She had seen it, too.

Mrs. P. quickly closed the drawer, opened another, and found the glasses.

Laurie met Jill's eyes, daring her, and Jill as good as said, "Taken!" "Mrs. Primwell," she said, "didn't I see a gun in your desk?"

Mrs. Primwell looked as if she had been caught stealing the silver. It was all Laurie could do to keep from laughing while Mrs. P. stumbled through fragments of explanation. "When I first came here—being from Boston—stories about Chicago—gangsters—Al Capone—friend gave me a gun—just a little one—licensed, of course—silly in this intellectual atmosphere—ah, shall we resume?"

An hour later they filed out, Mrs. Primwell keeping Dewey a moment to inquire sycophantically about her father. They were quiet until they were certain they were out of earshot, and then all of them—even the Fawners—started talking about the gun. There was speculation that she had used it to do away with Mr. Primwell. Em thought that Mr. Primwell had used it to do away with himself.

Carol held up a hand, stuck out a finger, and made like a gangster with a machine gun, sweeping them with bullets. "Next time we're late to dinner," she said, "that's what we'll get from Mrs. P.!"

"Oh, Danny's not so bad," said Laurie, and she and Carol rocked with laughter.

"You dolts!" said Louise. "What's so funny?"

CHAPTER EIGHT

The University of Chicago
The following day

Blue skies, smilin' at me—Bing, on the record player.

"Nothin' but blue skies, do I see"—Carol, as she entered the room. "Where are you going, Laurie?"

"Bi. Sci. Aren't you?" Laurie pulled a sweater over her head and looked around for her notebook.

"I thought about it—but it's such a gorgeous day. Laurie, let's cut class and go to the C-Shop."

"But I'm so behind in the reading. The least I can do is— hey, what are you—" Carol had pulled her into a wild lindy.

Her clever face lit with laughter, her plaid skirt flying, Carol whirled Laurie out and back to the lilting notes of "Blue Skies." "Come on—these are the best years of our lives. Why waste an hour in class?"

Laurie said, what about notes, and Carol said, notes shmotes, they'd borrow Louise's.

"Oh, all right." They broke off the dance. Laurie redid her lipstick, and Carol combed her mussed-up bangs. You never knew who you'd find in the C-Shop.

"Let's go," said Carol.

"One minute." Laurie ran to the bathroom. A few minutes later, she called out, "Flushing!"

"Thank you," said a voice from the shower, someone she had saved from being scalded.

Laurie loved the C-Shop, the graceful beams that arched to the tall ceiling, the cozy wooden booths that lined one long wall, the pointed Gothic windows that lined the other. She loved the din, the shouts, and the laughter. And she loved the way the afternoon sun streamed in, sending ribbons of light through the clouds of smoke over the center tables, where students were snacking, playing bridge, playing chess, and otherwise proving that college would be so much fun if it weren't for classes.

They surveyed the room. "He's cute," said Carol, pointing out a boy who was playing chess, "and I saw him looking at you. He's a PD, Laurie"—*PD* being the Gang's abbreviation for Potential Date, one of the few concepts they had applied from Phy. Sci.

"I don't need PD's. I've got—" She stopped. There was Abe, playing bridge, bare feet on the table. And he had said he couldn't see her after class because he intended to spend the afternoon in the library!

To reach the soda fountain, they had to make their way along the narrow space that ran past Abe's table. "Laurie!" he said. "How the hell are you?" She looked straight ahead, though she could see he was wearing his argyle sweater in a blue that matched his eyes. "Isn't that the girl you're pinned to, Abe?" she heard a bridge player say.

"Very much so."

"Not very friendly, is she?"

When they returned with their drinks, Laurie chose a booth

well away from Abe's table. He was dealing. The jerk! She took a big pull on her chocolate Coke.

"Nevertheless," said Carol, looking from Laurie to Abe, "there are invisible bonds between you."

"The hell you say—can't trust him. Let's talk about something else."

"Let's talk about Dewey. I'm so sick of her, Laurie. I hate living in darkness all day. And then, when she does get up, the Fawners are always around. Speaking of which—"

Lana was approaching, looking very *Mademoiselle* in a red blazer with white piping. She stopped when she saw them, a strange look on her face. "Nice blazer," said Carol.

"Like it?" said Lana. "It's yours."

A second of silence. Then Carol said icily, "Take it off, Lana. Now."

"Why are you so possessive about material things?"

"Take it off!" Carol looked as if she could kill Lana.

Lana removed the blazer. For a moment Laurie thought she was going to throw it on the floor. Then—"Oh, if you're *upset*—" She threw the blazer at Carol. "Can I sit down?"

What nerve, Laurie thought, and started to say so. Then suddenly Abe was there, taking her hand. "Want another Coke?" he said, his voice deep, his tone saying, forgive me. She pulled her hand away.

Lana, who had taken the opportunity to sit down, said she would love a marshmallow Coke, and Carol said to make hers chocolate.

"Invisible bonds," Carol said, as they watched Abe move away.

"He's so smooth," said Lana. "Don't you love his eyes? Sort of happy and sad at the same time. *And* he's a BMOC!"

"What makes *him* a Big Man On Campus?" said Laurie, somewhat resentful of Lana's overly intimate comments.

"Well, he writes for the *Maroon*. Rebecca loved his article about quotas in medical school."

"Do BMOC's go barefoot?" said Carol.

"That's another thing—he's sooo unconventional," said Lana.

"A fraternity man, unconventional?" said Carol.

"He only joined," said Laurie, "because the food was so much better than in his dorm."

Abe returned with the drinks and sat close to Laurie. "Thought you were going to study," she said.

"I was. I got waylaid—by friends. Thought you were going to class."

"I was—but I got waylaid."

"By a friend," said Carol. "Me."

They sat talking, rather haltingly, then somehow—no, not somehow, the topic was always present when Lana was around—Locke and Hobbes came up. They were the villains who kept preventing her from passing Social Sciences. "I'm so *upset*. Everyone says Locke and Hobbes are different, but I don't get it."

They all jumped in, trying to explain the differences. Ideas were tossed around—"The state of nature has a law of nature." "The state of nature is a state of war." "The chief end of government is to preserve property." "The chief end of government is to end war." Lana looked more confused than ever.

"Think about it this way," said Abe. "Take Hobbes. If you, Lana, weren't living in the genteel society of Dall Hall, if all you girls were living in a Hobbesian state of nature—you'd be getting more and more out of control."

"Yeah," said Carol. "We'd all be so *upset* we might start stealing clothes."

"You'd be at war with each other," Abe went on, "fighting each other for power. You'd degenerate. Your lives would be—"

"I know," said Lana, "nasty, British—I mean brutish—and short."

"Right, and according to Hobbes you'd be in continual danger of violent death."

"Violent death! In Dall!" Lana giggled.

"Now, Locke," said Abe, "sees the state of nature and the state of war as entirely different. You could say he has more trust in—"

"Trust?" Laurie stared at Abe.

He got up. "Come on, Laurie—we have things to talk about."

"But Carol and I—"

"Dig you later," said Carol. "Remember—invisible bonds."

"What's that about?" said Abe.

"Oh, something," said Laurie, thinking how great Carol was. After all, they had planned an afternoon together.

They went to Hutchinson Court. The four sets of steps that converged below, at the fountain, were crowded with people sunning themselves. They moved between Zoology and Botany, saw a few students sneaking out of the labs, premeds, headed for the C-Shop. They entered Hull Court, Abe, as always, humming a Pearl Bailey song under his breath. As they circled Botany Pond, he stopped and took her hand. "Graceful long fingers," he said, "curving up. An artist's hand. So beautiful."

Another of his flowery compliments, exactly the kind you'd expect from a future writer. She loved them, but they embarrassed her. "I use Jergens," she said.

"When we're married, we'll live on the millions you'll make from modeling your hands."

Married? Did he mean it? Sometimes it was hard to believe that she had attracted Abe. He was so sure of himself, as Lana had said, so smooth. He was so brilliant—he understood everything about chain reactions and nuclear fission. And so witty—she would have expected him to be interested in someone equally witty, like Carol. Yet he had chosen her—and he always made her melt.

They returned to Hutchinson Court and sat on the steps. A few steps down a couple was necking. Laurie stared ahead at the fountain, wondering if she let herself be influenced too easily. Carol had talked her into cutting class—and now she felt guilty. Abe had made it seem as if his lie—well, it wasn't really a lie—didn't matter. Then Abe leaned over and she forgot her doubts as they exchanged a long kiss that made her dizzy. He started to breathe heavily—like what Jill had talked about. She wasn't sure she liked making him breathe that way. She drew away, searching for something to say. Abe pulled her toward him.

"Funny," Laurie said loudly, "what you were saying about Hobbes and violent death."

"Why?" he murmured.

"Guess what Mrs. Primwell keeps in her desk."

CHAPTER NINE

Midwestern University
Midafternoon—the same day

"We were so young to have this sudden burst of freedom. We—I—loved it. In high school, I'd been labeled the Brain—and you know what happens when you're typecast. That changed at the U of C. How could I be typecast when everyone was a brain?" Her mother smiled, almost a smile of triumph. "For the first time in my life, I felt popular. For the first time, boys were interested in me. I got used to the idea that I wouldn't be at the top the way I was in high school. It wasn't that I couldn't get good grades—but to get the grades, you had to work, and I was having too much fun. The classes—" She paused at a yell from a nearby table.

"It sucks! I waited two hours, and when I got to the head of the line this old lady goes, 'It's filled!' " Students, Beth told her mother, talking about advance registration for next fall. "Did you get a good number? . . . I'm way down. . . . There'll be nothing decent left. . . . That sucks!"

"Our classes didn't suck," her mother said. "But they were so tough. They had this idea that to understand a concept you had to read the originator. So to understand how the heart worked, we read Harvey on circulation of the blood—in chickens. We never could convince Lana that the human heart had more than two parts."

"Continental Drift? . . . Highlights of Astronomy? . . . They're micks."

"What's a mick?" said her mother.

"Mickey Mouse," said Beth. "Meaning an easy course."

"Feminist Theory and the Movies? . . . Sounds good. . . . Jazz Dance? . . . It's filled. . . . That sucks!"

Her mother laughed. "Makes me think of how we were taught Chemistry. We had to read Lavoisier—the original text with the long *F*'s for *S*'s. You can imagine what it was like every time we came to a passage that said 'Suck up a tube.' "

"You're getting away from the theft," said Beth, trying not to sound impatient.

"In Humanities, we looked at slide after slide of cathedrals— I never did understand what a flying buttress was. And the reading! We read *The Brothers Karamazov*. 'So profound,' Abe said. It put me to sleep. We read Thucydides. It was weeks before I figured out he was writing about the war between Athens and Sparta."

"Mother! The theft! The murder! The love triangle!"

"The love triangle. Funny, as things start to come back more clearly, remembering starts to—hurt."

"You can't stop now!"

"No . . . I guess not. All right. The love triangle. Looking back, I can see that it really started the night that Abe and Carol got into a discussion about Machiavelli. . . ."

CHAPTER TEN

The University of Chicago
Early May

Outside the dorm the grinds straggled by, headed for Harper Library to study. Inside, in Great Neck and Little Neck, appropriate to the names, couples were necking, scooched down in the love seats, coming up for air when an assistant head strolled past.

In Oyster Bay, some girls were reading, others were sprawled on the floor, playing bridge. Someone was playing the piano softly, and very competently. Laurie looked—Dewey, of all people!

Of the lounge lizards who had arrived for the evening, Tony Valentine had garnered the most girls. He was sitting on the rug in front of the fireplace, surrounded by girls, lying on their stomachs, gazing up at him. They listened, enthralled, while Tony talked about his fraternity's Spring Fling, each hoping she would be the one he asked.

On the broad window seat of the bay, Abe was stretched out, his head in Laurie's lap. Carol was seated next to them, reading Machiavelli. "I love this," she said suddenly. " 'But when the prince has soldiers under his control . . . it is extremely necessary that he should not mind being thought cruel.' Then he says that Hannibal had an enormous army, but he never had a problem with dissension. 'This,' " she read enthusiastically, " 'could not be due to anything but his inhuman cruelty.' "

"Oh yeah," said Abe. "Then he says that the reason Scipio's armies rebelled was because he was so excessively kind."

"You admire that kind of thinking?" said Laurie.

"When it's necessary," said Carol. "As Machiavelli said, the end justifies the means."

Abe sat up. "Where's the passage about the lion and the fox?" He took the book and started flipping pages.

Giggles from the Tony Valentine group. "Tony, can't you ever stop talking about sex?"

"Natch. Has anyone seen the fetus exhibit at the Museum of Science and Industry?" More laughter. More adoring gazes.

Tony Valentine. Laurie watched him as he laughed and reached out to stroke a girl's hair. She was drawn to him, not because she had a crush, but because his perfection fascinated her. He, she thought, was the male counterpart to Jill. With his perfect blond looks, his perfect clothes—not too dressy, not too grubby—his ready laugh, and his snappy comebacks, he was the epitome of smooth. She could see him in a magazine illustration for a story about college. It would have to be a romantic story because Tony was crazy about girls, and girls were utterly crazy about Tony. She could swear that even Letitia Dallworthy above the fireplace was ready to leap out of her portrait to flirt with him.

Her attention shifted to the bridge game, which had just lost a player. A passing girl was asked to fill in. When she said she didn't know how to play bridge, someone said, "Take a hand anyway. You'll learn." Wonderful. Laurie loved the calm assumption that all of them were capable of doing anything they wanted to do.

"Here it is," said Abe. " 'One must therefore be a fox to recognize traps, and a lion to frighten wolves. Those that wish to be only lions do not understand this.' Meaning, he says that a prudent ruler doesn't keep his promises when it goes against his interest—"

Carol grabbed the book. " '—and those that have been best able to imitate the fox have succeeded best. But it is necessary to be a great feigner and dissembler; men are so simple that one who deceives will always find those who allow themselves to be deceived.' "

"So great," said Abe. "He understood the masses."

"You're such cynics," said Laurie. "I don't believe people are so easily duped as he thinks."

"You're such a romantic," said Abe, patting her cheek fondly and, it crossed her mind, condescendingly.

"The thing is," said Carol, "he understood how to get things done."

"So did Hitler," said Laurie.

"Why bring him in?" said Abe and Carol, and they were off again, praising Machiavelli's discussion of a prince's justification for doing evil.

They didn't really mean it, Laurie thought. They just liked to be shocking.

Dewey had switched from classical to "Moonlight Serenade,"—Jill's favorite. Then a pounding down the stairs and Jill was there. Ignoring Tony—was she making an obvious effort to ignore him?—she went up to one of the lounge lizards, someone new, Laurie hadn't seen him before. She had the impression of a narrow body and a handsome evil face. Evil? She was beginning to think like Machiavelli. Jill stretched out her arms and pulled Evil up to dance.

"Who is that guy?" said Carol.

"Don't know."

"Looks like a drip," she said, and returned to Machiavelli.

Evil had drawn Jill close to him. They glided around the bridge games, the players taking no notice of them.

"This is my favorite," said Carol, "about exploiting cruelties. Well-committed cruelties, he says, are those 'perpetuated once for the need of securing security in one's self and which afterward are not persisted in—' "

"And you think," said Laurie, "that it's okay to commit a cruelty just to be secure? Would *you* do it?"

"I might."

"He said only once," said Abe.

"Isn't once too much?" Laurie asked.

"The end justifies the means," they said together, and looked at her challengingly.

No—she wouldn't take the bait. She looked away. What was this? What was happening? Someone else was at the piano, playing "In the Mood," and Evil was whirling Dewey around the floor. Where was Jill? Evil swung Dewey out and back, out and back. How graceful Dewey looked—and how divinely happy. Then the dance came to a halt—Jill had returned. She had changed to a tight red T-shirt and jeans. She held out her arms to Evil, and they began to dance. Evil gave Dewey a brief nod, and, head high, she walked out of the room.

Jitterbugging in her tight T-shirt, Jill had never looked sexier. The music got louder. More people got up to dance. "Too noisy," said Carol, and left.

Evil swung Jill out, and she stretched out an arm and arched her body, chest pointed toward the ceiling. Amused, Laurie saw that Tony Valentine was staring at Jill's T-shirt. She turned to Abe. Less amused, she saw that Abe was staring, too, as if he were seeing Jill for the first time, as if . . . as if . . . she were a hot-fudge sundae he'd love to devour.

Louise passed through, carrying books—on her way to Harper, probably. She waved at Jill. Now Tony was dancing, too, and Laurie saw Jill looking thoughtfully from him to Louise. "You're dangerous," Laurie heard Evil say, and he pulled Jill closer. With practiced ingenuity, she escaped his embrace. "I'm not dangerous," she said, "but our housemother—" She leaned forward, talking in his ear. Tony steered his partner forward. Laurie could tell he was listening.

Abruptly the music stopped. Not now, Tony said, they couldn't stop now, and he asked Jill to dance. "Can't," she said. "I have to study."

And that, Laurie thought, if the truth were known, was the biggest laugh of the evening. She turned to tell Abe. He was still staring at Jill.

CHAPTER ELEVEN

*The University of Chicago
Mid-May*

"It's going to be hideous," said Louise. "I never should have agreed to this."

"Don't be silly," said Jill. "It's going to be yummy."

"But he's so—so—what will I say to him?"

"Tony Valentine?" Em said contemptuously. "You don't have to say anything. Just listen—then sigh at regular intervals, and say, 'Oh, you were *so* wonderful.'"

Date night at Dall. The Gang had stationed themselves in Jill and Louise's room to help Louise get ready for her big night. She had invited—been forced to invite, she said—Tony Valentine. Jill had suggested she ask him, but it had taken their combined efforts to get her to make the call. She had to study. "You can take one night off." (Laurie.) What if he said no? "Then you can study." (Carol.) No, really, what if he did say no? "So what? You can ask someone else. For a change, the woman is in command." (Em.) She had given in finally, and they had listened to her phone Tony, and then they had run back to the room just as she hung up.

She had come in looking dazed. "I can't believe it! He said yes!"

Later Laurie and Carol had cornered Jill and asked her how it really happened.

"I don't know—he must have just decided to say yes."

"Sure," said Carol, "and if I believed that I'd believe that Mrs. P. is Albert Schweitzer in disguise."

"Okay. I did call him. I asked him as a very special favor to say yes when she called. But for God's sake, don't tell Louise." Jill gave them her irresistible smile. "She'll never know, and this will be so good for her—she needs confidence."

All day the fourth floor had been preparing furiously, ironing their dresses and hanging them over doors, putting their hair up in sock curls, skipping showers in favor of long bubble baths, studying their makeup more intensively than they had ever studied Aristotle.

For Louise it was different. They almost had to tie her down in a chair so they could fix her up. Carol had been assigned the makeup. "Now, I don't want a lot of glop on my face," said Louise, moving her arms in a gesture of protest.

"Hold still!" said Laurie and Em. Sitting on either side of her, they were giving her a manicure, despite Em's initial objection that polished nails were symbols of women's sexual slavery.

"It's not glop," said Carol. "Just a touch of pancake," smoothing the sponge over Louise's face.

"What's that?" Louise glared at a small red case.

"Mascara," and over Louise's protest that it would drip under her eyes, Carol held her head in a vise, rubbed the brush into Maybelline black, and applied it to Louise's lashes. "Eyelash curler," said Carol, like a surgeon asking for a scalpel.

"It looks like a torture device," Louise wailed.

"Don't move," and a few sweaty moments later the operation was complete. "Now lipstick," said Carol.

"My God! It's black!"

"Russian Sable—perfect for your coloring."

Laurie sprayed her with Arpège, and then Jill took over the hair. Ignoring Louise's complaints that the pins hurt, that it would droop, Jill brushed her hair into an upsweep, letting a few curls fall around her ears.

When Carol and Jill finished, they were all quiet for a moment, gazing in awe at the transformation. Louise was not what you would call beautiful, Laurie thought, but her square intelligent face had a glamour she would never have dreamed possible.

Maggie walked by and looked at the dress hanging over the door. "Drool, drool," she said. "Dream dress, Louise." They had tried to talk her into wearing Carol's drop-shoulder velveteen, but Louise would not hear of anything so revealing. So they had settled for Laurie's draped black with a sunburst rhinestone brooch in the V neck. "No, Louise. It's not too low."

Then the big moment. Time to put on the dress.

"Wait," said Jill. "You need a different bra—wear my Hi-Lo."

"Yeah," said Carol, "the one that gives daring separation."

"No, not that way." "Bend over." "Let them fall in." When she had put on the new bra to their satisfaction, they stood back. "Maybe stuff in some socks?" said Jill. At that, both Louise and Em had protested so vigorously, though for different reasons— Louise, fear of fall-out; Em, degrading and dishonest—that the others were forced to give in.

They helped her slip the dress over her head—"Watch out for her hair!"—and pulled up the zipper. They stood, looking at Louise peering into the mirror. She looked—not wonderful— but very, very good, definitely better than she had ever looked, thought Laurie, wishing Louise had not insisted on wearing glasses, or at least had something zippier, like harlequins, and wishing most of all that she had let them use the socks strategically.

Jill was looking at her critically. "She needs something else. I know—earrings. Someone run and borrow Lana's Eisenberg Ice drops!"

"I'll get them," said Louise. "I'm sick of staying in here like a prisoner." They watched her pad off. "Her seams are crooked," said Carol.

What had taken so long? they asked when she came back. "Did Lana give you a hard time?" Jill said.

"Said it was perfectly okay."

The seams were straightened. The earrings were clipped on. Louise giggled and shook her head, watching the earrings swing.

"I don't like those shoes," said Jill. "You can wear my platforms."

Louise groaned. "I'll be limping all night."

"Tony's tall. You need something to give you height." Jill searched for platforms, thought back to who had them last. "I know—Rebecca."

Em went to get them, and when she returned, Jill said, "They're a mess! Where the hell was she keeping them?"

"Under her bed," said Em.

"That's the last time for Rebecca," said Jill, working with the suede brush. "Okay, put them on. See! We are the same size!"

Louise tottered around the room. "I feel so high up. And the ankle straps are digging in." She would forget all about it, they told her, when she was dancing with Tony. "Yeah," Louise breathed, "Tony Valentine."

Lana came by and stopped to admire. "You look super. Love your earrings—I have some just like them."

"They're yours," said Louise. "Hope you don't mind."

Carol gave Lana a look, and Lana said no, of course not, and asked Louise who her date was. "Tony Valentine!" she screamed. "But how—"

"Shut up, Lana—and tell Rebecca she can forget about borrowing my platforms."

Strange, Laurie was thinking. Louise had said Lana had been in her room. Then she thought, oh, Louise is so excited she can't even say what she means.

"It's chilly," Jill was saying. "Borrow my lynx jacket in case he asks you out afterward."

Em stroked the fur and helped Louise into the jacket. She strutted around the room, hugging the fur to her face. "But what'll you wear if Evil asks you out?" she asked Jill. Evil— they all used that name now, even Jill, who thought it made him sound dashing.

"I'm going to wear my mouton—okay, take off the jacket and let us look at you."

Still in bras and panties, they stood in a circle, admiring their handiwork. Jill hugged her toy Scottie and told Louise she looked perfect.

"I feel like Pygmalion," said Carol.

"It's Jill who should feel like Pygmalion," said Laurie, thinking how pleased Jill looked, how dedicated she had been to recreating her roommate.

"Look at the time!" said Carol. "And we're not dressed!" She, Laurie, and Em started to leave. "Oh for God's sake!" They shrank back and slammed the door.

"It's only Herman, girls. Why you stop up the bathtub?"

"Drop dead, Herman."

CHAPTER TWELVE

The University of Chicago

In Little Neck, the lights were turned down low. In Great Neck, the punch bowl brimmed with something pink. In Oyster Bay, the carpets were rolled back, and couples were cutting a rug to "Straighten Up and Fly Right." Maggie, in charge of Dewey's flashy new record player, had been instructed to shift from fast music to slow until late evening, and then keep it slow.

A stag line of extra boys had crashed the party. But Mrs. P., who was being two-stepped around the floor, didn't seem to care. "Either someone spiked the punch," Carol told Laurie, "or the guy she's dancing with is from a prominent family." They had come down before their dates arrived, so they could be sure to catch Tony's reaction when he saw Louise.

"Look," said Laurie. "That must be Rebecca's premed."

"He looks like an elephant who just took his first dancing class," said Carol.

True, he was pudgy and he danced heavily, but Rebecca looked as if she were in heaven.

Dewey was dancing with a boy half her height, a brain from B-J, Carol said, referring to Burton-Judson, the men's dorms. "Dewey says he wants to write for a newspaper and have his own column someday. Draw your own conclusions."

Lana whirled by with the president of Alpha Delt. Her outfit, a combination of appropriations and borrowings, looked terrific. Em was dancing with the first-year law student she had met at the law library. She was wearing an *LY*, Last Year's in Gang lingo. "Not as bad as Mrs. P.'s—definitely *EA*," said Carol, and Laurie asked what that meant. "Eons Ago," said Carol—and they doubled up.

Jill came down the stairs and Evil went over to meet her. She looked devastating in the drop-shoulder velveteen and nailhead platforms, even higher than those she had lent Louise. All the boys were ogling her. Rebecca's premed actually stopped dancing to stare, until Rebecca tugged him back into the throng. Tony came in, told the maid he was there, and immediately his eyes were riveted on Jill. Oh, God, Laurie thought, get a move on, Louise.

The elevator doors opened, and Louise walked out unsteadily. Her platforms, Laurie thought. She didn't want to risk the stairs. She would look marvelous, if only she were walking more confidently and didn't look as if she were about to have a nervous breakdown. And Tony—his eyes on Jill—was staring right through Louise. *Oh, God, he doesn't know who she is.*

Louise took a deep breath and tottered up to Tony. "Hi," she said. "I'm Louise Hallman," and gave a loud giggle. Tony turned, took Louise in, and a look of horror crossed his face.

"Oh, no," Laurie whispered. "He looks like he wants to shoot himself." Carol said to give it time, and they watched them move onto the dance floor, saw Louise stumble over Tony's foot—Laurie turned away. "I can't look."

Then in quick succession Abe arrived and then Carol's date, a fourth year, said to be an expert on *OII* (Observation, Interpretation, and Integration), the course that panicked everyone.

Soon Laurie and Abe were dancing, taking occasional breaks

for punch. Maybe the punch *was* spiked, Laurie thought. Everyone seemed so uninhibited. Evil and Jill were dancing, arms around each other, when Laurie saw the premed guide Rebecca close to them. He must have suggested a double cut, because now Jill was dancing with the premed. Rebecca stood and glowered, but Evil cut in on Dewey and whirled her around the floor. Carol said she had never seen Dewey so wide awake. They danced until Dewey's budding columnist cut back in.

Laurie asked Abe to dance her by Louise and Tony, so she could check on Louise. She heard Tony say, "Where have you been all my life?" and saw him pull gently at one of Louise's curls. Louise gave him a push, said, "Oh, you"—and giggled loudly. Oh, no. Tony was automatically turning on the charm, and Louise had no idea how to respond to his line. The music switched to "Embraceable You." "Oh, Frankie!" said Louise— God! They should have told her not to giggle. They turned and she saw Louise nestling in Tony's arms, her eyes closed, her face dreamy. They turned again and Laurie caught a look of boredom on Tony's face.

Then they were out of sight, and Evil and Jill dipped and glided into view. "How about a double cut?"—she could hardly believe it—Abe had said that. And almost before she realized what was happening, Abe was dancing with Jill. Laurie looked at Evil and by unspoken agreement they moved to the side of the floor. Evil waited a few seconds, then cut back in. When Abe returned, Laurie made no comment. She had always known he couldn't really be attracted to her.

Now the whole evening seemed a failure, as if everyone wanted someone else. She saw girls pointing to their partner's back, signaling a friend in the stag line to cut in. And what was this?—Tony pointing to Louise's back. She had never seen a *boy* do that. Now someone from the stag line was taking over for Tony, Tony giving him a look that said I'll do something for you someday. Then—oh, cruel to Louise—Tony was cutting in on Jill and Evil. But Jill shook her head vigorously and Evil looked as if he might pull out a stiletto.

Midevening someone turned the lights down low, so the room was almost pitch black. In the dim light, Laurie saw Jill, mouton over her arm, race past the table with the sign-out book and dash toward the door with Evil. She hoped Jill knew what she was doing. Then she was caught up in the caressing notes of "Stardust." Abe drew her close. She closed her eyes and tried to forget about Jill.

"I have to leave—" Tony's voice punctured Laurie's dream. She drew away and moved to the side of the floor, Abe following, asking what was the matter. "Shhh—I want to see."

At the foot of the steps, Louise stood facing Tony. "You really—you don't really have to leave?" She sounded ready to cry. Tony said he really did have to hit the books. Laurie whispered to Abe that Tony had never hit the books in his life. "Oh, please stay a little longer," said Louise. This was hideous. She was humiliating herself. "But there was something I was going to tell you," Louise said, with pathetic archness, as if, Laurie thought, she were offering Tony a bribe. "Don't tell anyone, but Mrs. Primwell keeps a—"

"Oh yeah," said Tony. "She has a gun. I heard about that. Well—gotta take off." He kissed Louise's cheek, turned, and was gone.

Laurie knew she would never forget the way Louise looked as she watched Tony bolt out of the dorm. She stood rubbing her eyes, tears melting the mascara into inky pools, hair falling about her face in straggly mats. When Tony was out of sight, she started up the stairs, tripped, and fell. Laurie ran over and asked if she was all right.

"Don't look at me!" said Louise. She kicked off the platforms. Sobbing, she ran up the stairs.

CHAPTER THIRTEEN

Midwestern University

Having been driven out of the Student Center by a surfeit of soaps, culminating with *All My Kids,* as the students called it, Beth and her mother strolled past the library. The rain had taken a break, and the sun gleamed on the sweet-smelling lilacs.

"Professor Austin!"

They turned. A girl in a RUTH BADER GINSBURG SAYS SAFE CAMPUS FOR MEN T-shirt was approaching as rapidly as a book-loaded backpack would allow. "Your . . . Dickens . . . course . . ." She paused for breath. "I'm desperate to take it, and it's filled." Couldn't she take it another time, Beth asked, but it seemed the girl would be a senior next year. Her last chance, and she had done all the reading. "Even *Edwin Drood*—I can't wait to hear what you say about it."

"Neither can I," said Beth, fervently wishing that Dickens had had the decency to write a better unfinished final novel. She told the girl to come to the first class, as some students were certain to drop when she announced she was assigning four papers.

"Four!" The girl blanched—recovered herself, thanked Beth, and said she would be there. When she turned, the back of her T-shirt revealed—AND WOMEN.

"A ween," said Beth, "or, as you used to say, a grind—like Louise."

"Louise was much less of a grind after that party."

"What did she—help!" Beth had spotted her colleague Arthur Hewmann. "Quick!" She steered her mother down a different path, explaining the Hewmanns had just bought a place on Martha's Vineyard, and if Arthur caught them they were in for a lecture on the joys of the intellectual East. "And I want to know what happened to Louise!"

"Poor Louise," said her mother. "At first she was devastated, but then she talked herself into believing that Tony's attentions meant something. She didn't understand that Tony was like Pavlov's dog—see a girl, any girl, and he was conditioned to respond. The flattery, the holding her close, the kiss on her cheek—meant nothing to Tony. But Louise! She had it bad, maybe because she'd never had a heavy crush before. She let her studies slide and spent all her extra time chasing Tony. I think," said her mother, "that Louise approached Tony the way she approached a course."

"Meaning what?" Beth asked.

"She studied his habits, she memorized his schedule. Then, just when Tony was due to leave, Louise would be walking past his fraternity house. When one of his classes was due to end, she'd be waiting outside the building. When he was due to arrive, she'd be sitting in the C-Shop. She went to his baseball games—"

"I thought there were no athletics at the U of C."

"Nothing Big Eleven, but they had intramurals. Tony played first base for his fraternity. Louise would stand on the sidelines cheering him. Tony was driven off his nut by all this, including the ribbing from his fraternity brothers. He tried ignoring her, but she was obsessed. Louise even fooled herself into thinking he would ask her to Spring Fling. Of course he didn't. He asked Jill, but she turned him down and—" Her mother paused to watch a group of book-toting students, commenting that they took their studies seriously.

"Wait till Reading Week," said Beth. "They'll be pulling all-nighters at the library."

"What about going home so late? Is that safe?" Not entirely, Beth said, and her mother said that she and her friends never had those worries—"maybe because we had hours."

"That reminds me," said Beth. "Did Jill get in trouble for not signing out?"

"No. She stayed out all night, but Louise covered for her. What was strange, though—"

"Give us escorts! Give us light! Make the campus safe at night!"

They had reached Fraternity Row. Girls marched back and forth, carrying posters—WE WANT AN ESCORT SERVICE; END CRIMES AGAINST WOMEN—their chanting almost drowned out by the rap music blasting from the fraternity houses. In a show of brotherhood—they had not pledged sisterhood—fraternity men hung out the windows, jeering, and sat on the roofs, dumping water balloons on the parade. Sirens sounded and University police cars sped their way.

"A real ivory tower, this campus," said her mother.

Oh, if she wanted an ivory tower, said Beth, she was in the wrong place—she should try the Board of Trade. "Let's get out of here," and they changed direction. "You were saying that something was strange."

"What was strange was that after that night Evil disappeared, never to be seen again. It turned out he'd never been a student at the U of C."

"How did Jill react to Evil's disappearance?"

"Didn't seem to bother her—but she was in a strange mood."

"Ah, Beth, and your delightful mother. What luck!" Trapped—and Arthur Hewmann lived up to Beth's worst fears. A perfunctory "What are *your* end of the summer plans?" and he was off, relating Tales of His Vineyard Neighbors—the Supreme Court justice, the New York newspaper mogul, the Pulitzer Prize–winning poet. "For me it is truly *similis simili gaudet*—like taking pleasure in like." They might have been there still, had Arthur not spied the Dean, to whom he must, simply must, relate the exciting news.

"God!" said Beth. "If only he'd stay in the East . . . What do you mean Jill was in a strange mood?"

"More thoughtful—not as lively."

"Mother, you're still not getting anywhere. What about the love triangle? And the murder?"

"You didn't ask about the thefts." She looked at her watch. "I've missed my appointment."

"Mother! Thefts, plural?"

CHAPTER FOURTEEN

The University of Chicago
Mid-May

1.

"I wish they had raisin bread," said Laurie. She put two slices of white in the big rotating toaster that always made her think of a ferris wheel.

The Saturday after mid-quarterly exams, and Dall's kitchen was crowded with girls staggering in to breakfast, just under the wire. They were in pajamas and robes, except for Louise, dressed in sweater, rolled-up jeans, and saddle shoes. "Move it, Jill," Louise said. "You're blocking the oatmeal."

Jill, who had been leaning against the broad counter, came out of her trance. She took a cup and peered into the vat of cocoa. "Ick—skin."

"You can push it away," said Em, reaching in with the ladle, but Jill shook her head. Em said she wished they had Ovaltine and that she had her Little Orphan Annie shaker-mug.

"The brave little girl detective and her loyal dog?" said Carol. "Barf, says Sandy."

"Don't you dare slam Annie," said Em. "She was my hero.

It took months to save up for my secret code ring." Didn't she mean heroine? Carol asked. "No, hero! Name any other girl on radio who doesn't need to be led around by a boy to have an adventure!"

Carol turned to Jill, who was studying the cereal boxes. "Have you triieeed Wheaties?" she sang, and everyone groaned and told her to shut up.

"Jill," said Laurie. "Why did you reverse your robe?"

"Why not? Time for a change."

"But I loved the plaid side—hands off my toast!" This to Em, who insisted it was hers, and they argued amicably until the next rack came around the bend. They buttered their toast, sprinkled it with sugar and cinnamon, picked up silverware, and left.

"I hate those stupid birds!" Louise scowled at the dining-room wallpaper with its endless pairs of white lovebirds, perched on nests, beaks touching.

"But they're so *sweet*," said Carol.

"Sweet!" said Louise, grabbing a carton and pouring milk over her oatmeal. "They look as if they're going to peck each other's eyes out!"

Everyone stared at Louise.

"What are those round things supposed to be?" Laurie said to break the silence.

"They're eggs, Dumbo," said Carol. "Don't you know what happens when lovebirds get together?"

"It's too bright in here," said Jill, and went to draw the venetian blinds. Returning to the table, she lifted a spoon of cereal to her mouth and put it down untasted. She moved a tea bag up and down in her cup and said idly, "Has anyone seen my bracelet? The one with the football charm."

The one from her high-school boyfriend? they asked. Was

Jill sure it was missing? She was. "I keep it in a certain place. Louise, you know—" She stopped. "It doesn't matter."

"But it does matter," said Carol. "It was real gold, wasn't it?"

"Forget it," said Jill.

Rebecca and Lana came in and started a new table, complaining the cook had tried to tell them the kitchen was closed when they still had five minutes before ten. "Did you—uh—borrow—Jill's football bracelet, Lana?" said Carol.

No, she had not, Lana said indignantly, and as a matter of fact she was very *upset* because someone had stolen money from her wallet. "I know I had three dollars—and one is missing."

"Me, too," said Rebecca. "I had at least five and now I've only got a dollar and some change."

Carol gave Laurie a significant look and asked them if there were pennies left. Rebecca said she didn't remember. Lana said, oh, all right, there *were* pennies, but that didn't prove anything. Laurie reminded them about the theft of her money and instantly Carol asked if any pennies were left. Laurie said she didn't have any change, just bills. Then Em said she was missing money she'd counted on to pay her gym fee. "Any pennies left?" Carol asked.

"Yeah. How did you know? What's the big deal about pennies, Carol? Did you get new loafers?"

"Didn't you know?" said Carol. "Dewey throws them away—and Dewey's the only one who's not missing anything."

Lana said Dewey was too missing something. "I was going to borrow her gold evening bag—that cute one, like a little envelope—and she couldn't find it."

"I bet she's hiding it," said Carol. "When could anyone steal something from Dewey? She never leaves our room."

"That's not true!" said Rebecca. "She's out in the evening—

and sometimes in the afternoon. What about you, Carol? You're her roommate, and you're not missing anything."

"So what? Neither is Louise—not yet. Our thief needs more time to roam at night." Louise, unperturbed, dug into her oatmeal, but Lana and Rebecca said furiously that Carol should stop trying to give everyone the idea that Dewey was the thief.

"Then why didn't either of you report it?" said Carol. "Protecting Dewey?"

Rebecca shrieked that Dewey didn't need her protection. Lana said she had thought of reporting it to Mrs. P.—"Then I remembered it didn't help Laurie. But now, with everyone missing something—"

"Almost everyone," Jill reminded her.

Louise looked at her watch. "Have to scoot"—and she rushed out.

"Where's she going?" Laurie whispered to Jill.

"Tony—natch," Jill said loudly and unsympathetically. "He plays baseball at eleven."

"Maybe we should all go to Mrs. P. together," said Lana.

"Terrific idea," said Carol. "We'll tell her we think it's Dewey."

"I don't think it's Dewey!" said Rebecca in a voice that brought the other tables to attention.

"Neither do I!" said Lana. "You only want to see Mrs. P. pin the blame on Dewey"—her voice rose to a scream—"and I'm not going!"

"Well, praise the Lord and pass the ammunition," said Em. "Don't you know it never does any good to talk to Mrs. P.? And before you rush around hanging the dreadful crimes on Dewey, you'd better have proof. How do you know it's not one of the maids? Or maybe"—she gasped with laughter—"maybe Public Enemy Number One is It's Only Herman!"

2.

Later, in Carol's room—for a miracle Dewey was out—Carol told Laurie she was sure Dewey was the thief. "I heard her allowance is only ten dollars a week." Laurie said that was pretty darn good. "Not if it's supposed to cover all those taxis and dinners at the Hut—she always pays. And the pennies left behind! That's what clinches it!" Laurie protested that not everyone had pennies left. "Lana and Em did," said Carol. "I bet Rebecca did, too—only she's not admitting it. It's got to be Dewey. I'm going to Mrs. P. right now. Wait for me."

"Here? What if Dewey comes back?"

"Relax. She's not dangerous—she's only a rotten thief," and saying she could hardly wait to see the last of Dewey, Carol slammed out.

A few minutes later Dewey came in. She looked like a spook, Laurie thought, her face dead white, dark circles under her eyes. And the way she acted—so creepy, not even saying hello, just going straight to her trunk. Dewey's back was in the way, but Laurie could tell she was taking something out. She stuffed whatever it was into her blazer pocket. At that moment Carol returned and Dewey walked out without speaking.

"Well?" said Laurie.

"Mrs. P. is a stupid idiot!" For once ignoring Laurie's *oh, Danny's not so bad*, Carol burst out, "Mrs. Idiot knows her dear little Dewey would never do such a thing, and it was very, very improper of me to make such an unwarranted accusation, in particular because I haven't had anything stolen, and in particular because my mid-quarterly grades—goddam her to hell! She's such a bag."

Carol yanked up the window shade and looked around furiously—at her own neatly made bunk, then at Dewey's bunk, strewn with clothes and half-eaten Oreos, at Dewey's desk with its overflowing Stork Club ashtray and empty Coke bottles atop the extravagant phonograph. Her eyes came to rest on the trunk. "Proof," she said. "I *know* it's in there." She tripped over Dewey's dangling bedcovers, swore, and got down on her knees in front of the trunk. She peered at the lock, tried turning it with a bobby pin. No good. She turned to face Laurie.

"I hate Dewey!" she screamed. "And I despise Mrs. P.! You should have heard her, Laurie. She's such a snob." They were still talking about Mrs. P. when Dewey returned.

"Out of my way," she said, and Carol, moving as slowly as possible, got up. They watched Dewey open the trunk, take something from her pocket, and put it inside. She relocked the trunk and put the key on the chain she wore around her neck.

She went to the window and tugged the shade down so hard Laurie thought it would snap off the roller. She stepped around Carol and flicked off the light. Shoving the things off her bunk, she climbed in, shoes and all, lay back, and closed her eyes. In the dim light, they saw a long ghostly arm reach for the makeshift hangings and draw them closed.

CHAPTER FIFTEEN

The University of Chicago

Midafternoon on a balmy Sunday about a week later. In the quadrangle outside Dall, students moved past the big window, some headed for the tennis courts, some for the lake and Promontory Point.

In Oyster Bay, the mood was more languorous. In one corner, the bridge game proceeded rather drowsily. In another corner, Rebecca and her premed were deep in a discussion with Em. On the window seat, the sun felt warm on Laurie's hands as she ran her fingers through Abe's hair. They talked idly about taking in the triple feature at the Tivoli.

"I'm not discussing it," said Lana, in response to a question about her Soc. grade, and began applying a second coat of Pink Lightning to her nails. She was seated in front of the fireplace, part of a group rehashing mid-quarterlies.

Someone asked Tony Valentine how he had done. "Preparation is everything," he said through a yawn. "Had to soften the parents up."

Lana finished her nails, waved her fingers in the air. "Tony," she said, "what actually were your grades?" No answer. She looked down and saw he was stretched out on the floor. "Oh, my God. He's asleep!" She blew on her nails a few minutes, then went to the piano and made a one-fingered effort at sounding out a tune. *"A man without a woman,"* she sang, hit a false note, and began again. *"A man without a woman, Is like a ship without a sail—"* She stopped, turned to look at Tony, saw he was still dead to the world.

In the fireplace group, a girl observed that Tony was back to being a lounge lizard and said she guessed he felt safe now that Louise had given up on him. Another girl shushed her and pointed to Great Neck, where Louise, sitting upright in a chair, appeared to be reading intently. She did not even turn her head when Em suddenly shouted, "We'll have it for sure—and we should!"

"Have what?" Jill strolled in, carrying her tennis racket. She looked sweaty and sultry, her T-shirt pasted to her body.

"Socialized medicine," Rebecca's premed said unhappily.

"Is that all?" Jill threw her racket down.

"Watch it," said Lana. "You'll hit him."

"Who?" Jill looked down and saw Tony. She laughed softly, sat down, and joined the conversation, her eyes returning, from time to time, to Tony. "He looks like a little boy."

"Cliché," someone said. "Ten-cent fine."

"A man without a woman," Lana sang,

"Is like a ship without a sail,
Is like a boat without a rudder,"

"Is like a kite without a tail—" Jill joined in. Suddenly she rose from the sofa and knelt beside Tony. She leaned over—he was breathing regularly—and put her face close to his. Conversation ceased. Lana stopped playing and swung around. Even the bridge players paused. Everyone waited to see what Jill was

going to do. She looked at Tony for a moment, then kissed him full on the lips.

Tony's eyes opened. He threw up his arms, almost as if he would push Jill away. Then, staring into her eyes, he moved up to receive the kiss. It was like a movie clinch, someone said later, only better, because it wasn't like those tight-lipped closed-mouth movie kisses. It seemed as if the kiss would never end.

Everyone stared at them—except Laurie, who studied the starers. Em looked contemptuous. Lana's face wore a why-didn't-I-think-of-that? look. Rebecca looked fascinated. Her premed—Laurie laughed to herself—looked envious. And Abe. He was spellbound, watching every move—and he looked even more envious than Rebecca's premed.

Laurie saw Louise staring, saw her start to leave her chair, then sit back, her eyes fixed on her book.

Now Tony's arms went up around Jill. He clasped his hands behind her head, pulling her down. It was almost unbearable, Laurie thought, to watch them.

A maid came in, stood watching them, expressionless, hands on hips. Then she said, "Telephone call for Miss Jansen."

Jill pulled away, jumped up, and ran out of the lounge.

"No—*wait*." Tony sprang up and tore after her.

Lana turned back to the piano. *"But if there's one thing worse—*

"In the universe,
It's a woman,
I said a woman,
I mean a woman,
A woman without a man."

CHAPTER SIXTEEN

The University of Chicago
Late May

Ever since what had gone down in Dall history as the Atomic Kiss, Jill and Tony had been seen everywhere together, necking on the Midway, drinking at UT—even at Harper, studying together. If you could call it studying, Carol had said. More like prolonged necking activity with an occasional time-out for a peek at the books. Tonight was Spring Fling and Tony was taking Jill. Laurie went down the hall to see how she looked. She raised her hand to knock. "No! If you want to stay out all night, find someone else to cover for you"—Louise, her voice almost a scream.

"You're still mad at me about Tony." Jill, surprisingly calm.

"I told you. I'm *not* mad. I never think about him anymore—typical fraternity jerk."

"Then why—"

"If I keep covering for you, I'll get in trouble, and then I'll never get into med school."

"That's only an excuse. You never worried about med school before."

"They never gave priority to vets before. And I'll tell you something else, Jill. You've been—" Laurie knocked.

Silence. Then, "Who is it?" and "Just a sec" from Jill. Then a call to come in, and as Laurie entered—"Ta-da!" Her closet door opened, and Jill stepped out. Oh, she looked dazzling. Her new dress, a black Ceil Chapman, had a tight-fitting lace top that showed off her gorgeous shoulders and molded itself to her perfect bust—like hot fudge over peach ice cream.

"What do you think?" Jill held up her fake-diamond drops. "Should I wear them?"

"Yes, they're perfect. You look—ravishing, Jill."

"Yeah," Louise said from her bed, a rat's nest of books and papers. "You look ravished."

Opposites, Laurie thought. Tonight that could be the title for a painting of Jill and Louise. Jill was like a movie star, and Louise—in ratty flannel pajamas—was like someone out of *Tobacco Road*. Her greasy hair was rubber-banded in a ponytail that bared her high forehead and exposed a fresh splattering of pimples—hideous.

"What do you mean, ravished?" said Jill.

"Just what I said."

The two glared at each other, the tension so terrible that Laurie could imagine comic-book daggers traveling between their eyes. She had to look away. The "Opposites" title, she suddenly thought, could be for their room, too. Even though both beds were covered with matching candlewick spreads (Jill had footed the bill), there was still a division, a Rich side and a Poor. Louise's side—bare dresser with a lone bottle of Coty cologne, half-empty closet with hangers to spare. Jill's side—dresser loaded with jewelry and perfumes, closet so stuffed she had extra hooks on the door. From one hook hung Jill's robe, the plaid side full of stains. Why hadn't Jill just told her that she had reversed the robe because she had spilled something on it?

Laurie saw them giving each other dirty looks. "That reminds me," she said, "Louise, can I borrow your Bi. Sci. notes from today?"

"What reminds you?" said Jill.

"She's changing the subject, Stupid," said Louise. "Do you really need them?" And when Laurie said she did—"When are you going to stop cutting and take your own notes? I'm not some notes maid!"

What was going on? This wasn't like Louise. "Gee," said Laurie, "I didn't think you'd mind."

"Oh, it's okay." Louise went to her desk, picked up a notebook. "Here they are, and don't forget to—what the hell? I'm sure it was here."

"What?" Laurie asked.

"My wallet." She opened a drawer. "Where the hell is it?"

Jill sat on her bed, hugging her toy Scottie. "It'll turn up."

"Easy for you to say," said Louise, raining paper clips, rubber bands, pencil stubs, as she turned drawers upside down. She turned out the last drawer and sighed. "Here it is. But how did it get in there?" She opened a worn brown wallet and started to cry. "It's all gone."

"Except for the pennies?" Jill said lightly.

"Yes"—through tears. "How did you know?"

Jill shrugged, went to the dresser, and tried on another pair of earrings.

How could Jill be so mean? "Did you have a lot of money?" Laurie asked.

Louise nodded. "I just cashed a check—my allowance. Mom and Dad said it has to last me through the quarter."

"Why don't you ask them to send you another check?" said Jill.

Louise gave her a look that plainly said her parents didn't have the extra money.

"When could someone have been in here?" said Laurie.

As it turned out, anytime. They had both been in and out all day, Laurie told Carol and Em later that night.

"And Dewey was here all day!" said Carol, and started her speech about Dewey being the thief and why wasn't something being done about it.

Laurie waited until she finished. Then she said, "What's really bothering me is—the Gang's falling apart."

"What are you talking about?" said Em. "We got together last night."

"Oh sure, we get together, but Louise isn't the same. Haven't you noticed she hardly talks? And Jill wasn't there. She never is now."

"She wants to be with us," said Carol. "But she's busy with Tony."

"I'll say she is," said Em. "He has her underpants hanging over his bed."

How did she know that? they demanded.

"Some of the guys told me. Jill's getting her wish—she's doing it. Is that what's bothering you, Laurie?"

Laurie said of course not, though she was bothered, she wasn't sure why. "It's just—I don't know—I always felt so happy here. And now I always have the feeling that everything is getting so—so dark. I keep thinking about that poem we read in Humanities. You know, about the *Titanic* and the iceberg, both of them growing, getting ready to meet each other—but they don't know it."

"How could they know it?" said Em. "They're things."

"I memorized how it ends—

"Till the Spinner of the Years
Said 'Now!' And each one hears,
And consummation comes, and jars two hemispheres."

"Consummation!" Carol and Em said together. "Now you're talking!"

CHAPTER SEVENTEEN

The University of Chicago
Early June

But everything did keep getting darker. The Gang had shriveled
to three. Now Laurie, Carol, and Em were the only ones who
got together, and without Jill and Louise half the fun was gone.
Dall wasn't much fun, either. The stealing had traveled beyond
Four—Two and Three had also reported thefts—and the whole
atmosphere of the dorm had changed. Announcements had been
made, notices posted. THIEF ABROAD! LOCK YOUR DOOR! But
sometimes the girls forgot and other times they were too hurried
to bother. The thing was, the thief seemed to be wise to all their
hiding places—inside boxes of dirty laundry, between pages of
Aristotle's *Poetics*, between records in Sinatra albums.

"How could it happen at the U of C?" Laurie asked Em.
They were in Laurie's room, waiting for an emergency food
package. "Stealing is so—irrational!"

"So far it's paid off," said Em. "No one's been caught."

"I feel as if we're living in *Ten Little Indians*."

"What's that?"

"You know, that Agatha Christie play."

"Oh, a mystery." Em made a face.

"Don't be a snob. It's super—ten people trapped on an island, and one by one they get killed off, poisoned, choked, axed. Everyone's terrified of everyone else—just like here."

"Hold it! Dall has a thief—not a murderer. We're not exactly terrified."

"Well, maybe," said Laurie. "But the whole dorm *looks* at each other now."

"What's the big deal? How can we not look at each other?"

"But we're looking at each other in a new way—you know, sort of suspicious, sort of scared. It's creepy! Yesterday that grind on Three—you know, the girl in the tower room—kept staring at me. I bet she thinks I'm the one!"

"Some people are looking at Dewey," said Em.

"I hate that, too. Carol has lots of the dorm thinking it's Dewey, but she can't know for sure."

"Better not let Carol hear you say that."

"Have you noticed how hideous Dewey looks? Bags under her eyes, and big black circles. I—I feel sorry for her," said Laurie.

"Carol doesn't look so hot, either. Who would, living in the dark all the time—like a mole."

"Special Delivery!" Maggie came in, back from International House, carrying a bag that sent off yummy smells.

"My treat," said Em.

"Are you sure?"

"Positive—I've been typing for the Business School all day."

Laurie climbed into the upper bunk, her favorite spot for spreading out. She took a swig of the Tiffin Room milkshake, so thick she almost needed a spoon. She unwrapped the hamburger, eyed the luscious transparent onions peeking out of the bun—

The door banged open. "Have I got great news for you!" Carol shouted.

"Quiet Hours!"—from all sides of the hall.

"Oh, can it!" Carol screamed, and slammed the door.

"What's going on?" said Em, hamburger juice dripping down her chin.

"I just went to the john," said Carol.

"That's the great news?" said Laurie, and she and Em were overcome with giggles.

"Morons! When I came back, my wallet was gone!"

"*That's* the great news?" said Em. They clutched their milkshakes and almost keeled over with laughter.

"Yes! Because in the wastebasket I found . . ." Carol paused, her eyes glittery, excited.

"*What?*"

"Exactly nine pennies—and they had to be from my wallet! I know I had nine because I almost had enough to buy fudge, but I had to use a dime instead. And Dewey! She's lying in bed as if nothing happened. She doesn't know she just hung herself with those pennies!" Carol hopped around the room, doing a crazy war dance, chanting, "I've got the proof! I've got the proof!"

"But everyone knows Dewey treats pennies like rubbish," said Em. "Why would she be so obvious?"

"Christ on a crutch! How should I know? Because she's off her rocker, dippy—just plain nuts! I always knew it was Dewey—and now I've got proof!" Carol grabbed Em's milkshake and took a big swallow. "First thing tomorrow I'm going right to Mrs. P. This time she won't dare give me the gate!"

CHAPTER EIGHTEEN

The University of Chicago
The following evening

"Beethoven's last movement!" said Em. "Not again!"

Groans around the table as the student waitress plopped down dessert plates filled with the Dall version of brownies. "Well," said Jill, "it helps my diet."

"I heard about a super diet," said Carol. "All you eat is celery. With the energy spent chewing, one stalk is minus-ten calories."

Carol wasn't really thinking about diets, Laurie thought. Her eyes were on the head table, as they had been all evening. Laurie looked over there, too, saying, "God, I wish they'd finish." But Mrs. P. was still puffing her after-dinner cigarette.

"Look at her with her Roosevelt cigarette holder," said Em. "And she's such a goddam reactionary."

"Poor Lana and Rebecca," said Louise. They did look miserable, Laurie thought, bored stiff, while Mrs. P. made genteel conversation with the assistant heads.

"Tough tomatoes," said Jill. "That's what they get for coming in late."

Jill could have been more sympathetic, Laurie thought, remembering how desperately Lana and Rebecca had tried to find empty places. But it was funny, seeing their phony smiles when, forced to give up, they had changed course. Slowly, slowly, as if they were walking the plank, they had moved to the head table, where the last empty chairs always waited. Late by a few seconds and you were stuck—though Lana and Rebecca had been way more than a few seconds late.

The waitress came around with coffee. Everyone refused, except Jill, who didn't drink coffee, but liked to play with it. Laurie watched her fill a spoon with cream, then edge it down so it just touched the coffee, then—

"They're leaving!" said Em.

"No, they're not," said Carol.

She was right. Only Maggie was standing. Mrs. P. and the other assistant heads were still in their chairs, looking at Maggie expectantly.

She stood there silently, not the usual Maggie. She was wearing a suit, for God's sake. "Funny," said Laurie, "to see Maggie looking so serious."

Carol nudged her. "This is going to be good," she whispered, and Laurie asked what she meant. "Just wait," Carol said in a low voice, her eyes glittery, triumphant, like last night when she had told them about her missing wallet.

Gradually, table by table, as each group became aware of Maggie, the talk died down. Maggie glanced at Mrs. P. Mrs. P. nodded.

Maggie straightened her shoulders. "We are almost certain," she said, her voice booming into the silence, "who is responsible for the thefts." She paused. "We want that person to turn herself in—now."

Bang! Jill's dessert plate crashed to the floor. No one looked at the damage. "Who?" "Who?" The murmurs echoed around the room. The waitresses had stopped stacking dishes. Like everyone else, they were staring at Maggie. And Maggie—she was just standing there, her eyes searching the dining room. Did Laurie imagine it, or did her gaze linger a few seconds at the next table? Dewey was sitting there, looking straight ahead, her purple Revlon lips turned up in a contemptuous smile.

"I am waiting," said Maggie.

No one spoke.

Carol raised her eyebrows and gave Laurie a what-did-I-tell-you? look. Laurie looked at the others. Em's lips were shut tight, as if she were keeping back a smile. Louise looked—almost scared—as if she were ready to run out of the room. Jill's face was indifferent. She played with the coffee, floating cream into a perfect circle.

"All right," Maggie said suddenly. Laurie jumped. "You give us no choice. You are to stay in your seats until you are told you can leave."

Immediately there were urgent whispered discussions at all the tables. "They're going to search our rooms," said Carol. "About time, too. I'm glad."

"Me, too," said Jill, looking up from her coffee. "What about you, Louise?"

"Why aren't they leaving?" said Louise.

Maggie was bending down, talking earnestly with Mrs. P. Then—"We want all keys," Maggie said. "If you have anything in your rooms that you keep locked—jewelry cases, footlockers, trunks—you must turn your keys in to Bridget." She nodded toward the hallway, where the maid stood with a basket.

Excited conversation. Nervous laughter. Light clinks as keys were removed from shoestrings, camp lanyards, ID bracelets. Saying they had left their keys in the room, a few girls started for the stairs.

Laurie saw Mrs. P. touch Maggie's arm and whisper something. "Wait!" Maggie called. "You can't go to your rooms alone. You must be accompanied by an assistant head." No one said a word. Everyone watched as a few girls went up the stairs with the assistant heads. When everyone had returned and seated themselves, they were told to leave, table by table, first turning in their keys. A procession formed, leading to Bridget. "Got your name on it, Miss? No? Here, now, you take this tag, and—"

Dewey's table was next. "Don't forget the one around your neck, Dewey"—a loud voice from the next table, a girl known for her bossiness.

Dewey's hand went up to clutch a thin gold chain. "That key is private—for my trunk," she said in a whiny drawl. "I have things in there that are extremely personal."

"They said *all* the keys," said the bossy girl.

They called her table. Dewey stood first. The same contemptuous smile on her face, she flounced over to the maid and, without bothering to unfasten it, yanked off the chain and dropped it into the basket.

"Oh, dear," said Bridget. "You've broken your pretty chain, Miss Conner."

A few minutes later Maggie said, "Do we have all the keys? Very well. You are to stay here until we return." All heads turned to watch Mrs. P., Maggie, and the other assistant heads as they left the dining room and started up the broad stairs.

At first the room was quiet. Then subdued conversations sprang up. And then there was a burst of talk, getting louder and louder, the way it got when a prof left the classroom. "They're crazy. I don't think it's any of us," said Rebecca. She and Lana had moved from the head table and pulled up chairs on either side of Dewey. Rebecca started to put an arm around her, but Dewey pushed her away and lit a cigarette. Lana was lapping up the leftover Beethovens.

At Laurie's table, no one was saying anything. The tension was terrible, Laurie thought, but—but—there was something delicious about it. Like watching a Frankenstein movie. Carol grinned at her, obviously enjoying herself. "What are you thinking about?" Laurie asked.

"Machiavelli. What he said about how the prince must above all abstain from taking the property of others."

"Oh yeah," said Em. "Because everyone hates the prince who usurps property. Machiavelli sure said it. He must have anticipated the great Dall burglary."

"What's with all the Machiavelli?" said Laurie.

"I was being facetious," said Em.

Laurie hesitated. She wasn't sure what facetious meant.

"You and Carol are so sure it's Dewey," Jill said suddenly. "It could be someone else."

"That's bull," said Em. "Of course it's Dewey."

"I wish they'd finish," said Louise. "I've got to study."

"You always have to study," said Jill.

Louise's face got very red.

It was so noisy now, it was almost like a party. At the next table, the girls' voices were so loud Laurie could hear every word. "Oh, God, the radiator!" . . . "Most popular girl in the college—twelve dates a week, *par exemple*." . . . "I'm praying, don't let them look under the radiator." . . . "She goes all the way." . . . "That's where we keep the fudge ingredients." . . . "If they look in her desk, they'll find her diaphragm." . . . "We'll be fined." . . . "That's where she always keeps her diaphragm." . . . "Won't help if she always keeps it in her desk—oh!" Who were they talking about? Laurie wondered. A sudden silence.

Mrs. P. had appeared in the hallway.

Surrounding Mrs. P., looking very grim, were the assistant heads. Mrs. P. stood perfectly still, a hideous smile on her face. She cleared her throat. "Someone," she said. "Someone in this room has information about the thefts. That person will come and talk to me about it after ten o'clock tonight. Otherwise—it will be a matter for the police tomorrow."

CHAPTER NINETEEN

Midwestern University

"So peaceful here," said Beth's mother. They were sitting on a bench in the Shakespeare Courtyard.

"Did anyone say anything?" Beth asked eagerly.

"When?"

"When Mrs. Primwell made the announcement about the police."

"Not a word. The only noise was chairs scraping when everyone got up at once—oh, and Maggie yelling at us not to push. We were all charging for the stairs, dying to get up to our rooms so we could hash over what had happened. It was like a stampede. And then . . . It was over so quickly I wasn't sure I had seen it." Her mother stared ahead, as if trying to recapture the scene.

Shrieking sirens from University Road pierced the quiet.

"Seen what?" said Beth impatiently, shouting over the clamor.

"When I try to remember, I see a bunch of disconnected images. Dewey just ahead of me—a foot on the first step. Someone—an assistant head?—reaching around me, her hand on Dewey's arm. Dewey being steered past the magazine table.

Dewey being walked toward"—she frowned—"I know—the office behind the phones."

"Then they must have found some evidence! Something to prove Dewey was the thief."

"I certainly thought so the next morning—what is this?" said her mother, as siren pursued siren with awful wails.

"Nothing important—just another lab error at Science. Mother, what happened the next morning?"

"Well, the bathrooms on our floor—on all the floors, really—were in two parts. On one side of the stairs was the one with toilets and a shower stall. On the other side was the sinks bathroom—"

"Mother! Why are you telling me about the bathrooms?"

"Because that's where I found out."

"Mother! Laurie! Found what out?"

"We had stayed up so late talking I missed my first class— slept through the alarm. I wouldn't have slept through this!"

"Don't worry. Just a teeny explosion—happens every day."

"But how can you have a teeny—" She caught Beth's eye. "All right, darling. Back to Dall. Anyway, I staggered around the hall to the sinks bathroom. I remember how quiet it was. No one around."

CHAPTER TWENTY

The University of Chicago
The next morning

1.

The huge sash window was open and a warm breeze wafted into the bathroom. Outside in the quadrangle, girls in shorts and T-shirts were sunning themselves. That's what I'll do, Laurie thought. I'll find Carol. We'll go out on the Midway. She rushed to the sinks, looked in the mirror—God! Huge bags under her eyes. Gloomily, she squeezed toothpaste onto her brush.

The door creaked and Jill came in, still in her nightgown, looking pale. At least she didn't have bags. Jill would never have bags, even when she was an old, old lady. Jill old—impossible—she could never be wrinkled and saggy. Laurie's thoughts came and went in an instant, while she brushed and waved hello with her free hand.

"Have you seen it?" said Jill.

"Seen whatsh?" said Laurie, talking through toothpaste froth.

"You look like a mad dog," said Jill, and started laughing so hard she had to sit on the floor. "Don't know—why I'm laughing," she said between gasps. "It's not funny."

"Whatsh not funny?" Froth flew and Jill collapsed again.

Laurie went on brushing.

"Come here." Jill was standing at the tub room, a strange expression on her face. "I've got something to show you." Laurie could tell she was on the verge of another round of laughs.

Laurie rinsed. "Just a minute."

"Now!"

"Oh, for—what's the big deal?"

Jill flung open the door to the tub room.

The toothbrush dropped from Laurie's hand. She screamed. Blood. Pools of it in the bathtub. Streaks of it on the walls. Wet splashes all over the linoleum and on the three-legged wooden stool. "Oh my God—what?"

"Dewey," said Jill. "She tried to kill herself. Tidy, wasn't she?"

"How? . . . Is she—"

"Slit her wrists," said Jill.

"With what?" Stupid, Laurie thought, as if it matters.

"I don't know—a razor? She must have sat in the tub without turning the water on."

"But how—is she—"

"She's okay. Maggie took her to Student Health."

"Does Carol know?"

"I'll say she does. She's the one who found her and ran for Maggie," and when Laurie asked where Carol was—"Went to Sixty-third Street to buy new heels. Said she can't face classes today."

Dazed, wondering why Carol hadn't told her, Laurie started back to her room. At the far end of the hall, the elevator door opened, and Dewey stepped out. But she looked so chic! New

Look skirt, studded belt, tucked-in sweater. Laurie stared. Peeking out under the sweater sleeves, wrapped around Dewey's wrists—bandages, so thick they looked like Kotex. Seeing them brought home what had almost—what if Carol hadn't found her in time?

Dewey was coming toward her, walking slowly, head down. When she saw Laurie, she picked up speed.

I can't just let her go by without saying something, Laurie thought. "Dewey," she said, "how are you?" immediately thinking, dumb question. "I'm—I'm sorry."

"*You're* sorry," said Dewey, the standard flip Dall reply. She brushed past and went into her room. The shades were down, but there was enough light so Laurie could see the mess—worse than usual. Shoes, nightgowns, pennants—all over the bed. Clothes and records all over the floor. Kicking a stack of records out of the way, Dewey went to the desk, grabbed her Stork Club ashtray, and flung it into the open trunk. She looked helplessly at the piles of clothes. Turning, she saw Laurie and gave her a look—a look that was rage on top but such aching misery underneath that Laurie could hardly stand it.

Dewey slammed the door in Laurie's face.

2.

"It's a miracle they didn't find this." Laurie reached under the lower bunk and brought out peanut butter and crackers.

"They probably did," said Carol, "and put it on the back burner. Bet you get fined."

"I'll worry about fines some other time," Laurie said, as she climbed into the upper bunk. "Okay, Louise—tell!"

"Well," said Louise, looking important. "I talked to Herman."

"Herman?" said Em. "When did Herman ever know anything about anything except copping a feel?"

"Yeah, sure, but Herman got it from Opal, and the maids always know everything."

"Tell, tell, *tell*!" shouted Jill, Em, and Carol, pounding the lower bunk until a cloud of dust flew up, and they roared with laughter. Like old times, Laurie thought, before all the hideousness—the Gang together, getting along, having fun. Fun was what she wanted. She couldn't get Dewey out of her mind—Dewey, her wrists bandaged, Dewey alone in her room . . .

"Well," said Louise, "it was in there."

"What?" said Carol.

"Your wallet."

"Oh that. I knew that. Maggie gave it back to me. And can you beat it? The money was still there. Guess she didn't have a chance to spend it yet."

"What else was in there?" said Laurie.

"Just Carol's wallet."

Carol looked bewildered. "That can't be. She *must* have had money stashed in her trunk. They didn't look hard enough!"

"Why are you so desperate?" said Louise. "Dewey's leaving—so what's to worry about? And they did look, Carol. There wasn't any money. Jill's bracelet wasn't there either. I asked Opal myself."

"That was nice of you," Jill said, "to ask Opal about *my* bracelet."

Louise's face turned an angry red.

Maybe things weren't the same with the Gang after all, Laurie thought. Oh, damn Dewey—no, she didn't mean that. But nothing would be the same now. Laurie felt a wave of sadness.

"I bet I know what *was* there," Carol was saying. "Dewey's gold evening bag. I just know she hid it to throw off suspicion."

"But it wasn't," said Louise. "I asked Opal."

"You thought of everything, didn't you?" said Jill.

Louise didn't answer. She got up from the floor, went to Laurie's dresser, and splashed herself lavishly with Tabu.

"Shut up, Jill," said Em. "What's the matter with you? Now, tell us, Louise. What else did Opal say?"

Louise turned from the dresser. "Opal said—she said—" What? they asked. "That the room is a mess."

"Big surprise," said Carol. "I just can't believe the bag and bracelet weren't there. I was sure—"

"Pounce!" Shouts from the hall, where a card game was in progress. *"Pounce!"*

"Quiet Hours! Quiet Hours!" they roared.

"You were sure of what?" said Em.

"Oh—nothing. Maybe she got rid of the stuff some other way."

"Maybe they should drag Botany Pond," said Em.

"They almost could have been dragging it—for Dewey," said Jill.

"Dragging for Dewey?" said Em. "What are you talking about?"

"You didn't know?" Jill told her about the suicide attempt.

"Oh, my God," said Em. "Why are we talking about the stupid trunk when Dewey almost died?"

Em was right, Laurie thought guiltily. The others looked guilty, too.

"Almost isn't the same as actually dying," said Carol, but she sounded ashamed.

The truth was, Laurie thought, that as long as Dewey hadn't—as long as Dewey was still alive—no one really cared. And that, she told herself, was Dewey's fault. But still, Dewey . . . the way she had looked.

"She *could* have died, Carol," Jill said.

"That's not my fault!"

"Who said it was? But Em's right. All you care about is ditching Dewey."

"*You* try rooming with her, Jill. Personally, I think the suicide thing was a big act. If I hadn't found her, she would have climbed out of the tub and made sure someone else did."

"If they're wrong about Dewey being the thief—" said Jill.

"They aren't wrong," said Carol.

"But if they are—think about Cob Conner, known for his hot temper and vengefulness. I read that in *Time*. Think about what Cob Conner could say in his column. He'll make Dewey a martyr—like Gandhi. 'My daughter, falsely accused, deeply depressed—' "

"Why falsely accused?" said Em.

"I have my ideas," said Jill.

"What ideas?"

"None," said Carol. "There aren't any other ideas. Dewey's the thief and that's that. And I couldn't care less about Cob Conner. Oh, it's going to be so super! I'll never pull the shades again."

The guys on the Midway would like that, they told her.

"Will you sleep in the lower now?" said Laurie.

Carol shuddered. "God, no—but I can't wait to shape up the S-H-I-T house."

"You mean Dewey's still here?" said Em.

"Leaving tonight," said Louise.

"On the Pacemaker," said Carol. "In a Pullman. She just had to tell me that."

"She must be feeling hideous," said Em. "Maybe we should—"

"Forget it," said Carol. "She's happy as a lark, says she can't wait to break out of this prison. And if you're thinking of going down to our room, last time I was there Lana and Rebecca were all over her—like vultures. She's giving them things."

What things? they said, and Carol said, oh, you know, clothes, shoes, too much trouble for her to pack. Was she giving away her cashmeres? said Em. Maybe she would go down there. Laurie told her to quit kidding, it was too sad.

"Does she act guilty?" said Louise.

"Are you kidding?" said Carol. "She doesn't care."

"She must care," said Jill. "Otherwise, why slice up her wrists?"

"Oh, stop," said Carol. "I don't want to talk about it any-more."

So they munched crackers and talked, circling carefully around anything connected with Dewey. They talked about sex, about boys, about the upcoming Open House—they were actually going to be allowed to invite boys up on the floors! Em was thinking of new posters—something really super. Laurie was planning to have classical music going on her record player— that would impress Abe. "Jill," said Louise, "we could rear-range the furniture and—" She stopped at Jill's look. Laurie felt a sharp response from Jill coming on. Why was she down on Louise?

"The girl of my dreams is the sweetest girl"—men's voices from below.

A serenade! They ran to the window. "Who is it?" said Laurie.

"A whole bunch of boys!"

"Each sweet coed, like a rainbow trail, fades in the after-glow—"

"Abe! I see Abe!"

Laurie jumped off the bunk, landed wrong, and felt a sharp

pain in her ankle, while from outside a voice called, "Laurie—
oh, Laurie—"

"Come on, Laurie. He's calling you!" They turned, saw her
lying on the floor, and screamed. "What happened?"

"Did something to my ankle." Painfully, she hauled herself
up and leaned against the dresser.

"Don't stand on it!"

"Maybe it's broken!"

"Come on! We're taking you to Student Health!"

And they did take her there, all of them except Jill, who said
she couldn't go, not now, but she didn't say why.

3.

Laurie was wowed by the doctor. Oh, but he was handsome.
"What's going on at Dall?" he asked them. "Emergencies every
night." He smiled at Laurie. "Guess you just don't want me to
sleep." Very gently he prodded her ankle. "I think it's just a
sprain, but we'll get an X-ray to make sure." He sent her into an
examining room and told the others to wait.

The X-ray showed nothing broken. Keeping up a flow of
conversation, the doctor wound a bandage around her ankle.
What courses was she taking? Did she ever take time off from
studying? "Oh, I'll have to start over"—unwinding the bandage—"not tight enough. So you do sometimes get away from
the books?"

They started back, all pronouncing the doctor a dreamboat.
An intern, said Louise. Who cares? they said. He's still a dreamboat.

"What were you doing in there with him for so long?" said
Carol. When Laurie said he was bandaging her ankle—"It
doesn't take that long! He must have dragged it out. Laurie!

He's a PD for you!" Laurie said to stop being silly. "How about the way he looked at you when we left?" Carol half closed her eyes, giving Laurie a sexy Charles Boyer look. "How about what he said—'I'll be seeing you!' "

"I'll be seizing you—in all the old familiar places," sang Em, and Laurie, who was leaning on her, laughed so hard she almost fell.

Oh, he was so cute, Laurie thought to herself. An older man, too—must be in his twenties. Did she dare ask him to the Open House? What about Abe? She forgot she was feeling depressed.

It was a wonderful night, delicious breeze, sky asparkle with shooting stars, a night for walks with boys, for necking. In the distance, lights played over the chapel. "Oh, look," said Laurie. "It's like a dream palace."

"You know what they say?"

"No, what do they say?"

"There are more souls conceived than saved in Rockefeller Chapel!"

Laughing and talking, they moved along slowly. As they neared Dall, they saw Dewey standing on the sidewalk, train case in hand. A Yellow Cab pulled up. The driver got out, stood hands on hips, staring at the mountain of suitcases.

Where was her trunk? they wondered. Must have shipped it, someone said.

"Bye, Dewey, bye," Rebecca and Lana waved from the window.

"Bye, Dewey. Good luck!" Waving frantically from another window—Jill!

Dewey didn't even look up. She gave a careless wave and disappeared into the taxi. They watched its red lights recede down 59th Street.

PART
TWO

CHAPTER TWENTY-ONE

Midwestern University

"I thought after Dewey left things would simmer down, but if anything there was more tension. Em had decided she wanted to go to medical school, and she got frantic about her grades. When she figured out she was due to get the Curse the day of the Bi. Sci. comp, she carried on as if someone had died. And Carol. I thought that now that she had the room to herself—she spent a whole day cleaning and rearranging the furniture—she would be delirious. But no. She was always complaining."

"About what?" said Beth.

"Everything. The Dall food—she said it was getting so bad it made her puke. The New Look—she had to let out all her hems. *The Brothers K.*"

"What about *The Brothers K*?" Beth asked. "Boring?"

"That, of course. But it was the agonizing, all the feeling guilty about nothing, that Carol said drove her crazy." Her mother chuckled. "She said that if the Karamazovs' mail came late, Ivan would probably jump into the Dnieper. . . . The whole Gang got strange. Jill had stopped snapping at Louise, but she snapped at everyone else. She was in a terrible mood. No one knew why. Em and Louise did nothing but study—it was Harper every night. The rest of us, especially Jill, were just the opposite—cutting classes, going out more, staying out later. We had developed a sort of I-don't-care attitude. It was almost as if . . ."

"As if what, Mother?"

"As if we were scared silly, waiting for something to happen."

"But why? Did you ever talk about it?"

"We barely talked at all." She paused as two girls, in PRO-CHOICE T-shirts, rollerbladed into the courtyard. "The thing is, we had become so separate. I thought we would be a Gang again after everyone helped me when I hurt my ankle, but—"

"By the way, Mother, what about the dreamboat?"

"What dreamboat?"

"You know—your intern."

"What about him?"

"Well," Beth asked, "was he a PD for you?"

CHAPTER TWENTY-TWO

The University of Chicago
Early June—a few days later

1.

The night entrance to the dorms, Laurie always thought, was the most romantic place on campus. She loved the way the lantern light just touched the low branches of the trees that surrounded the semicircle. She loved the way couples converged there, just before 1:00 A.M. Chancellor Robert Maynard Hutchins's house was across the street. Did he ever look out a window and watch the kissing couples, each in their own world, some standing in the full light, the more passionate staying back in the darkness?

And she loved the unspoken etiquette of the night entrance that ruled you did not peek at other couples. Who would want to peek if you were with someone you cared about? Could you love two men at once, she wondered, as she and Matt broke from a lingering kiss.

"How about tomorrow?" Matt whispered against her lips. "I think I can switch call."

"Oh, Matt—I can't."

"Abe?" he said so loudly that a couple turned to look. "I know it's Abe! How can you, Laurie? He's arrogant. He's a show-off. And he's uncouth—thinks he's being the rebellious intellectual because he runs around barefoot. Well, he's not as smart as he thinks he is. He's a temperamental little adolescent. All he has going for him is he has more time to be with you than I do."

"That's not fair. Abe is—" Over Matt's shoulder, she saw Jill's blond pageboy swaying in the breeze as she kissed—"Oh, no! Jill's with Richie!"

"Who's Richie?"

"Rebecca's premed!"

At that instant couples parted, and there was a general movement toward the entrance that meant time had almost run out. Laurie gave Matt a quick kiss and ran—she didn't want to sign in late.

At the door, she turned to wave.

"Tomorrow?" said Matt.

She shook her head.

"Tell him to wear shoes. I don't want you catching anything."

Laurie ignored him. The bells were ringing the hour—Jill would be late!

2.

Abe broke off the kiss. "You're thinking about *him*."

"Who?"

"Matt. How can you, Laurie? So he's going to be a doctor. Big deal. Do you know what doctors do? They learn which parts go where, and they fix people up—it's like fixing cars. He's nothing but a garage mechanic in a lab coat. And he's *old*. He must be at least twenty-five. How can you fall for such a fogey?"

"He's not. He's twenty-four . . . but I wasn't thinking about him."

"If you were thinking about me, you'd *show* that you care, instead of leaving me in this pain." She knew he meant when they were necking on the Midway and she had pushed him away when his hands had started to roam.

"Jill cares," said Abe. He looked meaningfully at the darkest part of the circle, where Jill and Tony were pressed so close they were like one person. Tony was rubbing his body against hers.

"Bizarre," said Abe. "Necking all night, and more for sure— and they're still—" Suddenly he took Laurie in his arms and kissed her hard, and all the time she knew he was thinking about Jill, probably wishing he was rubbing himself against Jill.

"Laurie," someone called. "You'll be late."

She lifted her face to Abe's. He was staring at Tony and Jill. She stared, too, fascinated. They must be—they were! She didn't know you could do it that way. God! Why do I feel so scared, she thought. It was Jill who would get a late.

CHAPTER TWENTY-THREE

Midwestern University

"We were so young, but oh, how we resented the hours—in by ten-thirty P.M. during the week, one A.M. on weekends. We said they were treating us like children. Silly in retrospect. Some girls—me for one—had to be in earlier than that when they were home. But we still moaned and complained. There was never enough time."

"Time for what?" said Beth.

"Use your imagination, darling. Anyway, we were all pushing the rules, getting in just under the wire—and that meant trouble."

"What kind of trouble?"

"Too many lates and you were—I forget what it was called, but you had to stay in every night for two weeks. An eternity!"

CHAPTER TWENTY-FOUR

The University of Chicago
A few days later

" '—and when the dead arrive, they have sentence passed upon them, as they have lived well and piously or not.' Your turn," said Carol. She tossed the book to Laurie, then reached under the bookcase for a Toll House cookie.

Hit by the horrible realization that comps loomed too close to be ignored, they were sitting on the floor of Carol's room, reading Plato to each other.

Laurie found the place and continued. " 'And those who appear to have lived neither well nor ill, go to the River Acheron and are purified of their evil deeds. But those—' "

Suddenly Jill exploded into the room. She threw herself into the one chair, felt the sharp edges of a pile of notebooks, and hurriedly stood. "Damn!" she said. "I'm restricted. What'll I *do* every night for two weeks?"

"You could get your laundry off the floor," said Louise, coming in with Em.

"Boring."

"You could study for comps," said Em.

"Double boring."

"Have you cracked a book this quarter?" said Carol.

"There's plenty of time. What's a comp—a mere six hours on each subject. The week before, I'll lock myself in with a supply of No-Doz and study madly all night. But not now." She looked around rather wickedly. "I just got another idea."

"I'll bite," said Laurie. "What are you going to do?"

"I'm going to play detective," said Jill, giving them the same wicked look.

"What are you detecting for?" said Carol. "Your books?"

"Don't be sophomoric."

"For what then?" said Laurie.

Jill looked at each of them in turn, a teasing smile on her face. "I'm going detecting," she said, "for the *real* thief."

"Oh, Jill," said Louise. "You're just looking for another way to waste time. You'll flunk out," she said, and Laurie could tell that she really was worried about Jill.

"I won't flunk out!" said Jill. "But who cares if I do?"

"You're proving it," said Em.

"Proving what?"

"That most women don't come to college to get an education. They come to snag a husband."

"Shut up, Em. I don't need you to nag me—or Louise either."

"Let's go, Em," Louise said. "Nat. Sci. awaits."

"Nasty Nazi," said Jill, after they left. "I mean Nat. Sci."

"Are you really going to—" said Laurie.

"Find the real thief? Of course."

"Don't be a moron," said Carol. "They've found the real thief. Everyone agrees on that."

"Do they? Do *you*, Laurie? . . . Laurie?"

"Yes," said Laurie, wondering why she had hesitated. "It must have been Dewey."

"Well, I know—I think it was someone else. And so a detective I will be, tra la, tra la."

"Where will you start?" said Laurie.

"That would be telling. But I can detect all right—" Reaching under the bookcase, she snatched some cookies. "Better get rid of the crumbs," she said at the door. "They're an obvious clue."

Carol got up and looked down the hall.

"Where's she going?" said Laurie.

"To her room. I knew she wasn't serious," and Laurie wondered why Carol sounded so relieved. "Jill hasn't done a thing this quarter," Carol went on, "except go out every night and steal someone's steady."

"Tony wasn't anyone's steady."

"Jill knew Louise was crazy about him," said Carol. "And she knew that Richie belonged to Rebecca. And why Richie? It's one thing to go after a Van Johnson type like Tony. But Richie is such a square. He's not worth hurting Rebecca. Jill's trying to set a record for collecting scalps, and she doesn't care who she hurts. I don't understand her at all."

Laurie said she didn't either—and they had to get back to Plato.

Darkness came just as Socrates was about to drink the hemlock. "Finally a good part!" said Carol, taking the book from Laurie. " '—raising the cup to his lips, quite readily and cheerfully he drank the poison . . . the man who gave him the poison pressed his foot, and asked him if he could feel; and he said, No; and then his leg, and so upwards and upwards. . . . And Socrates said: When the poison reaches the heart that will be the end. He was beginning to grow cold about the groin,' " Carol read enthusiastically.

"Open the window! Open the window!" A loud voice from outside.

"Sounds like Abe," said Carol.

"But why is he down at this end?"

They went to the window. Below Jill's room, the streetlight shone down on Abe, barefoot, swaying in the grass. "Open the window," he called. "Open the window, Jill, my luscious, my sweet"—it sounded more like "my shweet."

Jill's window opened, and she looked out, laughing. "What's up, Abe?"

"Whatsh up? Should I tell you?"

Laurie banged the window down.

"Want the hemlock?" said Carol. "Oh, come on, Laurie. Don't be sad. He's so stewed he doesn't know what he's doing. He probably thinks he's under your window."

"Stop rationalizing," said Laurie. "And I'm not sad. I'm *mad*."

"At Abe?"

Laurie shook her head.

"I told you," said Carol. "She doesn't care who she hurts."

CHAPTER TWENTY-FIVE

The University of Chicago
The following day

"Hey!" Laurie jumped out of the shower. "I just got scalded. Okay," she said to the two closed doors. "Who's the dope who did it? Why didn't you yell?"

"Me," said Jill, coming out. "Sorry. I forgot." She stood a second, looking uncertain, then rushed back in and slammed the door.

The other toilet flushed, and Rebecca came out. She looked at the closed door, taking in the unmistakable sounds of up-chucking. "Jill?" Laurie nodded. "Bet she's pregnant," Rebecca said loudly. "She's just a girl who cain't say no. She's in a turrible fix."

"I'm not!" Jill emerged again, her face ashy, but remarkably gorgeous anyway. "It was that creamed slop at dinner last night."

"Oh, sure—no one else got sick."

"You're the one who looks pregnant," said Jill, staring at Rebecca's hefty waistline.

"Who's the father?" said Rebecca. "Richie?"

"Oh, Richie," Jill said contemptuously. "You can have him back. I don't want him."

"Thanks for small favors. I don't want him, either."

"I don't blame you," said Jill. "He'll never get into medical school."

"You—you stinker! You don't know a thing about med school."

"I know you need brains to get in. And Richie—" Jill threw up her hands, as if to say he's hopeless. "And I know something else," she said, giving Rebecca a sharp look. "Your *friend* Dewey wasn't the thief!"

"Why are you looking at me like that? Are you suggesting I'm the thief?"

"If it fits—" said Jill, with a mean smile.

Rebecca drew herself up as much as her short figure would allow. "People like you—people like you," she said, looking and sounding so much like a sputtering Lou Costello that Laurie wanted to laugh.

"People like me—what?" Jill *was* laughing.

"Come to a bad end," Rebecca shouted, and ran out of the bathroom.

"Cliché," Jill called after her.

"Drop dead—stinker," Rebecca called back.

Immediately Laurie stepped back into the shower. It was Rebecca who was the stinker, she thought, but she didn't want to forget she was mad at Jill. She had hardly spoken to her since the night that Abe—Abe, hell! What about Jill? Jill didn't have to open her window, Laurie thought, and turned the water on full force. But when she pulled the shower curtain, Jill was leaning against the wall, crying so miserably that Laurie could hardly stand it.

She threw on her robe. "What is it, Jill?"—putting an arm around her. "What's the matter?"

"I *am* pregnant. *PG*. Knocked up."

Laurie heard the dreadful words and felt sick. Her arm around Jill's shivering body, her mind flew back to the year before she left for the U of C, when she was a high-school sophomore. She could still see the girl, thin and sort of bent over, never stood up straight. Her name—Darlene—was a little off, just as she was a little off—sweaters a little too tight, lipstick a little too heavy. Cheap, some said, when they talked about her, which was seldom. In the caste system of high school, she was at the bottom.

And then one day she was as famous as the school's star quarterback. Everyone—from the most popular cheerleader to the jerkiest jerk—knew Darlene was going to have a baby. "The father's a flunk-out." "Works in a factory." "Dirty slut." "Got what she deserves." Laurie could still hear the whispers.

Darlene must have heard them, too, just as she must have known that everyone was staring at her stomach. When she started to show, she left school. What girl could have stayed and lived through that hideous public shame?

"Oh, Laurie," she heard Jill say. "What am I going to do? Oh, God!"—she ran into a stall. Laurie prayed no one would come in.

CHAPTER TWENTY-SIX

The University of Chicago
The same day—evening

"Take a lot of real hot baths." "No! She should run up and down the stairs!" "How long?" "Till she drops." "She should jump off a wardrobe." "Too high—a table's better." "She should douche with vinegar and—" "What's a douche?"

"Tripe!" said Louise. "None of that stuff works."

Way after Quiet Hours and the Gang was meeting in Laurie's room, not sprawling as usual, but sitting upright, stiff—like a bunch of Primwells. But they didn't look like Mrs. P. They looked stunned—that *this* could happen to Jill. They looked terrified—what if it happened to them? Laurie knew that was what they were thinking, because she was thinking it, too. What if she had let Abe—

Carol was close to crying. "We've *got* to do something. It'll destroy Jill's whole life."

"Keep it down," said Laurie, looking at the door, which suddenly opened.

"Yeah," said Jill, coming in. "Keep it down. I could hear you all the way down the hall. Laurie"—reproachfully—"you promised."

"I had to tell the Gang, Jill. Otherwise, how can we help? I

promise—no one will tell." And when Jill looked at them
doubtfully, Laurie said, "Here, sit down," getting out of her
chair.

"Oh for chrissake," said Jill. "I'm not in my ninth month."

"I *want* to stand," said Laurie. "We are going to have a
ceremony." She suddenly felt confident—in command, a sensa-
tion that seldom hit her. But when it did she knew she would
succeed. She knew that she could make them do as she said.
"Now—everyone stand. Come on—get up! I mean it! No, Jill,
not you," as the others, saying this was so stupid, reluctantly
pulled themselves up.

"Okay," said Laurie. "Link arms and put up your right
hand!" How could they do both? they complained. "Link *left*
arms, you boneheads. Now—make the Girl Scout sign."

"I get it," said Carol, as she put up three fingers and joined
thumb and little finger. "We're going to do the Girl Scout oath:

"On my honor,
I'll do my best,
To help myself,
And cheat the rest."

"Cut it out, Carol. We are going to swear a solemn oath. Say
after me, 'On my honor as a member of the Fourth Floor Gang
of Dall Hall' "—after a grudging hesitation they repeated her
words—" 'I solemnly swear, on—' " Laurie hesitated. What
was the right symbol? Then it came to her. " 'I solemnly swear,
on the memory of Letitia Dallworthy, that I will never reveal
Jill's secret.' "

Half giggling, half serious, they repeated the oath.

"Why Letitia?" said Jill. She looked amused and somewhat
flustered.

"I just suddenly thought how noble she looks, and yet—there's sorrow in her eyes, as if she had to struggle. . . ."

"What struggle?" said Em. "You're always imagining, Laurie."

"I'm not!" Laurie said indignantly. "I know she gave the money for a girl's dorm. What I don't know is why. She *must* have had a reason. Who knows what she might have gone through?"

"Letitia pregnant out of wedlock?" said Louise. "I'll have to give her a closer look."

"Come on," said Em. "We have to talk seriously. Jill," she said, "who's the father?"

"Like Letitia—who knows?" said Jill. "I don't."

She knows, Laurie thought. She was sure Jill knew who the father was. The others must have thought so, too, because they started questioning her. Why won't she tell? Laurie wondered. Maybe because he won't marry her?

Tony? someone asked, and Jill said no. But Tony would fit, Laurie thought. He'd never get married now—he loved having loads of girls chasing him. Richie? someone asked. Jill laughed and said no. Richie would marry her, Laurie thought, but Jill would never marry him.

"Abe?" said Carol, with a please-don't-mind look at Laurie.

Of course I don't mind, Laurie thought, as she heard Jill say no. Abe had told her he was so tight that night he didn't remember what he did. But—had there been other nights?—nights when Laurie was in bed and Jill out on the prowl? Well, if it was Abe, he wouldn't get married, either. He was too—she wasn't sure what.

"Evil?" someone asked.

"Evil?" said Jill, looking thoughtful. "I'd almost forgotten

him—and no!" Evil! But he had disappeared long ago. Still—
Laurie counted back—it *was* possible.

"Why do you care who the father is?" said Jill. "I have no
intention of getting married." Laurie remembered the night Jill
had said she was having too much fun to get married. And she
had said something else—what was it?—oh, yeah, she wouldn't
force anyone to marry her.

"Because he can help pay for an abortion," said Em.

"Abortion! That's more like it!" said Jill.

"Listen to me, Jill," said Louise. She went over and clasped
her hand. Laurie almost expected Jill to push her away. But no.
Tears in her eyes, Jill was looking earnestly at Louise. "You
can't take a chance on abortion! No doctor would do one in a
hospital—he'd lose his license. That leaves the back-alley butchers—and their hideous, disgusting improper instruments."

Jill wiped away her tears and smiled. "What's an improper
instrument? One that misbehaves?"

"A coat hanger," Louise said grimly.

Jill's smile disappeared. Was she seeing in her mind what
Laurie saw—hairy hands, bending a hanger until it was long
and straight with the hook at the end. Laurie felt as if she was
going to upchuck.

There was a long silence.

"I know someone I could ask," Em said finally. "He knows
someone who does it outside a hospital."

"It has to be safe!" said Louise.

"It is. It's done by a doctor—under sterile conditions. I
know if I ask this person he can pull strings to get Jill to the
doctor."

"Can you call him now?" Laurie said, suddenly thinking,
how long before Jill starts to show?

"I can't. He's away, but he'll be back right after the Open

House. I'll ask him then. There's one hitch," she told them. "It could cost as much as two hundred dollars."

"God! I'm almost flat broke," said Jill. "I can't ask for that much extra money." They suggested she take it out of her tuition money. "For next fall? I don't get my allowance that far in advance."

"*We'll* get the money," said Laurie. "Carol, we can work in the mail room again." With a small wince, Carol agreed, thinking, Laurie knew, of the thousands of announcements to be folded and put in envelopes. Em said she would take some out of her savings and go back to her typing job. "I'll baby-sit," said Louise.

"Oh, Louise—Em—your studying," said Jill.

"I'll study while I'm baby-sitting," said Louise, and Em said she'd study Louise's notes.

Laurie still felt uneasy. She couldn't stop thinking about Darlene. When she roused herself, the talk—she wasn't sure how—had shifted to Jill's detecting.

"*Was* it Rebecca?" Louise asked. Laurie had told them what had happened in the bathroom.

"Couldn't tell you," said Jill. "I don't even know who the thief is."

"You know," said Carol, giving her a shrewd glance.

Jill looked mischievous. "I have been doing some detecting—in between throwing up." They asked where she had looked. "Oh—upstairs and downstairs and in the lady's chamber."

"You mean chambers," said Carol.

"Chamber. Chambers. It doesn't matter. I don't know why I got so excited about it in the first place—maybe it's a PG symptom. Thanks, guys, you've been so great." She got up and put her arms around all of them. "I feel much better."

Laurie didn't feel better. All right, they would get the money. But would Em do her part in time? Every day mattered. "Em," she blurted out, "you have to talk to this guy right away, before—"

"Before what?"

"Before Jill starts to show!"

"I will talk to him!" said Em. "Didn't I say I would?"

"Of course you will," said Jill. "I'm starved. Let's sneak down to the kitchen and get some bread."

CHAPTER TWENTY-SEVEN

The University of Chicago
Mid-June

1.

The boys were coming! All Dall was in a whirl of preparation for the Open House, girls frantically brushing out sock curls, changing from shorts to date dresses, putting finishing touches to their rooms. The boys would be *upstairs*!

Laurie, wanting to look erudite—one of Abe's favorite words—had her borrowed Brahms and Bach stacked up and ready for the record player. She hesitated over Tchaikovsky, then reluctantly pitched *The Nutcracker* in the drawer with her Sinatra albums. She looked around. The dresser needed something. Opening *Aristotle* to "Intellectual Virtue," she placed the book next to the Tabu, then stood back and appraised her work. She could already hear Abe saying, "I'm impressed." Excitedly, she went down the hall to see Carol's room.

"Think he'll like it?" Carol asked. She was hoping to impress her latest crush, a law student who kissed divinely. Her room was unbelievably neat, the bunks, with their new white spreads, so tightly made they could have passed an Army inspection. The only hint that Dewey had ever occupied the room was a sign taped to the wall: CAROL ROSS FOR SANITARY IN-SPECTOR. EXPERIENCE COUNTS. ROSS HAS HAD YEARS OF EX-PERIENCE WITH UNSANITARY CONDITIONS. "Well?" said Carol.

"He'll love it," said Laurie, "especially that—" She pointed to a bra hanging from a doorknob.

"Oh, God! I tried on so many!" Carol threw the bra into the closet and after several attempts succeeded in jamming the door shut.

"Hope he likes Fibber McGee," said Laurie.

Carol made a face at her and said, "The boys are coming! The boys are coming! Let's see what Em's doing!"

Em was finger-testing the underpants drying on the radiator. "Damn," she said. "Still damp." Swiping some thumbtacks from the bulletin board, she tacked the underpants to the back of the bureau. "Now—what do you think?" she asked, obviously proud of the way she had used her Bette Davis collection. On a poster from *Jezebel,* she had Xed out Henry Fonda and lettered MY HERO under Bette Davis. On a *Dark Victory* poster, she had written under George Brent, DO YOU WANT HIM FOR YOUR DOCTOR WHEN YOU COULD HAVE—and drawn an arrow to a framed photo of herself. Wonderful, they told her, she would draw a crowd, but Laurie secretly preferred her room's intellectual look. "Come on," said Carol. "I want to check out the competition."

Rebecca and Lana's room, with its sea of ruffles—spreads, curtains, pillows—made them pause. Carol and Laurie wondered if the feminine look would capture more boys. Only the ones, Em whispered, who liked bedrooms out of *Oklahoma!* The scene taking place was hardly out of a musical. Rebecca sat grimly in a ruffled chair, Lana working desperately on her hair.

"She peroxided her bangs," Lana said, seeing the girls in the doorway, "so she could be blond, like—" She caught Rebecca's eye. "Anyway, I can hide them. I'll just cut a little more." She picked up the scissors. "Wait!" Rebecca got out of the chair, giving them a full view of her bangs—a hideous orange—and ran to the mirror. "Onward!" Laurie yelled. She didn't want to hear Rebecca's reaction. "The boys are coming!" "Hey!" said Carol. "You're stealing my line."

Their procession of three wound up in Louise and Jill's room and stopped, electrified, staring at the walls. "She talked me into it," said Louise, rather shamefaced. "We did caricatures of each other." Jill had painted a huge Louise, wearing a surgeon's scrub pants and cap—and nothing on top but an enormous stethoscope, cleverly covering her bare bosom. Louise had painted an equally huge Jill as a cowgirl, out of *Annie Get Your Gun*—Stetson at a jaunty angle over her blond pageboy, leather bra revealing fantastically bulging breasts, and a pert leather skirt. But what caught everyone's eye were the objects dangling from the bullet belt—a flashy display of dance cards, fraternity pins, ID bracelets. All that was missing, Laurie thought, was a string of scalps.

"Love the stethoscope," Em said finally.

"How about me? Didn't Louise do a great job?" said Jill, seemingly unaware of the significance of the dangling trophies.

"Has Mrs. P. seen the walls?" Laurie asked.

"No," said Jill. "The old bitch was in her rooms all morning. Then she went out, looking very pleased with herself. She must be up to something."

Lana came in to borrow a headband and stood gawking at the painting of Jill. Wiggling her hips, she chanted, "Ashes to ashes, dust to dust, if you don't like my figure, get your hands off my—shoulders! Tony will just *love* the bra." Clearly, she was out to make trouble, but there was no sign of jealousy from Louise. She and Jill were giggling together like old times. Jill tossed the headband to Lana, and the Gang raced downstairs.

Great Neck and Little Neck were set up with punch and potato chips and all kinds of spreads. Would the boys ever leave the food and come upstairs? Oyster Bay looked gorgeous, flowers everywhere, on the tables, the piano, the mantel. "Now," said Louise, "for my look at Letitia. Oh, dear. She's crooked."

"Come on, Louise. Straighten the poor lady," said Jill. Smiling, she watched as Louise dragged the ottoman over and reached up to straighten the portrait.

"Jill," said Em. "I talked to him."

"Who?" she said, her eyes on Louise.

"You know—this guy who knows this doctor."

Louise turned. "You're sure it's safe?"

"I swear it is."

"See—it's safe." Jill grinned. "Now, hurry up," she said, "and straighten Letitia."

Louise gave Em a stern look and turned back to the portrait. She stood on her toes, reached, reached higher—

"Here come the boys! There's Mrs. P.!"

Louise jumped off the ottoman.

"They aren't that close," said Jill. "You had time to fix it."

"Where did Mrs. P. come from?" said Rebecca, who had been standing in the doorway, watching. "I thought she was in her rooms."

"She was," said Jill. "Then she went out."

Then the doors opened and a crowd of boys burst in. Barely holding themselves in check, they followed Mrs. P. as she went up the steps, oh so slowly, smiling her ghastly society smile.

2.

Midwestern University

"I can still see the boys swarming up the stairs, still hear the screams of laughter and girls yelling, 'Four! Four! Man on the floor!'

"Abe was late so I was wandering around. In the middle of the hall, I saw Tony, surrounded by a bevy of girls pleading with him to come see their rooms. He was saying he would—later—he had other plans for now. I pushed through the crowd and glanced in Rebecca's room. Richie was laughing and playing with her bangs. I heard him ask if she wanted to go with him to watch the Dodgers play the Cubs. Then I slowed down. Mrs. P. was just ahead of me, peeking in the rooms, reminding the girls that they should keep the doors open. 'She must think we have hot pants!' a boy shouted, but Mrs. P. pretended not to hear. I turned around and went back to my room and Abe was there, waiting for me."

"*Was* Abe impressed with your room?" Beth asked.

"Hard to say. Brahms's *Fourth* had hardly started before Abe had closed the door and dragged me to the lower bunk. We necked awhile, but I kept telling him we had to stop. I was really afraid Mrs. P. would come in.

"Then Abe said he had to go to the men's room—that day it was the fourth-floor bathroom.

"Time went by. No Abe. I got sort of lonely waiting for him, wondering what had happened. So I left."

3.

The University of Chicago

The Brahms was lovely, but the record was playing to an empty room. Laurie looked at her watch. Almost time. Everyone would be downstairs to watch the show the Dall girls were putting on. Damn, Laurie thought, I want to be there, too. She had worked so hard on the songs. She wanted Abe to—where *was* Abe?

Ahead of her, someone—a boy—was sidling down the hall. He tripped over a train case, caught himself—Laurie did a double take. She could hardly believe what she was seeing. Slicked-down dark hair, leather flight jacket—Evil! He darted into an empty room and closed the door. The return of Evil? That really would be funny. She ran to see. But as she passed the ironing room, she stopped abruptly.

Beyond the telephone and the drying rack were Jill and Abe, locked in each other's arms, kissing as if they would never come up for air. She heard Abe murmur, "Jill, Jill, let's go to your room." Laurie could not stop staring.

Just then the buzzer went off. Two longs and a short: Jill. Laurie wheeled around and ran.

Brahms was over. A Bach concerto was playing. The needle made a screech of protest as Laurie yanked off the record. Then she put the record on her knee and broke it over and over, until it was smashed to smithereens. One part of her mind told her she would have to pay for it. Another part said she didn't care. She flung herself on the bunk and lay there, sobbing, her arms around the pillow.

"Ain't no lift from the elevator,
Ain't no heat from the radiator,

But still we love our—Dall Hall!
Other halls must advertise,
But the girls from Dall they tantalize.
It's hard to keep the wolf outside the door."

Voices from the show—Laurie put her hands over her ears. Abe and Jill. Jill and Abe. They looked so—practiced, as if they had kissed like that millions of times.

She was still crying when she heard the door open. She turned her head. Abe was there. He looked strange, pale. "Laurie, I'm—"

"Where's Jill? Why aren't you with her?"

"She went to her room. I think she's meeting Tony."

"Don't let that stop you—go after her!"

"Laurie," he said again, "I'm so—"

"What? Sorry? Are you sorry about all the other times, too?"

He closed the door, went over, and sat on the edge of the bunk. "What other times? You're wrong, Laurie," he said, putting a hand on her shoulder. "Anyway, what about you and Matt?"

She shoved his hand away and sat up. "How dare you? That's not the same at all. We weren't sneaking around."

"All right," he said, "but—"

There was a horrible scream—not like in a horror movie. This was a real scream that moved forward and forward in anguish.

They looked at each other. Abe's face was startled. Laurie was filled with dread.

The scream came again. And again.

Abe got up, opened the door. Now the screams were louder

and closer—like a speeding fire truck when you might be the emergency.

"Is it true what they say about—Dall Hall?
Do the girls there look just like movie queens?
Do they all get A's in Phy. Sci.
And history and such?"

They raced down the hall, Laurie pulling ahead of Abe.

Louise! She looked as crazed as Rochester's wife, standing in the door of her room, giving out scream after piercing scream.

What Laurie saw first was the window where Jill had etched her name in the glass. Then she saw splatters of blood all over Louise's caricature of Jill. She forced herself to look down. *Oh, God! Oh, God! The bed!* The spread all blood-splashed. Jill's Scottie, drenched in blood, a big splotch where Carol had signed her name and written "Love you passionately." And lying there, horribly still, her perfect legs half off the bed, her arm around the Scottie, was Jill, blood, horrible blood, soaking one side of her pink angora sweater and all the way down one sleeve—

"We're geographic, mathematic,
Photogenic, pornographic—ooops!"

"Shut up! Shut up!" Laurie screamed toward the stairway. She turned back to the room. Then she saw it. On the floor, next to the bed—she knew it right away—Mrs. P.'s gun. Louise saw it, too. She moved her stony gaze from Jill to the gun and kept on screaming.

PART
THREE

CHAPTER TWENTY-EIGHT

Midwestern University

"It's getting chilly. Let's walk."

"Mother! You can't leave it at that! What happened?"

"Nothing."

"But that's ridiculous," said Beth. "There must have been an outcry. There must have been police."

Reluctantly, her mother sat down again.

"Well?" said Beth.

"Well?" She made a gesture of capitulation. "Well, of course everyone was devastated. Tony was in shock. He wandered around telling people, 'I loved her, you know. I loved that girl.' And Mrs. P.—I think it was worse for her because it was her gun that . . . Anyway, she was a basket case. I can still see her standing outside Jill's room. She had been crying and the tears had made silly white stripes through her rouge. She looked like a sad clown. 'Never, never,' she was saying, 'has there been anything like this at Dall. Never, never at Dall,' she said, wringing her hands. And then Em jumped right in front of her and started yelling that all Mrs. P. cared about was Dall's reputation, and what about Jill? We had to drag Em away. I guess I didn't mention the whole Gang—or what was left of it—was there."

"What *about* the Gang?"

"We were together constantly, talking and crying, crying and talking, asking each other, Why? *Why?*"

"Did you come up with any answers?"

"Never."

"Are you sure?"

"Well—we did think there must have been some connection with Jill's being pregnant. But we never got any further than that."

"Didn't the police question you?"

"Oh, yes. We were among the first. I suppose someone told them we were Jill's best friends. They talked to all of us— separately. When we compared notes, we found out they were especially interested in Mrs. P.'s gun. All of us had told them that lots of people knew about the gun—and anyone could have taken it."

"I thought Mrs. P. was in her rooms."

"Just in the morning. But then she left and didn't come back until the Open House started. Plenty of time for someone to sneak in and get the gun."

"What did the police say when you told them Jill was pregnant?"

Her mother looked surprised. "We couldn't tell them about that!"

"*Why* couldn't you?"

"Don't you see? We had made a solemn promise. We had promised Jill we would *never* tell," she said, her face such a mix of seriousness and innocence that Beth had a glimmer of how her mother must have looked as a girl.

"Not that it mattered," said her mother. "There was an autopsy, so of course the police did find out that Jill was pregnant. And then they changed their whole approach."

"Evil?"

"Oh my, yes. The police were desperate to find him. But no one knew his real name or even where he lived. So they concentrated on Richie and Abe and Tony."

"And then what?"

"They all had alibis. Rebecca said Richie was with her the whole time. A couple of girls said Tony had been down in the lounge watching the show."

"Do you think it was true?"

"What?"

"About Richie and Tony."

"I suppose so. It must have been."

"And Abe?"

"Abe?" Her mother rose. "Look—they have little labels for the flowers. *Feverfew. Dame's Rocket. Lady's-Mantle.* Don't you love the names?"

"Mother—what about Abe?"

She was leaning over a flower bed, her back to Beth. "Abe? I—I—provided Abe's alibi."

"You did *what?*"

Her mother stood and faced Beth. "I know it seems strange now that I would do something like that. But then—it just came naturally. I got that surge of confidence I had sometimes, and when the police questioned me about Abe, I knew exactly what I had to do.

"I pretended I was so embarrassed I could hardly talk. I made the police think they were dragging information out of me, forcing me to admit that Abe and I had been alone in my room. Doing what? they asked. Remembering to look embarrassed—it wasn't that hard—I said we had been necking. Had we heard anything? A gunshot? I looked even more embarrassed—I knew they would think we had been into some heavy necking—and said we hadn't heard a thing until Louise screamed. That part was true, of course. I never told them about when Abe left my room."

"How did you get your stories to jibe? Did Abe tell you what to say?"

"He didn't have to. We had a chance to talk before the police came, and I just told Abe I'd say we'd been in my room the whole time."

"Didn't Abe object? After all, you were perjuring yourself to save him."

Her mother stared straight ahead at the fountain. "No, he didn't object. But that doesn't make him—what you think. Anyway, the police never questioned me or Abe again. After it came out that Jill was pregnant—and after they heard about Evil— the police seemed very willing to believe that all three boys had alibis. I think they had made up their minds that Evil was the father—and the murderer."

"That doesn't make sense," said Beth. "If Evil was the father, why would he come back?"

"The word was that the police were sure Jill knew how to reach Evil—and that she had called and asked him to come to the dorm. But they never did find Evil. So the case was closed, or put on hold—or whatever it's called—dead by person or persons unknown . . . and that was it for Jill. Enough," she said, brushing a tear away. "I don't want to talk about it anymore. How did we get into this anyway?"

"Dickens—I think."

"Well, down with Dickens! Let's walk, Beth."

They left the hush of the garden and returned to the bustle of the campus. Dodging rollerbladers and sprinklers, they walked toward the library. In the library plaza, students were enjoying the late-afternoon sun, lying on benches, reading, sleeping. In the center of the plaza, a girl with a notebook was interviewing a bearded man Beth recognized—a new member of the English faculty, a star import from Yale. "But what *good* is deconstruction?" Beth heard the girl ask. She sounded as if she was having as much trouble getting answers as Beth.

They crossed the plaza and went down the steps, taking the path toward the lake. "But underneath," said Beth, "didn't you wonder if Abe was the father?"

"You don't give up, do you, darling? You're like a mastiff. Oh, all right, I did wonder. But I told myself even if Abe was the father—so what?"

"Mother, I think—"

She met Beth's eyes. "You think what?"

"I think you're still protecting Abe. I think you believe he was the murderer."

Her mother stopped short. "No! I *knew* Abe could never have done a thing like that!" A rollerblading professor with briefcase turned to stare.

"How could you be so sure?" Beth asked. "Wishful thinking?"

"No! Instinct—insight—call it what you will. I knew Abe Lowenstein didn't have it in him to murder. A brash New York boy who could behave outrageously—I see that now. But murder? Never!"

No, Beth thought. *It's impossible. It's too absurd.*

"You look so strange, darling. What is it?"

"Lowenstein," said Beth. "That was Abe's last name?"

"Still is. Haven't I mentioned it before?"

"You have not. And he was from New York?"

Her face reddened. "I think he still lives there."

They had reached the lakefill. Silhouetted against the gray-blue water, two girls jogged determinedly along the path. Beth watched them, thinking about what she would say next.

"Mother," she said finally, "this sounds silly, but do you know if Abe has children?"

She smiled. "One son—who must be the opposite of his father. Abe was such an intellectual. And his son writes popular novels—you know the kind—millions of highly forgettable pages."

Only Dickens, thought Beth, would have dared invent such a preposterous coincidence. "You mean Lincoln Lowenstein," she said.

"You've heard of him? I didn't think you left literature long enough to—Funny, I was just thinking. I'm the one who had an intellectual child, and Abe—"

"Have you read Link Lowenstein's novels?"

"Well—no."

"They're better than you think—and he's pretty much of an intellectual."

"Beth, you aren't saying that you know Abe's son?" For a moment her mother looked astounded. Then she smiled—slowly, nostalgically.

CHAPTER TWENTY-NINE

A few evenings later Beth turned the final page of *Edwin Drood*, left after this reading with the same feeling she always had—who cares who killed Edwin Drood? She did not. Shaw had said that Dickens's unfinished novel was "a gesture by a man already three quarters dead." While she resented the note of contempt for the great novelist, in the case of *Drood*, Beth was inclined to go along with Shaw. True, it was Dickens's first attempt at a mystery. But why would Dickens, master writer of page-turners, make the murderer so obvious?

Beth looked at her watch. Still early. She decided to emulate Anthony Trollope, who, having just completed a novel, but not his daily word quota, went on to begin writing his next novel. She reached for *Bleak House*.

Instantly Beth was transported from her brightly lit living room to Queen Victoria's England—and enveloped in a London fog. Now she was at the heart of the fog, where it was most dense, the High Court of Chancery. Ah, this was the Dickens she loved. Once again, she was in the dim courtroom, looking on, as the case of Jarndyce and Jarndyce trudged along to nowhere.

Scores of persons have deliriously found themselves made parties in Jarndyce and Jarndyce . . . whole families

> *inherited legendary hatreds . . . The little plaintiff or de-*
> *fendant who was promised a new rocking-horse, when*
> *Jarndyce and Jarndyce should be settled, has grown up*
> *. . . Fair wards of the court have faded into mothers . . .*

Mothers. Beth thought of her mother and the murder that still had her in its grasp, a murder, like the case of Jarndyce and Jarndyce, that stretched back to the past and blighted the present. Why was her mother still so troubled? . . . No! Resolved to put the Dall Hall murder out of her thoughts, Beth found her place and continued to read.

Now she was in the world of fashion, a London town house, the pied-à-terre of nobility. Here, sitting before the fire, were Sir Leicester Dedlock and the elegant Lady Dedlock, too well-bred to take the slightest interest in anything. And here was the cunning solicitor, Tulkinghorn, reporting on my Lady's cause before the court.

My Lady only appears to listen—until she sees some papers on the table. Then, looking closer—then closer still—she asks impulsively: "Who copied that?"

> *Mr. Tulkinghorn stops short, surprised by my Lady's*
> *animation . . .*
> *"Is it what you people call law-hand?" she asks . . .*
> *"Not quite . . . Why do you ask?"*
> *"Anything to vary this detestable monotony. O, go*
> *on, do!"*
> *Mr. Tulkinghorn reads . . . Sir Leicester dozes, starts*
> *up suddenly, and cries, "Eh? what do you say?"*
> *"I say I am afraid," says Mr. Tulkinghorn . . . "that*
> *Lady Dedlock is ill."*
> *"Faint," my Lady murmurs, with white lips, "only*

*that; but it is like the faintness of death. Don't speak to me.
Ring, and take me to my room!"*

Only a faint, but as Beth knew too well, Lady Dedlock, having
shown interest in the handwriting, had placed herself in
Tulkinghorn's clutches. Only a faint—*like the faintness of
death*—and the reason stretched back to Lady Dedlock's past.
. . . The past. Beth thought of the long ago Open House . . .
of Jill. *"Oh, she was so cute. Everything about her—"* Stop! Beth
turned back to the book.

Now Ada Clare, ward of the court, makes her appearance.
Beth watched Ada's new friends fall under her spell. "Such a
beautiful girl!" Esther thinks, such a "captivating, winning man-
ner." Her cousin Richard, instantly enamored, compares Ada to
a summer morning—"With that golden hair, those blue eyes,
and that fresh bloom on her cheek."

Jill. She's Jill! The same extraordinary blond beauty, the
same bewitching personality. Who did murder Jill? *No!* Call it
quits for tonight, for *Bleak House*—and for Jill. Beth threw the
book on the table.

Lying among the books was the latest issue of *Prairie Gust*,
Midwestern's student newspaper. A caption from the "Letters"
column caught Beth's eye: SHOWERS FROM HELL ARE REAL
DANGERS TO STUDENTS:

> *A few days ago I emerged from my morning shower with
> a long red welt up and down the side of my body. I thought
> I had learned so well how to sense the subtle change in
> pressure that warns of the impending scalding.*
> *You see, in Sheridan House—at least in my wing—the
> showers scorch you when anyone on the entire floor flushes
> the toilet. There is often no warning and—*

"Flushing," Beth remembered. And "Thank you" from the shower—someone saved from a scalding. Just like the fourth-floor shower at Dall.

That did it. Unless she looked into this murder, she would never accomplish anything. Now—tonight—she would phone her mother.

She showered, thankful she need not fear a scalding, and got in bed.

CHAPTER THIRTY

"It's you—I thought so."

"Why did you hang up?"

"I want to forget, Beth. I should never have told you. I'd put it out of my mind—and now everything's come back again."

"Mother, I've got to pursue this."

"Can't you pursue Dickens instead?"

"I tried"—Beth told her how she had tried. "Can't you see? Unless I pursue this, I'll never get anything else done. Do you want your daughter to lose her tenure?"

"Lose your tenure! You've only been distracted from your work. You haven't committed moral turpitude."

"Not yet. You can't tell what I'll do. Right now I feel so thwarted I might run through the library naked!"

"If you must—but don't take coffee into the stacks. . . . Okay, darling, okay. But I don't know how I can help."

"To begin with—where is everyone? What happened to the Gang?"

"Oh—the Gang. After—after Jill—the Gang broke up. I moved to another dorm. So did the others. We were scattered all over campus. I hardly saw them—I guess they didn't want to see me either. Too painful. And after graduation, I lost touch with everyone."

"You don't know where they are?"

"Well—I read the alumni notes."

"Then you do know where they are!" Beth searched for a nonthreatening name—"Where's Lana?"

"Lana is dead," her mother said flatly.

"Lana! But that's horrible!" Beth felt as if she had lost a friend. Lana, the brazen borrower, so shameless she was funny. Gone now. Had she ever passed Soc.? "When? What happened?"

"Oh—years ago. A car crash."

"What about Dewey?"

"She never graduated."

"What about the others?"

"I don't know. They never send in news."

"There must be some list somewhere. Mother, you're holding out."

"I suppose I could—"

"Could what?"

"Have a look at the alumni directory. But it's ancient!"

"Come on, Mother. We're not talking about the Middle Ages."

"Let's see," her mother said a few minutes later. "Carol. Carol lives on the North Shore." She named a suburb not far from Beth and gave the address. Warning that they could be out of date, she read off addresses for Em, Louise, and Rebecca. "Strange," her mother said, "I didn't even know they all live in the Chicago area."

"That is a bit of luck," said Beth, or she thought, another Dickensian coincidence.

"Beth, I have to finish these notes. Everything's piling up." And the conversation had ended before Beth realized she had forgotten to ask for the men's addresses. She would have to get them later.

Meanwhile—Beth looked over the list. Where to start?

CHAPTER THIRTY-ONE

Late August

A week later Beth stood in front of a handsome old Astor Street building that made her think of the Dedlocks' London town house. Narrow, curving driveway. Arch of awning covering the red carpet that led to the entrance. Guarding the entry was a brass-buttoned doorman who said that Dr. Hallman was expecting her. He took her up in a paneled elevator that opened to a parqueted foyer. As Beth looked for a button to push, the door opened.

"Hello. I'm Louise Hallman." Beth introduced herself, and they shook hands.

But she's *old*, Beth thought, still clinging to her image of a gawky, giggling Louise. On the other hand—Beth brought herself back to the present—Louise looked younger than she had expected—and more expensive. Good haircut, and a good color job—chestnut brown with highlights. Tasteful makeup. Perhaps a little too much eyeliner—it gave the brown eyes a hard look.

Louise led her through the apartment, moving at a pace that allowed only fleeting impressions of silky fabrics, highly polished tables, deep pile rugs. They walked down a hall lined with silver-framed photographs. Beth slowed to look at a candid of a young dreamy-eyed Louise in a wedding dress. Here she was again, she and the groom—kissing. Here they were coming down the aisle, Louise all smiles, the groom, a handsome blond who wore tails well, looking more dazed than blissful. Here they were cutting a wedding cake topped with miniature bride and mustached groom.

Turning, Louise saw Beth looking at the photos, but made no comment. "I thought my office," she said, opening a door.

The office was all business—framed diplomas on otherwise bare walls, furniture of the modern leather and metal variety— except for a huge mahogany partners' desk. Louise gestured Beth to a chair and seated herself behind the desk, as if to put a professional distance between them. After all, Beth thought, looking around, it's not as if I'm a patient.

Louise caught her eye. "You're looking for the couch," she said, allowing herself a smile. "I don't use a couch." She asked about Laurie, said it was too bad they had lost touch, though she didn't sound all that regretful. Then she said abruptly, "So why does Laurie's daughter want to see me?"

Beth had anticipated this question and had thought of saying she was doing research into dormitory life. One look at Louise and she had known the story would never go over. "I'm investigating," she said.

"Investigating what?" Louise sounded annoyed.

"Jill Jansen—her murder."

"Jill! That was settled long ago."

"But it wasn't really—settled, I mean. And something came up."

"What came up?"

"Some unfinished business that still troubles my mother," Beth said, praying her contrived answer would appeal to a psychiatrist.

"Still troubling Laurie? That seems remarkable." Louise

frowned and sat thinking. Then she said, "I don't have much time. I'm expecting a patient. What is it you want to know?"

So the watchword was brusqueness. All right. "First—what was your impression of Jill in the weeks before—"

"Before she was murdered?" Louise said briskly. She opened a drawer, took out cigarettes, fished for a packet of matches whose logo Beth recognized as that of a plush New York hotel. Louise lit a cigarette, drawing in so deeply that Beth wondered if the smoke would ever come out.

It did come out, and with it—"Jill. Yes, Jill. I would have to say that during that period she was emotionally unstable."

Beth asked in what way unstable.

"She had mood swings," said Louise. "Jill and I always got along well, but suddenly she was hostile to me. I never understood why. Then, sometime later—just as suddenly and for no apparent reason—she was friendly again."

Beth started to ask a question, but Louise held up a hand. "In addition," she said, "Jill was behaving obsessively. Jill was always an extrovert, but never so extreme. She started dating every boy in sight, poaching on other girls' boyfriends. Openly poaching—almost as if she wanted everyone to know." Louise waved a hand to indicate she had finished and was ready to take questions.

"To what do you attribute this—unstable behavior?" said Beth, thinking she sounded as clinical as Louise.

"One can't be certain, of course, but I can't help speculating that Jill was severely depressed. Her pregnancy, you know," said Louise, looking closely at Beth. Louise nodded, as if a question had been answered. "The severe stress reaction," she continued, "may have been the source of Jill's obsessive pursuit of boys—an escape into fantasy. As to her mood swings—no doubt they were due to hormonal changes during pregnancy. Is that all?"

"Not quite. What do you remember about that day—the time before the murder?"

"Before the murder?" Louise hesitated a moment. "I remember being downstairs, standing on an ottoman, trying to get a look at a portrait over the fireplace. Then someone warned me that Mrs. Primwell was coming in—and I jumped off the ottoman. After that, I don't remember anything distinctly—no doubt for Freudian reasons—until the sing."

"How did you come to find the body?"

Louise lit another cigarette. Long pause, as she drew in. Then, her words mingling with dragon puffs of smoke, she said, "I was downstairs at the sing, watching for someone. Tony Valentine. You may have heard of him?" Again, she looked closely at Beth, who said, yes, she had. "I thought so," said Louise. Pause. Another deep drag. "I was a very silly girl then," she said. "Well—Tony finally did come down. I had hoped he would sit next to me. He did not. Silly to think he would, but when he didn't even say hello . . . I rushed up to our room, and—and I saw her. . . . I'm sorry, but I'm afraid I don't remember the details of what I saw. Surely they're unnecessary?"

"Hello, darling. Am I interrupting?" In the doorway stood a graying handsome man in golf clothes. He strode to the desk and kissed Louise on the cheek.

"You finished your round early," she said, receiving his kiss as her due. Frowning, she stared at the drink in his hand, started to say something—

"Aren't you going to introduce me?" he asked.

"Oh, yes—I want you to meet Laurie's daughter, Professor Beth Austin. This is my husband—Anthony Valentine."

Tony! Beth tried to appear indifferent, but Louise's eye was on her and Beth knew she had picked up on her astonishment.

"So you're Laurie's daughter," said Tony. He pulled a chair close to Beth—unnecessarily close. "Professors have certainly improved since my day." He gazed at Beth admiringly.

"Don't you want to question Tony?" Louise said icily.

Tony looked alarmed. "Question me about what?" he said, rubbing a small bald spot on the back of his head.

"She's investigating Jill's murder, darling," Louise said with some pleasure.

"Good God!" Tony downed his drink. "That was eons ago. Why go into it now?"

"Something came up," Louise said happily.

"What came up? Something about me?" His face was ashen.

"No," Beth said. "Something else. Your mother," she said, glancing at Louise—a look from the steely eyes—"I mean, your wife. Your wife has been telling me about the afternoon of the murder. Perhaps you could—"

"Yes, darling. Tell her your version," said Louise.

Tony looked at Louise. "You don't mind?"

"Why should I?"

"It was earlier," Tony began. "I mean, I had seen Jill earlier in her room"—he met Louise's eyes—"I mean, your room, both of yours—oh, forget it. This was—you know—before—"

"Before she was murdered," said Louise.

"Yes—before—and Jill sent me down to the sing, said she'd be there right away. So I did go down. Later—after—when the police came, some of my friends—"

"Girlfriends," said Louise, with a cracking noise that might have been a giggle.

"Oh all right—girlfriends. They told the police I had been at the sing the whole time." More rubbing of the bald spot. "But I wasn't."

"Where were you?" said Beth.

"I waited and waited, but Jill never came down. So I went up to find her. When I got to her room, someone was there—the guy they called Evil. They were—on the bed—"

The phone rang and Louise picked it up. It was clear from the conversation that she was talking to a patient.

Tony made wigwagging motions, mouthing, "We can go."

Louise shook her head vigorously. "I'll call you back."

"We could have left," Tony said.

"Unnecessary," said Louise.

"Anyway," Tony continued, "they were on the bed. When Jill saw me, she jumped up and said, 'It's not what you think, Tony,' and she told Evil he had to leave."

"What did he say?" Beth asked.

"He didn't say anything. I was surprised he didn't put up an argument. He just sort of sidled out. Then Jill and I had a fight—about Evil. She kept saying it was all a joke, she could explain. But I was so damn mad I didn't want to listen. I ran down the stairs, back to the sing."

A distant buzzing sound. "That's my patient," said Louise. "I'm afraid I can't give you any more time."

Beth stood, and Tony said he would see her out.

"Tony," said Louise, "I want to talk to you. You can find your own way out, can't you, Beth?"

Beth turned as she left and saw Tony standing in front of the desk, rubbing his bald spot. Louise was talking, her voice low and angry. "Oh, all right," Beth heard Tony say. "And how many cigarettes have *you*—"

CHAPTER THIRTY-TWO

"Tony and Louise? I can't believe it!"

"Believe it," Beth told her mother, and was immediately deluged with questions. How did they look? "Tony? He's not a dreamboat, but he's still handsome. Louise looks . . . chic." Louise, chic! Her mother couldn't believe that, either. What were they like with each other? "Hard to say, Mother. I think she worries about his drinking." But did they seem to care about each other? "Hard to tell. Maybe." And what about the murder—did Beth learn anything? "I'm not sure. Mother, I need to think!"

Beth put down the phone. At last, the moment she had been waiting for. Now she could focus her thoughts on the visit to Astor Street. Slowly, she told herself. Take it in order.

First, Tony. If Tony was telling the truth, Evil left before Jill was murdered. That meant Evil was not the murderer. It also meant Tony knew he was not. So why didn't Tony tell the police? The answer was obvious—Tony had to protect his alibi. But the fact remains, Beth thought, he had no alibi. So where did that leave Tony? What if his story of finding Jill and Evil on the bed was just that—a story? He saw Evil somewhere—and dreamed the whole thing up. What if Jill was alone when Tony went up to her room? Tony wouldn't want Louise to know that.

Beth turned her thoughts to Louise. Louise knew. She knew

Tony didn't have an alibi. How long had she known? Since before they were married, Beth thought. Tony—in his fear—must have confided in her. If that was the case, did Louise believe that Tony murdered Jill? Surely she would never have married him if she believed that. But why was Louise so eager to get Tony to tell his version, as she had put it, of what happened? Wouldn't Louise want to protect Tony? Or did she simply want the truth?

Restlessly, Beth rose from her chair, went to her bedroom, changed to a robe. In so many marriages, she thought, as she put out her clothes for the next day, there's one who loves more than the other. And, considering the history of their romance, Louise was the one. Beth returned to the living room and stretched out on the sofa. But if Louise was the one who loved the most, wouldn't she be softer, more submissive? Here Beth almost laughed. One could hardly call Louise submissive. On the contrary, Louise was assertive—as commanding, Beth suddenly thought, as Lady Dedlock. And Tony, the one who loved less—or not at all?—was as deferential to Louise as Sir Leicester to Lady Dedlock.

Beth pictured Louise, earlier that day, guiding her through their elegant apartment. Definitely the high-rent district, and a far cry from Louise's impoverished student days. Louise—always short of money. Could it be that she was the thief? And was Louise, like Lady Dedlock, keeping this secret from the past from her husband? Beth's thoughts moved on. Convenient that Louise had a Freudian amnesia for much of the afternoon when Jill was murdered. What if after Tony arrived, Louise had left the sing—unnoticed? Could it be that Louise was keeping a different, more dangerous secret? Lady Dedlock had kept a secret that allowed another to exert power over her, to subtly threaten her.

Lying on the table was Beth's worn copy of *Bleak House*. Impulsively, she picked it up and paged ahead: evening at Chesney Wold, Sir Leicester's Lincolnshire estate. The villainous Tulkinghorn is relating a story to the Dedlocks and their house party. "I speak of a really great lady," says Tulkinghorn, "married to a gentleman of your condition, Sir Leicester. . . . The lady was wealthy and beautiful." To Lady Dedlock, but to no one else, it is clear that Tulkinghorn speaks of her and that he intends her to understand his meaning.

> *"Now this lady preserved a secret under all her greatness, which she had preserved for many years. In fact, she had been engaged to marry a young rake . . . She never did marry him, but she gave birth to a child of which he was the father."*

Lady Dedlock rises; "graceful, self-possessed," she leaves the room.

But we know it's an act, Lady Dedlock. We know you are pretending indifference. We know you gave birth to a bastard— a profound violation of Victorian morality, a disgrace, if revealed, that automatically exiles you from polite society—and still a disgrace, nearly a century later, in Dall Hall.

Oh, stop, Beth told herself. Her thoughts were becoming muddled. Everything led her to *Bleak House*—then back again to Dall. Face it. For tonight, she had gone as far as she could go—and if she was going to think about Dickens, why not push on and continue where she had left off.

Beth paged back and was soon immersed in the Jellyby household, disorderly in the extreme. Neglected rooms—fires out, ashes in the grates. A curtain fastened up with a fork. Neglected children, one getting his neck caught between iron railings, another falling down the stairs. A chaotic dinner—potatoes mislaid in the coal scuttle, Borrioboola-Gha correspondence in the gravy. At the center of the disorder, Mrs. Jellyby, who neglects home and family to oversee her beloved African project—educating the natives of Borrioboola-Gha. Suffering admidst the disorder, Mr. Jellyby, who sits in a corner with his head against a wall and never speaks a word.

Interesting, Beth thought, the way Dickens moves his story from abode to abode. It struck her that, in investigating Jill's murder, she, too, would move from abode to abode. Interesting, too, the way Dickens characterizes people through how they live. Could she have learned more from her visit to Louise and Tony's home? Beth had the uneasy feeling that she had overlooked something.

She closed the book, drew a bath, and lay in the bubbles, thinking of Louise, of Tony, of Link—that was nice—of Link's father. No! No more returns to Dall—not tonight. Back again to Link—she leaned forward to soap her toes. The soap slithered out of her hand, and Beth reached into the bubbles to retrieve it. But the soap seemed determined to elude her, forever slipping through her fingers. Just as she had the soap in her grasp—she remembered.

Dewey. They had never talked about Dewey. Stop it, Beth. Dewey was never even on the scene. Long before the murder, Dewey had left Dall. So Dewey—as they say—had been made redundant.

CHAPTER THIRTY-THREE

What with explaining to a student why he had received an A—
and not an A, it was something of a rush for Beth to keep her
appointment. She drove past the Museum of Science and Industry, went to 57th Street, and turned into Harper, a street of turn-
of-the-century wooden houses, all well-kept except Rebecca's,
which needed painting.

On the porch a swing dangled by one chain. On the pink
door was a crumbling Christmas wreath, under it a nameplate
that read RICHARD RICE. MS. REBECCA RICE, B.A. Beth looked
for a doorbell. Finding none, she picked up the tail of the piglet
door knocker and rapped. The door swung open.

"You're here! Hello! I'm Rebecca," and Beth experienced the
same time warp she had felt when she saw Louise. Her mental
picture of a young, feisty Rebecca had to be adjusted. Still feisty
perhaps, but now the short curly hair was entirely gray, and the
body, enveloped in a warm-up suit, could have posed for
"mass" in an art class.

"Come in, come in"—ushering Beth into a living room that
suffered from a surfeit of cuteness: dried flowers in rooster
pitchers, cat-shaped rugs, cow-shaped tables.

"Interesting house," said Beth.

"Yes, like all of Hyde Park. That's why we could never bid
adieu to the U of C. We loved it here so much that even after

Richard"—the smallest pause—"left medical school we decided to stay."

A noise from a corner, and for the first time Beth noticed a child in stained overalls, who looked to be about two, standing in a playpen observing them. His nose needed wiping, and a rim of what looked like chocolate circled his mouth.

"Oh, this is my granddaughter. Say hello, Portia." Portia looked at Beth contemptuously and blew bubbles out of her mouth.

"No, no, Portia. Be nice. *Grand-mère* went to school with her mother."

Shoving several months of magazines off a rocking chair, Rebecca motioned for Beth to sit down. "How is your mother?" she said, dropping into an overstuffed chair whose gingham was fraying. "I know Laurie married her doctor, but what does she *do*? I suppose she's active in the hospital women's auxiliary," she went on, without waiting for an answer. "*I* substitute teach—nursery school—and I do research into how girls are forced into nurturing roles, don't I, Portia?"

Portia hefted a fire engine over the side of the playpen.

"No, no, Portia—girls *like* fire engines, remember? They're fun," said Rebecca, flinging her arms around in steering motions and yowling like a siren. Turning back to Beth, she said, "I understand you're a professor. *My* daughters—Phi Betas all, but don't dare tell them I told you—have gone into the fundamentals. A weaver. An apiarist. And one—Portia's mother—designs outdoor gear. She's meeting with her patent attorney today—about a backpack. That's why I have you, don't I, Portia? But let me get us some tea."

Over Beth's protests, Rebecca disappeared, leaving her alone with Portia, who eyed her suspiciously, then dropped a rubber football out of the playpen and stood staring at it.

Rebecca offered herb tea and ancient cookies out of a box. "Now, what is it you wanted to talk to me about? You said something about Jill."

As Beth explained her detective work into the past, she saw Rebecca's face tighten into obstinacy, and some instinct made her add, "My talk with Louise was very helpful."

Instantly Rebecca's expression changed to eagerness and curiosity. "You've seen Louise? You know she married Tony Valentine—that was a shocker. We'll never have to take up a collection for *them*. Tony's rich as Croesus—family money, you know. Not to mention what Louise must make from her practice. Richard and I have tried and tried to get together with them, but Louise always puts me off. I suppose her apartment is very grand," said Rebecca, giving Beth a sharp look. "Richard and I prefer *simplicité*—"

"About the murder," said Beth.

"I'm all ears," Rebecca said gaily.

"What do you remember about that afternoon?"

"That afternoon? Oh—the afternoon of the murder. Let's see."

A loud wail from Portia, who had emptied the playpen of its contents. Rebecca lumbered over, picked up a toy stethoscope, and gave it to Portia, who flung it out again. "Now, Portia— *Grand-mère* is too busy for games." Rebecca disappeared and returned with a box of Cheerios, which she hurled into the playpen. And Beth, watching Portia finger her nose and shove cereal into her mouth, couldn't help thinking of the Jellyby household.

"What do I especially remember?" said Rebecca. "I remember being very angry."

"Angry about what?"

"The sing. They were going on and on with that stupid *'Oh, you can't get to heaven'* song, and I have to tell you I found all that *'Lord don't want'* talk very offensive. You'd think they would have been more sensitive—not everyone believed in their old Lord Jesus Christ. I told Richard we had to get out of there, so we left the sing and went up to my room and talked. At least we were talking most of the time," giving Beth an arch look.

"Do you remember anything special?"

"Like what?"

"Did you hear anything? See anything?"

"Well, the door was closed so we couldn't really see anything. I remember at some point hearing the elevator creaking, but that's all, until . . . Richard and I were—uh—talking about separation of Church and State—and then we heard this horrible scream. We ran down the hall. Louise was standing outside her room, screaming and screaming, like a banshee. We went to look inside—then Mrs. P. and Maggie made us stay back."

"But you knew—what had happened?"

"Oh, we knew. We had a chance to see before they pushed us back. I remember thinking—oh, this will sound terrible. Maybe I shouldn't say it."

"Oh, go ahead, say it," said Beth.

"I suppose it can't matter now. I remember thinking—that's one of them gone. That sounds terrible, I know, but I couldn't help connecting Jill with the others."

"The others?"

"You know—her whole bunch. Your mother—well, she was really the best of them. But I didn't like her friends. They thought they were so great—called themselves the Fourth Floor Gang and didn't let anyone else into their exclusive little clique. Louise and Em—so standoffish. They thought they were better than everyone because *they* were premeds. And Carol—she was the worst. She was so mean to Dewey. She railroaded everyone into believing Dewey was the thief. *I* never believed it!".

"Why not?"

"Cob Conner's daughter? Raised in the lap of luxury? I have to tell you, Dewey didn't *need* to steal anything. Oh, it was so terrible when she left. I cried and cried. See that?" Rebecca pointed to the bookshelves, where amidst miniature glass animals a black Stork Club ashtray stood out like a monolith. "Dewey gave me that just before she left."

Beth said nothing, but she was surprised. She had thought the ashtray was among Dewey's most precious possessions.

"I loved Dewey," Rebecca said, "and it's so sad we're out of touch. I wrote and wrote, but she never answered. Even recently, I've tried to call her, but she has an unlisted number— and who knows where she lives now? I blame Carol. If it weren't for her, I'd still be friends with Dewey. We'd be seeing her when Richard and I go to New York for my meetings—I'm sure she'd ask us to stay with her, and hotels are so expensive. Oh, I could kill Carol—"

"What about the other Gang member?"

"Who's that?"

"Jill. What did you think of Jill?"

Rebecca gave Beth a what-I-could-tell-you look. "Jill?" she said. "A real actress."

"An actress?"

"Always pretending to be Miss Femme Fatale."

"But wasn't Jill—"

"Popular with the boys? Yes—but she always had to make herself seem even more popular. I overheard a phone call once, when I was ironing. Jill used to pay one of the maids to do *her* ironing. Anyway, I heard Jill on the phone—putting on her usual act. It was a long-distance call."

"How did you know it was long distance?"

"When Jill didn't answer her buzz right away, I picked up the phone, and the operator said a long-distance call from—I think Jill's hometown. Then Jill came in, and when she saw me she gave me an absolutely filthy look—and just *snatched* the phone out of my hand. That's what I mean about that Gang—so rude. I was only trying to help—so she wouldn't miss her call.

"Anyway, she sat on the floor, crouched away from me—but I could tell she was talking to a boy. She was trying to make him jealous. Told him she'd been out the night before, was going out that night, and had a date for the next night. I happened to know she wasn't going anywhere that night—she was just putting on an act to drive one more boy wild. So—I suppose you could say Jill was shrewd. And kind of good-looking—I'll give her that."

"Kind of good-looking? Who's that?" In came a stocky man whose deep frown wrinkles gave him a look of permanent anger. "Hi," he said. "I'm Richie Rice. So you're Laurie's daughter. I remember how pretty she was."

"You can't possibly remember Laurie that well," said Rebecca. "You hardly knew her. And to answer your question, *Richard*, we've been talking about Jill Jansen."

"Jill? And you said she was *kind of* good-looking! My God, Jill was gorgeous. A Marilyn Monroe before anyone had heard of Marilyn Monroe."

"Speak for yourself, Richard. I thought she was overripe, cheap-looking—and a very jealous individual. Don't make that face at me, Richard. She *was*. She was jealous of the way we had our whole life planned out. You in medical school while I worked, then a practice on North Michigan Avenue, then children—"

"This is ridiculous, Rebecca. How many times did I tell you

that Jill wasn't interested in our plans? You're acting dumb—the way you did then."

"Well, I like that! When did I act dumb?"

Beth rocked back and forth nervously. They seemed to have forgotten she was there.

"You know," said Richie, "that afternoon when Jill was— remember? I walked out on you." And that, Beth thought, shoots two more alibis.

"I'd forgotten," said Rebecca. She looked at Beth. "Richard and I did have a little tiff. He left—but not for long. And when he came back, I told him Jill had gotten just what she wanted," said Rebecca, and Richie asked what she meant. "I'll tell you exactly. When Jill threw you over, you went into a funk. Because of Jill, you stopped studying—she made you think studying didn't matter. She even made you stop caring about medical school. All right—you got in. But I was right, wasn't I?"

No answer. Richie had gone over to Portia. He sat on the floor, leaning against the wall, making funny faces that had Portia giggling.

"All right, he won't say. But if it hadn't been for Jill," said Rebecca, "Richard would never have dropped out of medical school after one year."

"I didn't drop out," said Richie. "I flunked."

"That's right—flunked. I helped you study for tests. I looked through your microscope and did your drawings. And you still flunked. *I* would have passed," said Rebecca. "So now you're a pharmacist, but you could still be successful. You could have your own pharmacy. Yes, you could, Richard, if you joined organizations, if you learned how to network."

Richie made more faces at Portia, faces he probably wanted to make at Rebecca, Beth thought. Poor Richie. At least Mrs. Jellyby ignored her husband.

For some time it had been obvious that Portia's diaper needed changing. "For chrissake, Richard," said Rebecca. "Will you take that child—now!"

Gently Richie lifted Portia from the playpen and left the room.

"That reminds me," said Rebecca. "I knew there was something else about that afternoon."

"What's that?" said Beth, hardly caring what Rebecca might reveal next.

"The *odeur* of *parfum*," said Rebecca. "The hall absolutely *stank* of Tabu."

CHAPTER THIRTY-FOUR

The same day—evening

If she drove down to campus, Beth thought, she would find the Gang at Dall. They'd be at breakfast, fighting over whose toast was coming around. No—it would be night. She would take the stairs to Four, pass Dewey's room, see Rebecca and Lana there, trying on clothes. She'd wave, go on to Laurie's room—and find the Gang.

They would say hi, as Beth jumped on the bunk next to Laurie, and resume their discussion. Carol would be saying she absolutely positively could not take Dewey one more day. Em would tell Carol she was lucky not to have real problems—like the hideous discrimination against women who applied to med school. It was so hopeless, she would say. Louise would tell Em that they could do it—they just had to be *better* than the men. Then Jill, the delectable Jill, would say they were putting her to sleep, they should shove the problems to the back burner and— "Let's talk about doing it!"

"Jill, you have to be careful," Beth would say. "Careful about what?" Jill would laugh. "Come on, Beth, tell me!"

How would she answer Jill? Beth wondered. She didn't know. But somehow she would find a way to prevent—*bang!*

Outside her office someone slammed a door—and Jill was dead, long ago.

So why this sense of urgency, this feeling she had to find Jill's murderer *now?* Someone else was in danger. She felt it. She knew it. But who? And who should this unknown victim be afraid of?

Beth rifled through the mess on her desk, found her notebook, and added Rebecca and Richie-Richard to her list of suspects. After yesterday, she had to include them. She looked over her list: *Abe* jumped out at her. What if it was Abe? The thought that the murderer could have been Link's father made her feel sick. If she could just talk to Link—but that was impossible. Not the way things were between them. And the whole thing seemed absurd now—a minor mishap inflated to a major disaster. Who? Who? That was what mattered.

Outside, she could hear the janitor emptying wastebaskets. Getting late, and she had been so taken up with the murder that, except for teaching one class, she hadn't accomplished a thing today. Her desk was piled with letters to answer, recommendations to write, papers to grade. Maybe if she turned her mind to something else, her subconscious would take over. She picked up the first paper, an analysis of Browning's *Andrea del Sarto.* *"Ah, but a man's reach should exceed his grasp,"* the student quoted, and went on to interpret the poem as inspirational material for a basketball coach! Knowing she would regret it, Beth shoved the paper to the bottom of the pile, took up the next, and—the phone.

"Found you!" said Link. "I tried you at home. Hope it's okay I called the office."

"Perfectly. I'd just been thinking"—about you, she started to say, then thought better of it.

"Look, Beth, my last visit was a fiasco. I admit it." Beth said she had forgotten it entirely. "Then why didn't you answer my letter?" he asked.

Beth looked at the stack of letters—Link's on top. "I meant to, Link. I've been involved in—"

"You're still angry."

"I'm not. Really, I'm not. What's a panel discussion, anyway? A bunch of egos vying for attention."

"No, it was important. I see that now."

"Honest, it doesn't matter," and it didn't, she thought. What mattered was finding Jill's murderer.

"Beth—I'm coming to Chicago." She asked when, and he said a month or so, he'd check the date. "I want to see you, make it up to you. Start over."

"There's nothing to make up—is that why you're coming?"

"Actually, I have a signing," he said, sounding apprehensive.

Famous writer waiting for the hit? Did he think she would compare a signing with a panel? She wasn't in the mood. "That's fine," said Beth. "We'll find a time to get together."

"You're sure you're not angry?"

"Positive." This was perfect. She would much rather wait until Link was in Chicago to talk about his father. She picked up the notebook and drew a circle around Abe's name.

"Then why do you sound so strange?"

"I do?"

"Yes—why?"

"I guess because I've been involved—"

"Involved? With who?"

"Link, I've got another murder case."

"Another? What do you do—attract bodies?" he said, sounding amused, more like himself.

"I'm beginning to think so. And for what? I can't make

anything out of this one. I'm sitting here looking at my notes, and I haven't the faintest idea where I'm going."

"Want to tell me about it? I wasn't so bad in Hawaii."

"This is different." If he only knew how different. Different why? he asked. "A couple things." For one, said a voice in her mind, your father is a suspect. Aloud she said, "For one, the murder was years ago."

"How many years? . . . My God," he said when she told him. "That is a long time. Well—what have you got?"

How to begin? She wanted to dodge any mention of his father. "It started"—she took a breath—"at the University of Chicago."

"The U of C! That's where my father—"

"Let me tell you about it," Beth rushed in.

"So tell." He listened while she outlined the story, omitting the romance between her mother and Abe, ending with her visits to Louise and Rebecca. "See my problem? Nothing but suspects. And it gets worse. Louise and Rebecca aren't the only ones who gave false alibis."

"Who else?" She was silent, wishing she had never started down this path. "Come on, Beth. Who else?"

"My mother."

"Your mother! You think your mother—"

"No, no—I'm not saying my mother did it. She could never—"

"Then what?"

"She covered up for her hot and heavy boyfriend," and Beth filled him in on that part of the story.

"Hmm. Interesting case. You do have a load of suspects. When I'm in Chicago, we'll go over them. But you're holding off, Beth."

What did he mean? He couldn't know about Laurie and Abe. "Holding off?"

"I know you have an assignment for me. What is it?"

He was being so nice. Should she tell him about Abe now?

"Beth—are you there?"

"I'm here."

"What's going on? The assignment can't be that bad."

His antennae had picked up something. Better tell him. Later, if he found out she had waited, he would be furious. Oh, hell, get it over with. "Remember I said there were a couple reasons this case is different?"

"What's the other one?"

"My mother's hot and heavy boyfriend was—" The door opened, and the janitor came in. "Could you come back? I'll be out soon. Sorry, Link, that was—"

"The janitor. So tell me already."

"My mother's hot and heavy boyfriend was—just a minute." Her *Andrea del Sarto* student had strolled in, asking for his grade. She told him she hadn't read his paper yet.

"Is there some conspiracy," said Link, "to prevent you from finishing your sentence?"

"My mother's hot and heavy boyfriend was"—she told him the name.

"Abe Low—what Abe Lowenstein? You mean—He's never mentioned a Laurie or a—Hey, are you saying my father is a murderer?"

CHAPTER THIRTY-FIVE

Mid-September

A couple of weeks passed before Beth found the time for her next visit.

"Coffee?" Carol said, then looked at her watch. "It's after eleven! Let's have Bloody Marys," she said with a mischievous grin. That was how she must have looked when she was coaxing Laurie to cut class.

Her expression, that is. Beth's picture of a saddle-shoed teenager, bangs flying as she jitterbugged, had been revised. She hadn't expected Carol to be so petite—or so stylish. Her improbably jet black hair tied back in a smooth chignon, she was wearing a long red and yellow tie-dyed dress that would have been a disaster on a figure with the smallest outlaw roll of fat.

"Come out while I make them," and Beth followed her into the kitchen.

A strange kitchen, Beth thought, witty with its framed *New Yorker* covers, but otherwise oddly uncluttered. Not even a note on the refrigerator door.

"I miss Laurie," Carol said, as she sliced a lime. "Whenever I called her, she put me off. So—I stopped trying."

"She's very busy with—"

"I know she's busy, but she must have *some* time. "Oh, well." She opened a cupboard filled with liquor bottles.

"That's a lot," said Beth, as Carol poured vodka recklessly.

"Not really. The tomato juice dilutes it."

The orderliness carried over into the living room. On the sofa, black and white pillows balanced each other exactly. On the shelves, the books seemed to be organized by color, rather than author. Artfully arranged on the mantel was a collection of gold objects, among them a miniature Chrysler Building, which Beth went over to examine.

"Like it?" said Carol. "I picked it up in New York. My work takes me there a lot. I'm an interior decorator," she said. "I help Chicago's North Shore achieve the Eastern Yankee look. I am becoming slightly sick of Chippendale."

She set the tray down so it was on a precise diagonal with a stack of art books, and they seated themselves on the sofa.

Carol raised her glass. "Let's see. We need a U of Chicagoish toast. Define your terms? Everything is relative? I know—ontogeny recapitulates phylogeny—and here's to the U of C!"

They clinked glasses, Carol downing almost half her drink. "So," she said, "how in the world will you ever find out who the father was?"

"What father?" said Beth, caught short by the question.

"The father of Jill's baby, of course. Isn't that why you're here?"

"That and other things," Beth said, surprised that word of her search had preceded her. "But as long as you mention it, do you have any ideas?"

"Me! I don't know. Tony, I suppose—but it could have been almost anyone. There was a slew of candidates." She sighed.

"And then came the hideous day when one of them decided against marriage."

"Tell me about that day," said Beth.

"That day?" Carol settled back, looking thoughtful. "I remember waking up feeling absolutely wonderful. I could see sunlight pouring all over the room—because the shade was *up*," she said, "not like when Dewey was there. And the room looked wonderful, everything neat and orderly, because I'd fixed it up to impress my date—*and* because Dewey's crud wasn't all over the floor."

"Mother mentioned that Dewey was a difficult roommate."

"Difficult! Rooming with her was sheer misery." She took a long drink. "The payoff came when Dewey, who had been lifting stuff from all over the dorm, started stealing from *me*." Carol still seemed indignant at the memory. " 'When neither their property nor their honour is touched, the majority of women live content.' That's Machiavelli, except I changed *men* to *women*—and I was far from content *before* Dewey stole my property." She took another long drink and emptied the glass.

"But sometimes, sometimes, I feel . . . not guilty exactly. It's just that I wish I hadn't been so hard on Dewey."

The question popped out of Beth almost reflexively. "Do you think you feel guilty because Dewey might not have been the thief?" She watched Carol's face turn red and redder. Why did I say that?

Carol sat perfectly still, and silent—angrily silent. "I didn't mean—" Beth started.

"Dewey definitely," Carol broke in, her voice icy, "very definitely, was the thief." Then with a bewildering change of mood she gave Beth her appealing grin. "I'm being ridiculous. Why should I be defensive?" She jumped up. "It's such a wonderful day. Let's go out on the terrace." She put glasses and coasters on the tray, wiped invisible rings off the table. "An-other drink? You're hardly into that one. I'll make us a fresh one."

When Beth refused, she said, "Oh, come on. How often do we have days like this, beautiful days when we can go out in the sun and celebrate being alive—and drink Bloody Marys just for the hell of it?"

Beth gave in, thinking she'd nurse her drink.

"Go on," said Carol, opening a French window. "I'll just be a minute."

The flagstoned terrace overlooked a sweeping lawn, punc-tuated with flower beds as weed-free and geometric as the Lux-embourg Gardens. Beth was trying to remember how to say "Keep off the grass" in French when Carol returned with drinks and a telephone.

"I think I need to explain," she said. "First of all, Dewey *was* the thief. Don't have any doubts about *that*. But when I found out her parents were getting a divorce, I did feel I might have been too hard on Dewey. It couldn't have been much fun for her at home. Her father was a famous columnist—he was also a well-known bastard. Always getting sued for libel. But *yes*," she said, "or no—there was no doubt that Dewey was the thief and that rooming with her was gruesome."

"Mother never mentioned the divorce."

"I may not have told her. I didn't know myself until after she left, read it in a gossip column, probably, or—" The phone was ringing.

Carol answered and, when she recognized the voice, made a face. "You want to use the whatnot? . . . "Yes. Yes, I know it was your grandmother's—and it is a beautiful piece"—another face. "But in the foyer?"

Shouting at the other end.

"I see. I see. I know"—brightly. "What about the butler's pantry?" Her voice became enthusiastic. "Your Staffordshire! We can fill it with your collection. I can just see the dogs—yes, darling, you *do* have wonderful ideas. Yes, tomorrow at ten. Eleven? All right. I have the swatches for the dining room. Oh, and *good* idea!"

Carol put down the phone and sighed. "Thank God that's over, but at least"—the grin—"she thinks she's running the show. Where were we?"

"I wanted to ask you about that day—before the Open House."

"Another?" Carol pointed at Beth's drink. Beth shook her head, surprised to see she'd almost finished it. "Well, I'm going to," said Carol.

"Before the Open House? I don't remember much. I know the Gang was downstairs. And I vaguely remember a discussion about abortion and something going on with Louise and a picture. That's about all."

"How about the Open House? Any memories?"

"Some. I was with the boyfriend I mentioned, a law student—who was always saying he made wonderful pineapple upside-down cake. Funny, I can't remember his name, but I do remember that. We were at the sing, and he got bored or something. So he jumped up, without even an apology, and went into Great Neck and started talking with one of the older girls—a sexy assistant head. I'll show him, I thought, so I left and went out in the quad. I stayed there quite a while."

"How long?" Beth asked lazily. She wondered when Carol would start showing the effect of all the drinks.

"Oh, I don't know. Long enough to be sure that he would feel plenty worried. When I did go back, he was all apologies.

Where had I been? He was desolate, he'd make me a pineapple upside-down cake, and then—screaming, terrible, terrible screaming. It was awful," she said, putting her feet on the wrought-iron table.

Let's see, Beth thought. *Now what do I ask?* Then it came to her—"What did you think of Jill?"

"Jill? Nice enough, but thoroughly boy crazy. I'll tell you something funny. One day I found her in the bathroom." Carol giggled. "She was rubbing cream on her boobs—to make them bigger, she said. Some people are never satisfied." Carol looked down at herself and shook her head. "The thing is, Jill loved attracting boys. She loved the effect she had on them." She grinned at Beth.

The grin seemed to disengage itself from Carol and float between them—like the Cheshire cat, Beth thought. "Anything else you think I should know?" she asked woozily.

"What else could there be?" said Carol, stretching out her arms. The sun glanced off her gold bracelets.

CHAPTER THIRTY-SIX

How she had made it through the rest of the day, submerged in a Bloody Mary haze, Beth did not know. When at last she fell into bed, too tired to sleep, she picked up Dickens.

So many domiciles in *Bleak House,* she thought again, all reflecting the people who lived there. Bleak House itself, anything but bleak, reflected the domestic bent of the orphan Esther Summerson. Esther, who sets herself to learn the contents of each cupboard and then apologizes, calling herself "a methodical old-maidish sort of . . . person." Methodical indeed. A regular nineteenth-century Martha Stewart—or a Carol. Carol's house shouted her obsession with order.

Other than discovering that she could have murdered Jill— *had* she been out in the quad?—what else had she learned about Carol? A manipulator, Beth decided, remembering how Carol had handled the call from her client.

The phone sounded through the quiet like an alarm. Beth reached for the receiver; *Bleak House* slipped out of her hands and crashed to the floor. When she finally disentangled book, phone, and cord, she learned the caller was Link, who wanted to know what the hell she was doing.

Reading *Bleak House,* she told him. She certainly read boisterously, he said, but the novel did pack plenty of power. "*Bleak House* is loaded with potential for a miniseries."

"Somehow," said Beth, "I don't see the Court of Chancery beating out *Monday Night Football*."

"Forget Chancery. Every first-year law student knows about it—and no one else cares. The case drags on and on and—"

"Wasn't that Dickens's point?"

"Sure, but it's not as if he's writing Turow-type courtroom scenes."

"So why a miniseries?"

"Easy. You play the Dedlocks to the hilt—they're perfect miniseries material. Titled people—living high. London town house. Country mansion *with* a Ghost Walk. You center the script around Lady Dedlock. She has everything: Money. Glamour. Arrogance. Like that Wallace Irwin poem—'Of all the fish that swim or swish/ In ocean's deep autocracy,/ There's none possess such haughtiness/ As the codfish aristocracy.' Isn't that Lady D.? She's so wonderfully snooty."

"You're being unfair," said Beth.

"She's not snooty?"

"She acts haughty, of course, but that's what it is—acting. She uses a mask of haughtiness to hold people at bay because she's terrified that someone will discover her secret."

"Yeah! Her mysterious past. The script could make a big deal out of her secret."

"It is a big deal! The disgrace is so terrible—" She broke off, thinking how Jill's disgrace paralleled Lady Dedlock's.

"Hey, don't take it personally—it's fiction."

"I'm not. It's just that I keep being reminded that a secret from the past can—"

"Can what?"

"Hold someone—everyone—prisoner forever."

"Now I know why you're in a strange mood. You're thinking about your latest case. How's the detecting?"

"Terrible. Too many suspects."

"I can't wait to help you narrow them down. Beth—I'll be in Chicago tomorrow for a few days. I could be persuaded to stretch it to a week."

"Your signing?"

"Signings, plural now—and *Oprah*."

"*Oprah?* Is your new book about dysfunctional families?"

"Yeah, families. Listen, Beth. About my father. He didn't do it."

"You seem so certain."

"I am. He told me he didn't—and I believe him. Don't you?"

Why should I? she thought, after the way he treated my mother. "We'll talk about it when you get here," she said.

"Let's talk now."

"Not now. I want to wait till you're here so we can really talk. Tell me about *Oprah*."

"What do you mean—really talk?"

"You know—*tête-à-tête*. Tell me about *Oprah*."

"Oh, if you're going to resort to French. Okay—*Oprah*. I'm going to be on with two sisters who traded lives."

"Marvelous! What kind of lives?"

Conventional, he told her, rags and happiness for one, riches and misery for the other—and they joked about the show. But after the conversation ended, Beth found she was so unnerved by his assumption of his father's innocence—how was she going to tell him he needed proof?—that she gave up on sleep and returned to *Bleak House*.

Poor Lady Dedlock, Beth thought. All the signs are against her. Outside, the Ghost's footsteps sound on the terrace—foreboding the disgrace that is coming to Chesney Wold. Inside, the cold sunshine casts a menacing light on Lady Dedlock's portrait.

Worse, the conniving Tulkinghorn is closing in. Earlier, the sight of someone's handwriting had so agitated Lady Dedlock that she nearly fainted. Now Tulkinghorn delights in telling her that the person whose writing she recognized is dead—took poison. And now, though Tulkinghorn professes the matter is ended, my Lady watches him mistrustfully, wondering how much he knows.

Yes, Beth wanted to tell her. You *should* fear Tulkinghorn! Look at his home to learn what he is—a house rented out in sets of chambers, where "lawyers lie like maggots in nuts."

Beth paused. She knew maggots were something small and disgusting, but what exactly? She crawled out of bed. *Maggot*, said the dictionary, "a legless grub." And what was a grub? As a noun, "an insect larva." Beth preferred the verb—"to dig, work, or search in the dirt; to be occupied meanly"—as horribly suited to Tulkinghorn, who, in his maggoty way, loves to dig up the secrets of his aristocratic clients—and confront them when he can do the most harm.

Tulk the Torturer. Tomorrow, Beth thought, she would be seeing Em—also a lawyer. Would she find any resemblance to Tulkinghorn?

Beth slept fitfully, dreaming that Tulkinghorn was outside her window, pacing the Ghost Walk. Then he stepped through the window, stretched a hand out of his black sleeve—and pointed a bony finger at her. "Divulge Carol's secret," he said, "or I shall ring the alarm and rouse the house!" Beth cowered, tried to scream—then sat up, wide awake.

But how do I know, she thought, what Carol was drinking? After the first, I never saw her making drinks. She could have poured straight tomato juice for herself—and flooded my second drink with vodka!

CHAPTER THIRTY-SEVEN

Late September

A far cry from the wormy Tulkinghorn school of architecture, Em's office was in a soaring Chicago building that flaunted three sets of elevators, each a new phase upward to Em's high floor. Yes, said an ultrasmart receptionist. Professor Austin was expected. Aware of a hush, as of high-priced work in progress, Beth followed the receptionist past vast conference rooms and bays of earphoned secretaries, typing away on PC's, to a corner office.

For a moment Beth felt as if she had stepped inside the skyline, that if she reached out she could touch the Sears Tower. Then her eyes moved from the windows to a sleek desk where a woman sat talking on the phone. She smiled and indicated that Beth should sit down.

Beth had prepared herself for another age warp, but Em looked remarkably young. News-anchor young, Beth decided. Television hair, blond as her desk, cut short to curve around her face. Television eyes—a lurid contact-lens blue. Television clothes—bright jacket, dark skirt, and around her neck one heavy piece of modern jewelry, which she played with as she talked. "We're prepared to consider a settlement," Em was say-

ing. Beth turned her eyes away, trying to ignore the conversation.

Someone had once told Beth that personal-injury lawyers
made more money than God. Em's office proved the point.
Forties furniture—not repro—the real thing that was commanding high prices at auctions. Rich old Oriental rugs with Art
Deco designs. A door left ajar revealed the marble and frosted
glass of a private bath. Lined up on tall shelves was the founda-
tion for all this opulence—big leather-bound law reports marked
CASES WON. She glanced at the bindings: *Jones* v. *Allstate. Smith*
v. *Lakeside Nursing Home.*

She felt Em watching her, so she looked away at the paintings that covered the walls. A Frankenthaler, a Hartigan, and—
whose was that?—the high-stepping strutter, one booted leg
kicking the air.

"Of course we are always ready to go to trial." Em's voice,
modulated, unrelenting, broke into her thoughts. "We're well-
prepared and looking forward to trying the case." Em caught
Beth's eye, winked, and said, "Our client will be very appealing
to the jury." She ended the call, and rose. "I'm Em Greenberg."
She gripped Beth's hand firmly.

After a few minutes of conversation, Em told Beth she had
noticed her interest in the paintings. "Let me give you a tour,"
she said, taking Beth's arm. "That's a Helen Frankenthaler.
That's a Grace Hartigan." Beth asked about the strutter. "Mir-
iam Shapiro. Isn't it wonderful?" Em frowned. "Crooked," she
said, reaching up. As she straightened the painting, a white
paper dropped from behind it and fell to the carpet. Beth bent to
pick it up, saw the words *CLIENT COMPLAINT* before Em
snatched the paper from her hand.

Mumbling she had forgotten it, Em threw the paper on her

desk and resumed the tour. "Sonia Delaunay. Lee Krasner. Jeanette Sloan."

"Are they all by women?" said Beth.

"Yes," said Em. "I swore I would make it big and that when I did I would focus on women. We still have a fight ahead of us," she said, her eyes on the paintings. "Look at the movies—women are still sex objects. Why? Because men want it that way. Look at the abortion clinics. Blockades. Shootings. Engineered by men. We're still under scrotal control."

"Thank God they haven't bombed them yet," said Beth.

"The scrota? Might be a good idea."

"I meant the clinics," said Beth.

"I know, I know," and Em roared with laughter, just as she must have, Beth thought, in the old days with the Gang.

Em stopped laughing and gave Beth a searching look. "So you're Laurie's daughter. Yes, I see her in you—you have her determination. How is Laurie? Strange we never get together. But I think about her, I really do. What's she doing?"

Beth started to answer, but Em was too fast for her.

"Laurie must have done something. Well, obviously, she produced you. I understand you're a professor—and a sometime detective. But—you know what I mean. I always thought Laurie's boyfriend was holding her back, making her think she was dumb. What was his name—Abe something?" She interrupted herself and strode to the ringing phone.

"What is it? . . . No, I do not want to talk to him. . . . Tell them to take whatever action they want, and I'll take whatever action *I* want. And they'll be sorry when I do. Got that? Now, hold the rest of my calls.

"What were we talking about? Oh—abortion clinics. How different life would have been—life. Jill would still be here." She grinned. "You're surprised I mentioned Jill. Louise told me you're investigating her murder. I admire you for that. I always thought it shouldn't have been left an open case."

"I agree"—Beth seized her chance—"and that's exactly why I wanted to see you."

"I'd love to help," said Em. "But how?"

"I have a few questions—maybe you can help me put the puzzle together."

"What kind of questions?" Said nonchalantly, but Em's eyes were wary.

"Oh—like, what did you think of Jill?" Em asked what she meant, and Beth said, "Just that. What did you think of her?"

"I don't see how my opinion of Jill fits with—Let's sit down."

They sat opposite each other in Knoll chairs, Em upright, as if prepared for an inquisition.

"What did I think of Jill?" Em stared out the windows. "Mischievous. Not brilliant, but bright—well, everyone was that. And beautiful," she said, turning back to Beth. "So beautiful. It wasn't fair for one person to be so gorgeous. You should have seen Jill on a party night. Party night, hell. You should have seen her in a T-shirt."

Fending off a recitation of outfits, Beth asked, "Do you know if anything had been worrying Jill just before—"

"Before she was murdered? Well, obviously that she was pregnant. And if you think that wasn't a worry, read Dreiser, or see *A Place in the Sun*. Worry—it was a catastrophe!" She paused then, deliberating. "There *was* something else."

"Something else?"

"Something else worrying her—if you're interested."

"I'm interested in everything," said Beth.

"Spoken like a true Sherlock. All right, I'm not *sure* it was worrying her, but she was on the outs with Louise—and they had been so close."

"I thought they made up," said Beth.

"Did Louise tell you that?" She shrugged. "Then I suppose it must be true."

"Do you remember the afternoon of the murder?"

"Very well. I was going to invite someone to the Open House, but I'd just broken up with—it doesn't matter. So I went down to the sing. It was hideous."

"Hideous?"

Em laughed. "Maybe *depressing* is a better word. It was what they were singing."

Beth waited, wondering if she was going to hear another denunciation of "Can't Get to Heaven."

"They were singing 'Man Without a Woman,' and when they got to the chorus, they just *threw* themselves into it. Jerks. They didn't even understand what they were saying. *'If there's one thing worse, in this universe'* "—Em broke out in raucous voice—" *'It's a woman without a maan.'* " Behind her the gallery of women painters seemed to echo her indignation.

"And what happened then?" Beth said.

"After two more choruses of *'a woman without a maaan,'* I'd had it. I ran outside."

"Did you see anyone?"

"Aha! Sherlock again. Is there some confirmation of my movements during the time in question? Of course I saw someone. You were always seeing someone in the dorm quadrangle, so I must have—I don't remember who. I sat on the steps—"

"Did you see Carol?"

She hesitated. "I don't think so."

"You're sure?"

"Yes—I would have remembered Carol. Does it matter?"

"No," said Beth. "Just a thought. You were on the steps?"

"Yes, I sat there, smoking, listening, worrying. The windows were open and I could hear the singing so clearly. They'd switched to 'Can't Get to Heaven.' "

Beth watched Em play with her jewelry. "You were worried about something?"

"About med school, as usual. It turned out I didn't need to worry. I got in. Louise and I both got in." She looked at Beth closely. "Then why am I a lawyer? I know you think it's strange. I suppose it is. I'd only been in med school a short time. I was in the OR. They were letting us watch them work on a child—she'd been hit by a truck. I watched them sew up her arm, and I passed out cold. You can imagine how my jolly male classmates sniped at me after that."

"Was that why—"

"Why I left? My sexist classmates? Don't you believe it! I gave it right back to them. That wasn't the problem. My squeamishness—it got worse. So—I finished out the year and switched to law school. Why PI? Because someone else does the patching up, and I can make sure people who are injured get a full measure of justice from the people who hurt them."

Sounds good, Beth thought. But she must like the money. "And—back to that afternoon?"

"I was out there, smoking, worrying—and then all hell broke loose. Screaming. Sirens. Police. I ran back in, pushed my way to the center of all the racket. Louise was outside her room, crying, screaming, flailing her arms. I could see blood, blood everywhere. It was—" She broke off.

"You said something about Jill before," Beth said gently.

"What was that?" Em wiped away a tear.

"That she was mischievous. I wondered what you meant."

"You know, that's funny. I think I was connecting with a

memory of Jill that same afternoon—before the Open House. We were all downstairs—the whole Gang—in Oyster Bay. Louise was standing on the ottoman, reaching up—she was going to straighten a picture. And I was telling Jill about a doctor for—" She hesitated.

"An abortion?" said Beth.

"You know about that? That's right. But Jill didn't seem the least bit interested in what I was saying. She just kept watching Louise. She had the strangest smile on her face—a mischievous smile, as if she were playing a trick." The phone rang. "Now what?" Em went to her desk.

"He says it's a matter of life and death? Just a minute." She turned to Beth. "Sorry I have to cut this short. Call me—we'll have lunch."

As Beth went out the door, she heard Em say, "Put him through, but goddammit, it better be life and death—or it might be *his* death."

She was hardly a Tulkinghorn, Beth thought, as she moved downward from one elevator to the next. Tulk the Torturer was far smoother. Yet, yet—there was something. Like Tulk, Em gave the feeling she was watching you closely, judging your reactions. Was she, too, determining when would be the right time to close in?

CHAPTER THIRTY-EIGHT

Early October

Just as she stepped out of the shower, Beth's bell rang. "It's Link," the speaker announced. She threw on a robe—the *yukata* she had bought in Hawaii—ran barefoot to the door, and stood listening to him run up the stairs. When he dashed around the corner, she felt a tug of delight—she always forgot how good-looking he was, how he gave off New York energy.

"Thought you were coming tomorrow," she mumbled against his lips.

"Couldn't wait that long to see you," he mumbled back. A long pause. "Aren't you going to invite me in?"

A door clicked—a ray of light extended across the hall carpet.

"What's that?" said Link.

"Retired prof," she whispered.

"Prof of what?"

"Philosophy."

"Oh, in that case"—another long kiss.

"In that case what?" she murmured.

"Philosophy, you said. Don't want the professor to think we have a platonic relationship."

What was she doing? she asked herself as they went inside. How could she have allowed herself to fall into his arms?

"Love that robe," he said.

She looked down, saw her *yukata* had fallen open. "I meant to put on a business suit"—hurriedly retying the robe.

"This"—stroking a sleeve—"makes a much better fashion statement. Makes me think of Hawaii." Arm around her, Link moved to the sofa and looked startled when she slipped away and sat in a chair.

"Did you have a good flight?" she asked, drawing another startled look.

"I sense a definite coolness," said Link. "It's last time, isn't it?"

She nodded.

So they went over Link's last trip to Chicago, and he said it wasn't that he objected to her being on a panel. It was that the panel cut into the little time they had together. How dare he say that, Beth asked, when the topic was so urgent?

"What's urgent about the scandalous condition of women in the nineteenth-century novel? Weren't you forgetting your twentieth-century sisters? What would Gloria Steinem say?"

"If she's been reading Dickens, she'd say we can trace the condition of our twentieth-century sisters right back to the nineteenth century. Look at the way Dickens fawns over Esther because she's so domestic. Look at the trouble Dickens cooks up for—"

"Did Dickens cook?"

He was laughing now, and she couldn't help laughing, too. "The real question," she said, "is—did Lady Dedlock cook? It's clear Dickens has it in for her—obviously because she never sees the inside of a kitchen."

"Must we talk about Lady Dedlock?"

"Of course not. We can talk about the panel you wanted me to abandon."

"What I wanted was to spend the afternoon with you."

Silence. Through the open window, she could hear a child crying, a mother calling.

"By the way," she said, "when's *Oprah?*"

"We're taping tomorrow morning."

"That's when I'm going to the U of C."

"Can't you put it off? I want to go with you—and I can't change *Oprah.*" He caught her ironic smile. "Okay, okay, I get the point." He moved to the chair, took her hands in his. "Forgive me? I promise to call my next book *Revenge of the Nineteenth-Century Women.*" He leaned forward, looking at her in a way that made her close her eyes.

"Now what?" said Link, when she drew away.

"We have to talk."

"About what?" he said, kissing her.

"Your father," she murmured, wondering if his father had been as attractive as Link, "and Jill's murder."

"Oh, that," he said. He returned to the sofa. "I told you. He didn't do it."

Oh didn't he? Beth thought. The old lecher—he deserted my mother to neck with Jill. "Can he prove it?" she said. "He can't be counting on his alibi."

"You know about that?"

"That my mother covered for him? Yes."

"All right. Dad admits his alibi was phony. But he didn't murder anyone."

"Why are you so certain?"

"He gave me his word of honor."

The word of a deceitful lecher—what was that worth?

"Okay," she said, "we'll set the murder aside. Could he have been the father of Jill's baby?"

"Absolutely not." Beth asked how Link knew that. "I asked," he told her. " 'Dad,' I said, 'did you ever have sex with Jill?' He laughed so hard I had to stall off a call from one of his patients."

"What was funny?"

"*Have sex*—he thought the expression was hilarious."

"Well, did he?"

"What? Have sex with her? No." He left the sofa, pulled an ottoman in front of her chair, and put her bare feet in his lap. "Let's have sex, Beth. Or we could make love," he said playing with her toes.

She longed to say yes. Had his father had the same effect on her mother? No wonder Laurie had been so attracted to Abe. "And you really think they—he—didn't?" she asked regretfully, tucking her feet under her.

"Let's get off my father," said Link. "Let's get off fathers in general. Tell me about the Dall girls. Do they have alibis?"

"No," said Beth, and she told him about her visits. "So you see," she finished, "no one has an alibi. Not Rebecca. Not Em. Not Carol. Not Louise."

"And not your mother."

"Why bring my mother in?"

"If Dad loses his alibi, she loses hers."

He said it lightly, but that didn't matter. She was furious. "You think my mother could have committed murder?"

"That's what you think about my father"—not so lightly now.

"If you knew my mother, you'd see how absurd—"

"And if you knew my father—"

She glared, waiting for his next outrageous accusation against her mother.

"I guess," he said, "this means you don't want me to stay over?"

"Good guess," she said, and collapsed in laughter.

"That's better," Link said, grinning. "One more thing. I insist on going with you to the U of C. Can't you wait until afternoon?"

"I suppose so—but why?"

"There could be a murderer running around loose on the campus."

"Really! Who is this loose murderer? A disgruntled student?"

"Someone who doesn't appreciate your research into Dall history."

"Don't worry. If the murderer appears, I'll outrun him—or seek refuge in Rockefeller Chapel." Seeing that Link was about to protest—"You're being silly," she said. "No one cares about Jill's murder anymore."

"You care. You can't be sure no one else does. And too many people know what you're doing. Beth, call me a sexist—"

"Sexist!"

"—but *please* wait for me."

"Seriously?"

"Seriously."

So she agreed to wait.

"Great," he said. "Right after my signing we'll go out there and detect." He drew her to her feet. "It'll be like Hawaii," he said, putting an arm around her. "Remember?"

She linked an arm around him and walked him to the door.

"Think of Hawaii," he said, and kissed her. Across the hall, the door clicked open. "You, too," he said toward the door. "Think of Hawaii," and he ran down the stairs.

Beth rushed to the window. In the street, children were playing. At the curb, a limousine waited. She saw Link start to get into the limo, pause, and look up. Damn. He sees me.

"Tomorrow at three o'clock," he called. "Water Tower Books. Don't be late."

"Water Tower Books," the children chanted. "Don't be late."

Beth slammed the window down.

CHAPTER THIRTY-NINE

"Good. I caught you," Link said when she answered the phone.

"You can't make it today?"

"Doubter. Of course I can. Listen, Beth, I've been reading Dad's alumni magazine."

"What on earth for?"

"Thought we might do some detecting—and I wanted to be prepared. Anyway, I just found an item I want to read to you."

"A woman in the class of sixty-five has finally been promoted? How could that happen?"

"Go figure. It *is* about a woman—Dewey."

"Dewey! Where is she? I want to talk to her."

"Not much chance of that. She's dead."

Dead? Not to-hell-with-the-world Dewey, guarding her Vuitton trunk, tossing pennies in the trash. Not Dewey, defiant in disgrace, leaving Dall grandly, in a taxi. Dead! Why, she was only Mother's age.

"Beth, you there?"

"I'm here. What did she die of?"

"Doesn't say. Just 'Dewey Cobwell Conner, only child of the late Cob Conner, noted columnist, died on August twelfth.' "

Damn, Beth thought, I knew I should have talked to her. Or could I have? "Link, when does it say she died?"

He gave the date again. Beth thought back—when did Mother tell me the story? No, Dewey had died before—

"Beth, can you hear me?"

"Sorry—does it say anything else?"

" 'She had for many years assisted her father, and recently she edited a collection of his columns, *Wisecracks and Wisdom.*' Have to run—they're calling me."

"Where are you?"

"Water Tower Books—don't be late."

Wisecracks and Wisdom. She *had* to see it. Surely, Conner had written something about his only child. She picked up the phone.

Sold out, the local bookstore told her, the book had been out awhile. Could they order—No, said Beth, and, galvanized, she called Midwestern Library. In! Just time to get the book and meet Link.

Beth dashed past the library's bank of computers, glancing at the card-catalog files that still towered in the background. The files looked oddly threatening, as if resentful of the new system that was usurping their authority.

Minutes later, on Level Three, she pulled a book off the shelf. On the cover was Cob Conner. Wearing a fedora, 1940's style, he was crouching over a typewriter like someone out of *Front Page.* She couldn't resist a quick look at the table of contents, but the titles—"Joe McCarthy, American Hero," "Stork Club Drama," "People I Can Do Without"—offered little promise. Oh, well, too soon to decide.

At Circulation, Coleman Lenites, Librarian of the Damned, was the only one at the computers. *"Wisecracks and Wisdom?"* He raised his eyebrows. "Not your métier, surely?"

Hearing Coleman announce the title, someone at the computer gave a start, saw Beth, and instantly stepped behind the card catalogs. Casually opening a drawer, the person stood watching Beth intently. *What the hell is she doing with Conner's book?*

"Just research," said Beth, aware of a swift movement in the computer region. She looked around. Everyone pounding away, as usual.

"I heard you're deep into Dickens," Coleman said. Beth nodded. "So why—"

"Hey, Coleman"—handing him her faculty card. "Do you always require an explanation?"

Coleman's face reddened to the roots of his goatee. "I'm merely trying to do as our new president suggests—show interest, share goals."

"Hurry—please. *Now* what are you doing?"

"Merely making certain there isn't a prior call for the book."

"Coleman—let me share my goals. I'm rushing out to the University of Chicago to do some important research."

Look at Little Miss Professor. Standing there, so sure of herself.

"Ah, research—into what?"

"Living conditions at Dall Hall."

Dall! I know what you're up to! What makes you think you're so smart? Listen, it was eons ago—you'll never turn up anything. But . . . damn! What if she finds . . . She'll never . . .

"Dall Hall. Is that a literary institution?"

"Give me the book!"

As soon as Beth had run up the steps and disappeared, a catalog drawer was closed so violently that Coleman looked up, frowning. He debated going over to reprimand the—too late. He watched the vandal push ahead of the line at Book Check and tear out of the library. Well! Someone was in an unseemly hurry!

CHAPTER FORTY

Would that woman ever stop looking at the Chanel window? Beth honked. The car in front of her lurched forward, died— and Beth was stuck for the light. Traffic on North Michigan was at a creep—she was going to be late.

Three green arrows later she was at the head of the Pearson turn lane. Did she dare? she wondered, her eye on the policewoman directing traffic. Savagely, the policewoman motioned Beth forward, then ran to yell at a pedestrian—and Beth made a U-turn in front of Water Tower. A line of women stretched around the corner—was Field's having a sale? And where the hell was Link? She leaned over and opened the car door to a burst of excited talk.

"He told me he loves my hat. I'm going through again." "Me, too. He's so charming. He asked me where I'm from and then he said that Neenah is a wonderful name." "Truly a great author, a little naughty sometimes." Oh, God, the line was for Link, and the signing would go on forever.

"Move it"—the policewoman. "You're blocking a bus lane."

"I'm sorry. I'm supposed to meet Lincoln Lowenstein."

"And I'm the mayor of Chicago. Now, move it, or—"

"Just let me—"

"*Move* it—hey! Get out of that lane!" The policewoman tore after a wayward horse and carriage.

"—write a note." Beth searched for paper, finally scribbled a note on the back of a check. She looked over the line. The Neenah woman, carrying a stack of Link's books—she'd wait it out. "Will you give this to Link Lowenstein for me?"

"You know him? Fantastic!" She took the note. "Don't worry, I'll give it to him for sure. Hey! I was standing there!"

Where? Beth tried to remember as she moved through Outer Drive traffic. A face she had just seen, but where? In the line? No, not there. The policewoman—never! Then she remembered. In the Chanel window, a huge poster of Sargent's Lady X. White shoulders emerging from a low-cut black gown, pale face in elegant profile, the features icy, aloof, but so beautiful you wanted to keep gazing—exactly how she imagined Lady Dedlock in the portrait that hung at Chesney Wold.

The portrait. Dickens kept returning to it: the portrait, reigning supreme above the brilliant circle of titled people gathered in the great drawing room. The portrait, raising the spirits of Sir Leicester, who lies, stricken with gout, gazing at his favorite picture. The portrait, conveying mystery—why the uncanny resemblance between Lady Dedlock and Esther? The portrait, marked by foreboding—a shadow steals over it, as if waiting for the chance to draw a veil over Lady Dedlock's beauty.

Another portrait. As Beth turned off the Drive, she thought of the constant return to the portrait at Dall Hall. In her mind, all the Dall stories seemed to build to Louise, poised on the ottoman, about to straighten the portrait of Letitia Dallworthy. She wanted a look at that portrait.

Fifty-ninth Street was a tunnel, both sides packed with parked cars. She saw an open spot, started to back in. "Trust me," a student called, pointing to the NO PARKING sign. "The meter maids are here all the time." She kept on down the street, thinking she would park in the UC Hospital's lot. When she got there, she rejected the wait for valet parking and drove inside. The arm went up—she took a ticket and moved ahead, winding and winding upward, every level filled. Not until Level Eight did she find a spot—she darted into an obscure corner.

She cut through the hospital, past the gift shop, past the pharmacy, down the stairs to the lower level where the walls were lined with photographs of Medical School graduating classes. She found her father's year and stopped to admire his good looks. She found a later class—yes, there was Louise! But what a Louise—the heavy lipstick, the toothy grin, the Peter Pan collar—how different from today's sophisticate. Shouldn't Link's father be here? She searched through the L's and there he was, Abraham L. Lowenstein. Her father was much better-looking, no doubt about that. Still, she had to admit Abe was interesting: challenging eyes, thin mouth ready to spout quips. . . . She lingered, staring, imagining her mother strolling on the campus with Abe. . . .

The feeling of being back in time was so strong that when she crossed to the campus she half expected to see Sloppy Joe sweaters, pleated skirts, and saddle shoes. It was almost a shock to see that the students sprawled on the grass were wearing jeans and running shoes.

She gazed around her. Golden October trees, dropping the first leaves. Gray stone buildings, softened with ivy. Griffins and gargoyles surveying their university. Caught in the magic of the campus, she walked along, crunching leaves, swimming through conversations. "You have this data. . . ." "Nth state of matter, right?" "The nucleuses kinda converged; they had this, like, blob."

"Listen to this"—a girl, reading to a boy. " 'If you think someone is following you, don't tell yourself you're imagining

things. Yell, *leave me alone!* Or yell, *fire!* I'm going to try it."
"You're crazy, don't—" *"Fi—"* "Oh, don't, that's so to-
tally—" and Beth was out of earshot.

She passed Harper Library and headed toward the dorm.
Curious, she thought, as she entered the quadrangle. She had
never seen her mother's dorm, but she had known exactly where
to go. Here was Dall, so Gothic, with its turrets and pointed
arches over the windows. Just opposite one high window, a tree.
She imagined a boy climbing it, calling to one of the Fourth
Floor Gang. Silly, the tree would have been a sapling, if it were
there at all.

Inside and up the stairs, she halted. Her mother had told her
that Dall was now an office building. But what had they done?
They had raised flimsy walls, built ugly brown partitions. They
had debased the graceful entrance hall, reducing it to a utilitar-
ian passageway.

To her right—an open door. Beth walked in. Seated at desks
were three blond women—interlopers, Beth thought, in what
must be the remains of Little Neck. They looked up question-
ingly. "Just exploring," she said. "My mother used to live
here."

"Of course. Here in the Blond Office—that's what they call
us—we get lots of girls—uh, women—coming back." The
speaker, who introduced herself as Janet, asked if Beth knew
that Dall was the oldest building on campus. "The University
really keeps it up. They've replaced the roof, put in new copper
edges and whatdoyoucallems—finials. And they got rid of the
outdoor fire escapes." The women returned to their work, all
but Janet, who said she would show Beth around.

Down the shrunken hall they went, Beth ahead, trying to get
her bearings. Here on the left should be—"Go on in," said her
companion. "Big meeting today. Almost everyone's out."

Beth opened the door and entered a large high-ceilinged room. She looked for landmarks, saw a huge window facing the quadrangle. "This has to be Oyster Bay!"

"How funny. Why did they call it that?"

"Janet"—a blond woman in the doorway. "You have a call." Janet left, telling her to feel free to explore on her own, exactly what Beth wanted to do.

Yes, still there, behind the file cabinets—the fireplace. And over there, covered with cartons—the window seat. And there, behind the computers—that's where the grand piano must have been. As Beth looked around, imagining the room in dormitory days, the desks, the files, the hanging fluorescents faded away.

Evening. The big window was dark. Floor lamps and sconces cast a soft light over the window seat, piled with cushions, over the flower print that covered easy chairs and a skirted sofa. She heard music—a party!—that's why the furniture was pushed against the walls. She smelled gardenias—corsages! She saw boys and girls dancing.

The tall girl, jitterbugging away—Dewey! And the silly-looking woman in the dreadful satin shirtwaist—Mrs. Primwell, smiling her society smile. The boy dancing with her is making faces, gesturing for someone to cut in. Suddenly he looks up, staring—mouth agape.

Jill is coming in! God, she is gorgeous in her drop-shoulder black. And that impossibly cute blond boy—Tony!—is staring at her as if he will never tear his eyes away.

Here is Louise. She looks really nice, not wow like Jill, but nice. She is walking up to Tony, tottering on her borrowed platforms. *Why didn't they tell Louise not to look scared?*

Now everyone is dancing. Louise, eyes closed, is in Tony's arms, and Tony is asking her where she has been all his life. . . .

"I have to leave."

Oh, no—that's Tony.

"Please stay longer"—Louise.

Oh, please, Tony. Too late.

"Six no trump. Bid and made! I'm going to put it in my diary."

She was still in Oyster Bay, but now it was afternoon. Girls on the floor, playing bridge. Lana at the piano, singing. Stretched out in front of the fireplace, Tony Valentine, asleep.

Jill strolls in, fresh from tennis, sweaty, sexy in her tight T-shirt. She perches on the sofa, talking, her eye on Tony. Across the hall, in Great Neck, Louise sits in a chair, reading.

A silence. Everyone is looking at Jill. She's on the floor, bending over Tony.

Don't, Jill! Louise is watching!

She's kissing Tony! Tony's arms are going up around Jill— what a kiss! But Louise—the wounded look in her eyes. Now she's looking down, pretending to read.

The way Louise had looked at them! This is unbearable.

Beth left Oyster Bay and went down the hall. At the big table, the maids are sitting and talking. Beyond is the sunlit dining room, where girls in pajamas and robes are eating breakfast.

"Has anyone seen my football bracelet?"

"Are you sure it's missing?"

Was she? Please don't be sure, Jill.

"I'm sure—I keep it in a certain place."

Rebecca and Lana are saying they had money stolen from their wallets.

"Were any pennies left?"

"Oh, all right, the pennies were left."

"What's the big deal about pennies, Carol?"

"Didn't you know? Dewey throws them away—and Dewey's not missing anything."

"Yes, she is—she can't find her cute gold evening bag."

"Bet she's hiding it."

"Before you rush around hanging the dreadful crimes on Dewey, you'd better have proof!"

Em said that. *Good for you, Em.*

Beth ran up the stairs to the fourth floor, saw a sign, WOMEN, and went in. The same marble shelf, the same porcelain sinks . . . She jumped. Jill in a nightgown, standing at the door of the tub room.

"Come over here," Jill says. "I've got something to show you."

I don't want to look.

"Now!" Jill flings open the door.

Beth screamed.

Blood, pools of it in the bathtub, streaks on the floor, the walls.

"Dewey," says Jill. "She tried to kill herself."

Beth ran out of the bathroom.

She was in Dewey and Carol's room.

"It's got to be Dewey," says Carol. "I'm going to tell Mrs. P.!" Carol leaves.

Dewey comes in, looking right through Beth. Dewey looks terrible, her face dead white, dark circles under her eyes. She goes straight to her trunk, takes something out, stuffs it into her blazer pocket, and leaves.

Now Beth was in her mother's room.

Laurie is talking to Em. "We're all looking at each other in a new way—sort of suspicious—sort of scared. It's creepy!"

Oh, Mother, you're so pretty.

"Have I got great news!" It's Carol . . .

Laurie almost spills her milkshake. She and Em are giggling.

"Morons!" says Carol. "When I came back, my wallet was gone! . . . And Dewey's lying in bed as if nothing happened. She doesn't know she just hung herself with those pennies!"

The door opened and a man walked into the room. Bunk beds and dresser disappeared. Beth was in an office, on the desk a mug of coffee. The man stared at Beth. "Not another," he said, looking martyred.

"Sorry—this used to be my mother's room."

"Well, it's my room now!"

CHAPTER FORTY-ONE

About to leave, Beth suddenly remembered. She stopped in the office where Janet, alone now, was at the computer. "I forgot to ask—whatever happened to the portrait?"

Janet jumped. "You're still here! Portrait? Which portrait?"

"The one of Letitia Dallworthy. It used to be above the fireplace in Oyster Bay."

"Oh, I know the one. We took it out of storage and had it hanging in the main hall—until the night a student broke in and trashed a faculty office. Then, just to make sure *everyone* knew he hated getting a B, on his way out he slashed a knife right through the old girl. Terrible thing—we were fond of her. We're having the canvas repaired—and covered with glass, just in case another satisfied student turns up."

"Then it's out now?"

"No, it's still down in the Dungeons, waiting for someone to call the restorer."

The Dungeons, it seemed, was the Blond Office's name for the basement storage rooms. Beth asked if she could see the portrait, and Janet said, oh, why not, she would be working a while longer anyway.

The first thing Beth saw as she followed Janet down the stairs was a triple-locked cagelike construction surrounding machinery. KEEP AWAY. POWER FOR DALLWORTHY HALL. The threatening sign set the tone for the rest of the dismal area. Beth pictured It's Only Herman sweating and cursing as he shoved trunks down the dark narrow halls and wedged them into storage rooms.

"But which room?" Beth asked, after Janet had unlocked all the doors.

"Gosh, I don't have a clue—it's down here somewhere. Good hunting!"

The first room Beth tried was packed with old geography files whose narrow drawers were filled with maps. The next held the remains of high academic hopes—*Camelot Project, Dead File; Kennedy Conference, Dead File.*

The next room looked like an academic garage sale. Metal desks turned every which way. A stack of wooden swivel chairs. An ancient counter scales—to weigh what? Beth wondered. Brains? Leaning against the wall was a cracked dresser mirror, a Wash Prom dance card still tucked in its frame. She read the names, recognizing none, and, replacing the card, she turned to a beat-up wooden file. She opened a drawer and pulled out some typewritten sheets, the top one titled, "The History of Dallworthy Hall."

Beth started skimming. "Chicago Woman's Club . . . 1892 . . . notable meeting . . . President Harper of Chicago University . . . address on 'What Is the Relation of Women to the University?' " In 1892? Distant cousins, Beth thought, and read on. "Spoke of need for campus living quarters for women students . . . committee appointed to raise money. June 1892 . . . Mrs. Letitia Dallworthy gave a subscription of fifty thousand dollars for a third dormitory for women." Good for you, Mrs. Dallworthy!

Beth settled herself in a swivel chair and continued to read. "Told the dormitory could not be built for that sum, Mrs.

Dallworthy informed the board that if the University would go forward and erect Dallworthy Hall she would pay. On this encouragement the contracts were let and the beautiful building was constructed." Great, Mrs. D.! You gave my mother a place to live.

But did women belong on campus at all? Should there be a coeducational program? These were the worrying questions. Here the history moved ahead to 1916, quoting a Miss Dingee, who said, " 'The position of women was less assured in 1893 than now, and there was much question as to their status in the new institution.' " Mrs. Dallworthy must have wanted to make a strong statement about the status of women, because, somewhere along the way, "it was decided"—by Letitia, Beth was certain of it—that her hall would be taller than all the others. "Dallworthy Hall, when it was finished in October 1893, rose a full five stories"—one more than the other four-storied residence halls!

Letitia kept right on giving—"furnishing the house comfortably and with taste, so that the sixty-eight residents might live not in a 'dormitory,' but in a refined, dignified comfortable home." And you succeeded, Letitia! Mother's dorm had indeed been a comfortable home, less dignified perhaps and more crowded than in 1893, but still a home, until Jill . . . Beth read on. "Above the fireplace in the living room is a portrait of Mrs. Dallworthy by Anna Klumpke." *My God, the portrait!*

Beth jumped up and started ransacking the room. Inside one of the desks she found a pile of old bills. Laundry bills from the thirties. Food bills from the forties. From the fifties—a bill for tree removal. Footsteps sounded above. Janet. Better start looking. But what was left? Her eyes lit on the mirror, and on impulse Beth pulled it away from the wall. Behind it, a large cloth-wrapped package. She removed the cloth—*found it!* Now for a good look at the woman she felt she had come to know.

She leaned the portrait against her desk. Damn. The slash cut right through the center. She pulled the torn canvas together—facing her was a gray-haired woman. Straight aristocratic nose. Bold dark eyes. She must have been beautiful once. Regal, commanding, she sat erect in her chair, staring straight ahead, daring anyone to doubt her courage.

For some time, Beth stood gazing at Letitia, and then suddenly, she *knew*—Letitia was staring directly at her. *"I will* not *have unsolved mysteries in my residence hall,"* Beth heard a high thin voice say. *"You must see to this, young lady!"* Aloud Beth said, "I am trying, Mrs. Dallworthy. I am trying."

Beth turned the portrait around, picked up the cloth, started to rewrap—what was that? Behind the wooden slats that backed the portrait—a glint. She looked closer. Yes, definitely, where a knothole had fallen out, she could see something gold. Carefully, carefully, she reached between the slats. Her fingers touched something soft. She tugged—the brittle slats flew apart. In her hand she had a thin envelope bag covered with fraying gold silk. She looked inside, saw nothing, felt in the pocket— found a penny. Again, she reached between the slats, felt something metallic, gently pulled it out. A gold bracelet, dangling a football charm! Dewey's bag and Jill's bracelet—"You still down there?"

Janet!—coming down the stairs.

"Just leaving," Beth called, and thrust her finds away. She crammed in the Dall history, too, hoping her bag's new bulkiness would go unnoticed. Janet's heels clattering down the hall. Quickly, Beth turned the portrait around.

She was in the doorway. "You made your find!"

Oh, God. She knows. But Janet was staring at the portrait. "What do you think of our Mrs. Dallworthy?"

Resisting the desire to glance at her bulging bag, Beth looked at the portrait and said wildly, "Who was Anna Klumpke?"

"You noticed the signature! She's famous for painting gray-haired women. This portrait might be valuable—some museum wanted us to lend it for an exhibit."

Later, Beth thanked Janet and left, feeling guilty about the contents of her bag, rationalizing that she would, when the time was right, tell Janet what she had found.

Janet powdered her nose, searched for her comb—heard a cough. She looked up. Another visitor. Really peculiar, this one. This one made Janet want to come out with her favorite movie line: "Stop trying to dress like a woman. You don't have the face for it."

"I'm doing some research," said the visitor, "on Anna Klumpke—the artist."

No wonder this one was peculiar—an academic.

"I understand you have her portrait of Letitia Dallworthy here."

"How strange. Someone was just asking about it," Janet blurted out, instantly regretting her impulse. Now she would have to show it, and she wanted to get out of here.

"I would very much like to see it."

Well, maybe I could take the time, Janet thought, and then—no! Remembering her miserable failure on the Woman as Victim Quiz (Are you afraid to say no?), Janet diligently looked the visitor in the eye (Do people tend to ignore you when you talk?) and said, "It's not convenient now."

"I must insist. The portrait is crucial to my research."

Definitely an *OA*—one of the Obsessive Academics who

think their research will win them a prize. Plenty of Nobels on campus already.

"It's your responsibility to cooperate with researchers."

Her responsibility? That did it. They could offer her a cool million and she'd still never show this detestable OA one inch of the portrait. "Well, you can't see it now."

"Surely, if you let *her* see it—"

"No!" Janet said assertively—and at that moment something clicked. How did this OA know a *woman* had asked to see the portrait? Janet forgot angry—she was scared.

Stay focused, she told herself. Look stern. Janet stood. In the back of her mind, she saw her boxing class practicing hooks and uppercuts, heard chants of Stick it out! Stick it out! Jab! Jab! Jab! Power! Power! Power! She edged around the desk to get in position.

"Thank you—for nothing!" and the OA strode out.

Well! I must have made progress. Was it my stance? My look? Janet went into the hall, made sure the OA had left the building. As she locked the door, she watched the OA run across the quadrangle—*what's her hurry?*—and disappear into the darkness.

CHAPTER FORTY-TWO

Strange. Surely Dewey would have wanted to take the bag and bracelet before she left.

Or maybe it wasn't so strange, Beth thought, as she cut back through the hospital. Dewey must have been eager to flee from Dall, the scene of her hideous humiliation.

At the wall with the class pictures, Beth paused again, her eyes on Louise. Was she grinning like that when she stood on the ottoman and reached up to the portrait? And why did that memory keep cropping up?

"Where are you taking me?"

"X-ray, honey."

Beth moved aside to let the wheelchair go by, then followed it down the corridor.

Was that one incident so striking? Or was it part of a collective memory of pre–Open House excitement—girls competing for spiffiest room, for most glamorous getup, because hubba-hubba! Boys! Upstairs! Beth thought of Em, frantically tacking her wet laundry behind the bureau, of Carol, hurling a forgotten bra into the closet, of Lana, chopping off Rebecca's peroxided bangs.

"So I told him the orthopods already made their rounds for this month"—appreciative chuckles from lab-coated residents. Beth detoured around them and continued on to the exit.

How dark it was outside. Should have valet parked, she thought, as she made her way to the lot. She pushed the elevator button, her eyes on a guard patrolling with a dog that looked hungry to plant his teeth in someone's neck. Meant to be reassuring, she supposed, but that, coupled with a sign commanding her to lock her car immediately upon leaving or entering, made her jittery.

Just outside, someone headed toward the lot. Quickly Beth stepped into the elevator. Safer to go up alone.

Was that a man or a woman? Hell, thought the guard, he wouldn't bet either way. He watched whatever it was scramble up the stairs. And why didn't you wait for the elevator? You stood there looking long enough. Nasty-looking devil.

"Hold it! Please!" A man struggling with crutches, trying to reach the elevator. Beth held the door, giving him plenty of time to get inside before she stepped out.

Now, where had she parked? Looking to left and right, she walked down the incline. Sodium lights bathed everything in yellow, giving her a spooky feeling. She looked over her shoulder and shuddered. Anyone could be crouching behind one of the vans or behind that pickup truck. Where the hell was her car? She reached the bottom of the incline, her eyes on the convex mirror whose reflection expanded the parked cars into death-wielding tanks.

What if she saw a person in the mirror? What if she saw someone emerge from behind a van and move toward her? She imagined herself screaming, running wildly down the incline. Behind her, she heard a car engine. Calm down, she told herself, and moved aside.

A red Bentley pulled up next to her. A man leaned out the window. "Having trouble finding your car?"

"No."

"Sure? Want to get in with me and we can drive around and look for it?" He smiled—was he leering or flirting?

"No!" She edged back and hit a bumper.

"You're right," he said, looking amused. "Don't talk to strangers," and he screeched away. The license plate said DEEP CUT. Jack the Ripper? Oh, come on—a fun-loving surgeon.

Up and down she walked, up to the green electrician's truck, down to the convex mirror. Why were all the cars green? Next time she'd buy a red car—no, blue—no, red—oh, stop it. Then, almost at the end of the incline, she saw her car. How could she have missed it with the Midwestern sticker on the back? She must have passed it a dozen times.

Now, where were her keys? Angrily, she rummaged through the jam-packed bag—a *click*! From somewhere near her. A gun safety! Instantly her mind drilled back to Mrs. Primwell's gun. Absurd. The police had confiscated it long ago, and why think about guns at all? Probably someone popping a trunk.

The keys, dammit. Desperate, she turned her bag upside down on the car hood, grabbed a rolling lipstick, looked up, and saw, reflected in the mirror, something—*someone*. The convexity made it a fun-house picture, bulging, grotesque—but it was a person, lumbering toward her, getting closer.

"Fire!" she screamed.

Pounding feet moving away.

She heard a roaring engine, saw a huge car, threatening dark-glass windows, speeding toward her.

Beth leaped aside. "Help!" she yelled. *"Fire!"*

The car stopped. Slowly a door opened.

"Want a ride, lady?" It was Link.

CHAPTER FORTY-THREE

"You *were* being chased!"

"Really, Link, it was just my overactive imagination."

"But I saw someone—something—running away! Didn't you—"

A buzz—Beth was saved by Room Service. He took forever, spreading the cloth, polishing plates, aligning silver and crystal. Then he spent so much time insisting they tell him if they desired anything else that Link bribed him out with a tip so grotesquely large that he was back almost instantly with the next morning's *Tribune.*

Link lifted a silver lid. "You ordered a hamburger?"

"But it's a Ritz hamburger."

"And a milkshake? What's going on?"

"I feel as if I'm living at Dall Hall."

"Ah, a forties' coed—want to go steady?"

"With you? Wow! You're a BMOC!" Beth said, handing him the *Tribune.* "Look, there's an article about you."

They sat at the table, eating and reading. " 'Elegant and stylish writer,' " Link read, almost purring. " 'Brilliant, terrific, marvelous.' 'Jacket photograph somewhat pretentious.' Oh, for—what the hell does that mean?"

"I think it means your corduroy jacket," said Beth. "Listen

to these titles, Link." She was paging through the Conner collection. " 'Broadway Belles.' 'Congressional Commies.' "

"Adored alliteration, didn't he? What's wrong with my corduroy jacket?"

Beth didn't answer. She was reading intently.

CHRONICLE OF A COED

This is the story of a girl who attended a posh Eastern college. Was she pretty? A Venus De-Eyeful. Was she rich? Loaded. Selfish? Not a chance. She borrowed out her platforms, perfumes, and pearls to all the coeds in her dorm. She took her girlfriends out for real quizzine instead of dormitory pap—and she picked up the check.

So all the girls loved her? Who ya kiddin'?

They were jealous. They were mean. They called her the Rich B---h Who Walks by Night. Why? The poor kid couldn't sleep (no surprise), so she roamed around the dorm at night, while the real b---hes were getting their shut-eye.

And then these b---hes accused this kind beautiful *rich* girl of stealing gewgaws she could have bought for herself in a New York minute.

Was she treated kindly by the hoity-toity dame who ran the reformidormitory? *Nein!* Her Naziness told her to confess—or else.

Did she confess? *Nein, Fraulein!*

So Her Naziness told Miss Kind, Rich, and Gorgeous—Scram! Beat it! *Mock Shnell!* Much as Her Naziness loved rich girls, she couldn't keep a girl in her reformidormitory who committed billionous heinous heists.

But all along Miss Gorgeous knew who the real

thief was! Late at night Miss G. had seen her filching fripperies. . . . Get the picture?

Did Miss Gorgeous tell? Nosiree.

Why not? She was nobody's snitch. Anyway, she couldn't imagine any more ecstatic escapeapade than breaking out of that posh Eastern coop—uh, college— and never, never going back.

G. K. Oldchestnuterton said: "The essence of every picture is the frame." Miss Gorgeous was framed!

Beth looked up. "Link, you have to read this!"

"Would a tweed jacket be better?"

"No. I love the corduroy—come on, read!"

"Well, what do you think?" Beth asked, when he had finished.

"A father's prejudiced point of view. From what you've told me, Dewey wasn't that beautiful—or that sweet."

"Then you agree it's Dewey he's writing about?"

"Who else? He just changed the setting to an Eastern school to protect himself. As I recall, hordes of people were always suing Conner for libel."

"Then why write about the theft at all?"

"Revenge. He wanted to get back at the school and Mrs. Whatshername—Primwell—for a perceived injustice. You can't blame him for wanting to believe his daughter wouldn't steal. Of course, he was wrong."

"He wasn't! If Dewey was the thief, why would she tell him—and why would Conner go to so much trouble to show it?"

"Tell him what? Show what?"

"The real thief's hiding place, of course."

"What hiding place?" Link scanned the page again. "There's nothing here about a hiding place."

"But there is! Conner wasn't the literary type. Why do you think he went to so much trouble to work in G. K. Chesterton?"

"I give up. Why?"

"So he could work in 'picture' and 'frame.' He's almost shouting it! 'Get the picture?' 'Miss Gorgeous was framed!' " Link looked baffled.

"Wait!" Beth ran into the bedroom, returned with her bag, and dumped everything on the chaise. "Look what I turned up this afternoon!" She held out the purse and the football bracelet.

"The missing loot! Where did you find it?"

"I'll tell you in a minute."

"So this is the bracelet Jill's old boyfriend gave her." He picked it up. "Flat links," he said, "like the old ID's. Nice design." He studied the long clasp engraved with twining roses. "Must be solid gold."

"How can you tell?"

"Has to be gold—fourteen or eighteen karat—an alloy would have blackened long ago. So where did you find this?"

"Tucked inside the frame of Letitia Dallworthy's portrait," Beth said triumphantly. "Conner knew all about the hiding place! . . . Link!" He was staring ahead at the dark windows. "What are you thinking about? Not your jacket again?"

He gave her a reproachful look. "Very amusing," he said. "No. I'm thinking about Dewey. It's hard to believe she was as true blue as her father claims. If she wasn't the thief, and she knew the hiding place, why didn't she tell?"

"Good question," said Beth, as she reloaded her bag.

"What are all those papers?"

"More finds from the dorm."

"And you made off with them, too? I may have to report you to the Dean of Women. What is that stuff?"

"A history of Dall Hall, some old dorm bills—nothing important. Link, let me see that book again. Maybe I'll find something else."

He watched her page through—and suddenly stop.

"Find something?"

"I don't know—" She skimmed the column. "I might have."

"Yeah? Let me read it with you."

She moved over and he stretched out next to her on the chaise, the book open between them.

MADCAP MOMS

Anyone else had a bellyful of Hollywood's madcap moms?

Picture the big scene in *Stella Dallas*. Barbara Stanwyck stands outside a mansion, clutching the iron fence posts, shedding joyful tears, as she watches her daughter's High Society nuptials. Barb isn't allowed inside because she magnanimously passed herself off as an unfit mother—carousing, overdressing, using bad grammar—so her daughter wouldn't feel guilty about abandoning Mom to bunk with genteelfolk. Aw, c'mon. Would a dame smart enough to fake bad grammar really do that?

Or how about *To Each His Own?* Olivia de Havilland's in the family way, but—merciful heavens!—she has yet to tie the knot. Lest her babe be raised a marked child, Olivia gives him up for adoption. Meanwhile, she becomes a shrewd businesswoman, bankrolling her boy to teddy bears, tonsillectomies, and hard-to-get theater tickets, never telling him she's his mom. Olivia's ready to collect her pension before Sonny finally catches on. "Mother," he says, "I think this is our dance." He should have said, "I think you're a dunce."

Think I'll make my own movie.

Let's see—I'll make the dame a college coed, because she has to be smart. This plummy role goes to Gene Tierney—the only movie dame who shows brains (see *Laura*, readers).

Who'll play the boyfriend? Think I'll give the part to Johnny Weissmuller. He grunts. He's muscular. The perfect letter man.

I'll give Miss Coed the regulation plight. She's expecting a blessed event, and—unholy Toledo!—she's in a state of single bliss. Does she go off to a dirty scalpeller and die—nobly saving the father money and embarrassment? Does she give up her baby boy for adoption, pay his way through Groton and Princeton, even when he becomes President? Hell, no.

In my script, Miss Coed makes a date to meet her boyfriend and tells him, "You're going to be a proud papa." After she revives Mr. Muscles, she rejects his suggestion that she seek out an unwashed sawbones. "I'm going to have your baby," she says. "And guess who's going to take care of it? You—Daddyo."

"Me, bottles?" He howls. "Me, diapers?" He beats his chest. "Me. You," he grunts. "Let's get hitched."

"Forget it," she says. "I want my B.A.—not an MRS."

How to end this movie? I've got it!

Close-up to Mr. Muscles, rocking the little ape—uh, baby—watching proudly through the apse—or flying buttress—whatever—while Miss Coed is awarded her diploma.

Does Mr. Muscles kick about his sacrifice? Au Contrast. " 'Tis a far, far better thing I do . . ."

I have to polish the dialogue a little, but there it is, folks.

Don't try to steal it.

Hollywood has already made me a six-figure offer.

"There has to be a connection with Jill," said Beth.

"Because Conner has an unwed mother in his script?"

"That—and because this column and the other are the only two that were never published—until now."

"What's he saying then?"

"I don't know. But I'm sure Dewey must have told her father something about Jill's pregnancy, and whatever she told him was probably right. She was right about the hiding place."

Beth went to the window and stood watching the traffic winding down the Outer Drive, heading south, toward the U of C. She felt as if the girls were still there, at Dall, waiting for a phone call, waiting for the buzz that meant "Gentleman Caller," waiting . . .

"Do you think he's saying that Jill threatened someone?" Link asked. When she didn't answer, he went to the window and put his arm around her. "What's the matter?"

"I'm feeling so down. I think it was Conner's description of forties' movies—of forties' women, really."

"He was being satirical."

"But he had a point. He made me feel so bad for those women—those girls. They were always under pressure—to pretend they were dummies, to put themselves last, to capture a husband. They didn't need husbands! They were wonderful girls, talented—they could have been anything they wanted to be. Why wouldn't the world let them use their talents?"

"Hey," said Link. "You're crying."

"I feel so sorry for the whole bunch. And I know when I find the answer—it's going to be terrible. I'm sorry, Link. The whole day is caving in on me. I have to leave."

The next morning when Link called, she was feeling better—sad, apprehensive, but better.

"I've been thinking," he said. "What was the date on the Her Naziness column?" Beth said she'd look, and he said hurry, because he had to leave for O'Hare.

"No date for either column," she reported. He swore. "Why is the date important?"

"Say that the theft column was written after Jill was murdered. Say the thief killed Jill—or Dewey thought the thief killed Jill. Maybe Dewey told her father not to publish—because if the thief found out through the column that Dewey knew about her, she might—"

"Might what?"

"I don't know—rub her out. Teenagers get weird ideas. I have to leave. Watch yourself, Beth. There *was* someone running—I'll call."

Later it crossed Beth's mind—what if Dewey had been right, years ago, to fear for her safety if her father published the column? Years later, when the column was finally published, Dewey could still have been in danger.

CHAPTER FORTY-FOUR

In the underground vaults of Newspaper Microtext, Beth sat at a machine, winding out a *New York Times* microfilm. She whirled past last year's global crises, movie reviews, and Paris collections until she reached the date she wanted and "Obituaries." There it was! DEWEY CONNER, DAUGHTER OF NOTED COLUMNIST.

She studied the photo, dated some years earlier. Was this the Dewey who had prowled the dorm at night? How studious she looked. Probably the effect of the horn-rimmed glasses that overpowered her thin, eager face.

> Dewey Cobwell Conner, daughter of the late Charles "Cob" Conner, noted columnist, died yesterday in Manhattan Hospital. She died suddenly after a brief illness, said Ms. Evelyn New, her companion. Ms. Conner, who served for years as her father's assistant, was known for her support of feminist causes and worked with the National Organization for Women on behalf of the Equal Rights Amendment. For the past year, said Ms. New, she had been writing a memoir of her childhood. There are no survivors.

Suddenly! After a brief illness! Wait, don't get excited. Probably happens all the time. Still, it was something to follow up—and soon. She looked at her watch. My God, she'd be late for class—she ran, giving only a passing thought to Evelyn New and Dewey's memoir.

"I must see this one, too"—pointing to the microfilm Beth had turned in. Oily creature, thought the grad student behind the desk. Like someone out of Jacobean drama. He signed out the microfilm and resumed reading *The White Devil.*

Suddenly, after a brief illness. All day, the phrase haunted her. She thought *suddenly* while she graded papers that were choked with jargon and arrogant generalizations. She thought *brief* while she taught a class where her "What do you think of Tulkinghorn's unrelenting pursuit of Lady Dedlock?" drew blank stares and a gum bubble like a pink boil. She was thinking *suddenly* and *brief* at the English Department meeting that began with an interminable debate, which should have been postponed, over the janitor's Christmas present, then stalled, bogged down in a battle over the new course evaluations.

"What's your opinion, Beth?"

"About what?"

"Is it fair to ask students—'Rate the effectiveness of the course in challenging you intellectually'?" She had no opinion. What was her problem? they asked.

"Sorry—I was thinking about the nuances of meaning in *suddenly.*"

"As long as you're into adverbs, how about the nuances of meaning in *intellectually?* How can you quantify intellectual challenge?"

Someone groaned. "Listen to this—'Rate the effectiveness of the instructor in stimulating your interest in the subject.' "

"What if we tap dance the plots in class?" said Beth. Glares.

Reproachful looks. What if she just walked out on these—
these—asininities?

"I think we should write to the Dean, a polite letter—"

"A stern letter—"

"A chilling letter—"

"I think we should wait—"

"Wait! They're using these—these—"

"Asininities?" said Beth.

"That's it! They're using these asininities to make promotion
and tenure decisions!"

"I thought they were using them to help us improve our
teaching."

"Get real!"

"Without data, a letter wouldn't resonate—"

And the battle bumbled on until Beth wanted to stand up and
scream, How would you rate your effectiveness in making decisions?

The instant she got home, she ran to the phone.

"What's going on?" asked her mother, so Beth said just
some medical questions for her father. "It's something to do
with Jill, isn't it?" her mother said, with one of her intuitive
leaps that always startled Beth. "I'm sorry I ever told you. All
right, all right, I'll get him."

Her father came to the phone. "Daddy," she said, and why,
she asked herself, was she still saying Daddy, "I want to read
you an obituary."

"Not one of my patients, I hope."

"Of course not. Yours never die. Now, listen to this . . .
Anything suspicious?" she asked, when she had finished reading.

"Suspicious, meaning what?"

"Could she have been murdered?"

"What on earth makes you think that?"

"What about *died suddenly*?"

"Meaningless. Why was she in the hospital?" Beth didn't know. "Was her death unexpected?"

She didn't know that either. "But couldn't the *suddenly* be suspicious?"

"Yes and no," and Beth could see her father wagging a hand back and forth, the world's most annoying gesture. "Was it a serious illness?" he asked. "Don't know," she said.

"I'd like to help, darling, but I need more. I suppose—if it was a sudden death after a relatively benign illness—it could be foul play—or a gross foul-up. Too much intervention. Sometimes *MICCO* is better."

"Mike-o! What the hell is that—Father?"

"Hoped you'd ask. Medical Inactivity Coupled with Catlike Observation"—and he roared. "Yes, darling, it's a possibility. Hardly worth pursuing. But I know you will—Daughter," and shortly thereafter the conversation ended.

Yes, she would pursue it, but she felt like someone who had been waiting in line for hours and reached the front just as the box office—no, it was more like trying on bras for hours, with a salesperson who—no, it was like being a petitioner in *Bleak House*, pushed aside every step of the way, driven mad by the Court of Chancery. If only she had some solid facts.

She would pursue it—but how?

Impulsively, Beth called Manhattan Hospital, where she was Voice-Mailed from Pharmacy to Physical Therapy before reaching Public Relations and a voice so bloodcurdling she was ready to beg for the synthetic tones of Voice Mail. "We insist," said the werewolf, snapping his jaws, "on a signed permission from the family before we give information about the patient." But there was no family. "We cannot give that information." *Click.*

"If this is a medical emergency, press zero. If you wish to reach a physician, press two." And if you want to find out if Dewey was murdered—dial M for Maalox.

She called Link.

"Dewey murdered? Oh, come on." She reminded him of his reasoning about why Dewey had told her father not to publish. "But I meant years ago," said Link, "when Dewey was afraid of the thief."

"Oh, for—don't you see? The time doesn't matter! Once the column was published, Dewey was still in danger."

Pause. "You have a point."

"Right—and listen to this." She started reading the obituary, only to be interrupted after one sentence.

"Manhattan Hospital! That's where my father is on the staff."

"Wait," she told him, and read on. . . . "See?" See what? he asked. "You didn't pick up on *suddenly, after a brief illness?*"

"That's nothing to go on."

"My *father* thinks it's a strong possibility."

"*My* father would know. I'll get Abe to check it out."

"Give me his number. I'll call him myself."

"I don't know. He's—he's—" A low growl from Beth, who was beginning to feel a kinship with the hospital werewolf. "Well, okay, but let me call him to pave the way."

"Can't I do anything right away?" Beth heard herself scream. "Does everyone have to act like the Court of Chancery?"

"What's with Chancery? I'm talking a few minutes, not generations."

She waited. And waited. She picked up a crossword, filled in a few words, put it down. Too easy. She started a diagramless crossword that she had been saving. Asymmetrical yet. And no fair. The first definitions were too ambiguous. Ambiguous . . . Ambidextrous . . . Ambivalent—like Link. What was taking him so long? Was his father refusing to talk to her, refusing to take Laurie's daughter seriously? But I'm right, she thought, as she paced the room. *"Suddenly . . . brief illness."* It does mean something. And if I'm right—no *ifs*, I am right—one of them must have been in New York. Had anyone mentioned New York?

She thought back to Rebecca and Richie's house of kitsch. She saw Rebecca, chubby, self-important. Rebecca, who had been included in Dewey's coterie, but excluded from the Fourth Floor Gang, and still resentful. "Jill?" she heard her say. "A real actress . . . Always had to make herself seem even more popular . . . I overheard a phone call once. . . ." She saw Richie's frowning face. *"Kind* of good-looking!" she heard him say. "My God, Jill was gorgeous!" Then Rebecca, taunting him—"Jill threw you over, and you went into a funk. Because of Jill you stopped caring about medical school. . . ."

She saw the Astor Street apartment, saw the silver-framed wedding pictures, saw Louise, yesterday's ugly duckling, today's elegant professional woman. She heard Dr. Louise Hallman, the psychiatrist, evaluating her roommate of long ago. "Emotionally unstable. Mood swings. Jill and I always got along well, but suddenly she was hostile to me. Then, just as suddenly, she was friendly. . . ." Louise, whose friends had toiled to make her beautiful, whose every date had been a charitable fix-up, talking about the girl who had stolen her first love. "Jill was behaving obsessively, dating every boy in sight, poaching on other girls' boyfriends. . . ."

Then Tony had burst in. Handsome Tony Valentine, the campus heartthrob, the dormitory dreamboat. Beth saw Tony, pulling his chair close to hers, heard him saying that professors had certainly improved since his day. She heard Louise's "Don't you want to question Tony?" Then Tony, rubbing his bald spot, admitting he had gone upstairs to find Jill. "When I got to her room—Evil was there—they were on the bed."

Evil, Beth thought. She had forgotten him. Where was he? If he still was. She mused for a few moments. . . .

Then she was back in Carol's orderly North Shore house. She saw Carol, chic, confident, dispensing interior-decorating advice as nonchalantly as she dispensed vodka. How clever Carol was, still quoting Machiavelli. And how cheerful—smiling as she talked about the day of the murder. "I could see sunlight pouring all over the room—because the shade was *up*, not like when Dewey was there. . . ." Carol, drinking Bloody Marys, reflecting on the past—regretting? "I did feel I might have been too hard on Dewey." Carol, giggling about when she had found Jill in the bathroom. "She was rubbing cream on her boobs. . . . Some people are never satisfied. . . ."

Now Beth was high up in Em's office, where the shelves were packed with law reports and the floors were covered with Orientals. Em, the dropout med student, had made it big, and she had the clothes and the paintings to prove it. She listened to Em as she outmaneuvered an opposing lawyer. She saw Em staring out the window—afraid to meet Beth's eye?—as she talked about her friend. "Jill? Mischievous. Not brilliant, but bright. And beautiful. So beautiful. It wasn't fair."

Not a word about New York—nothing. Well, it wasn't as if New York was the Antipodes. They could have been in New York—any one of them. Any one of the friends her mother had loved . . . Beth stared at a vase of Fuji mums on the table, thinking . . . thinking. Was she right? Hadn't there been something about New York? What was it? The phone rang.

"Wow," said Link. "He really must have had the hots for your mother. He can't wait to talk to you."

Hots, indeed, Beth thought, after the play he had made for Jill.

His voice was so uncannily like Link's that at first Beth forgot to listen to the words. . . . "So you want to talk about a cause of death," Abe was saying. "Link says your father thinks murder is a strong possibility. What kind of medicine does your father practice?"

Oh, a putdown. Good medicine, Beth wanted to say. "He's an internist."

"Well, so am I. And I'm still surprised. Always told your mother I was going to be a writer. How is Laurie?"

"Wonderful."

"Is she . . . is she . . . what kind of shape is she in?"

"Do you mean is she fat?"

A chuckle. "I was inquiring into her health."

Oh, sure. "She's perfectly healthy. And she's not fat. She's gorgeous." So there.

"I knew it! She was so—she had the most beautiful hands. Have you looked at Laurie's hands?"

Had she looked at her mother's hands? What a question. Of course she had. Or had she?

"What's Laurie doing?"

"Not making the luncheon and benefit rounds," Beth said.

"I never thought she was. Not Laurie. Not with her abilities. But what is she—"

"I need to talk to you about Dewey Conner."

"Oh, hell, I'll look into her death. Tell Laurie I'd never say no to her daughter. And tell her—ask her—if she remembers the night we saw *Laura*."

"Laura who?"

Another low chuckle, rather charming. "I meant the movie. Oh, and tell her I'll always—no. Just ask her if she remembers the shooting stars on the Midway. Laurie will know what I mean."

CHAPTER FORTY-FIVE

Late October

Wearing backwards baseball caps, carrying water bottles, the students filed into the library seminar room, taking the seats they had claimed at the beginning of the quarter. The timid took corner chairs where they could duck behind the next person and avoid meeting Beth's eyes. The more confident took mid-table places. The supremely confident, in this case Future Rhodes Scholar, took the other dominant seat, opposite Beth, at the end of the long table.

Some students immediately opened *Prairie Gust* and started reading. Others were talking about Halloween. Beth caught whispers of a big bash that evening at *P-A*, meaning Parker-Andrews Dorm, a.k.a. Party Animals. "Sexy costumes?" "Yeah—required." "Like what?" "Like they have to, you know, slink, like Victoria's Secret. And masks—so everyone, you know, hangs loose." "They're going to have a great band, the—" Too low for Beth to hear the name, but someone awesome, judging by the gasps.

Dazzler came in and took her mid-table seat. A few boys stopped talking to gaze at her. Bubble Gum arrived, took her seat opposite Dazzler, glanced at her, then opened her backpack and peeked into a small mirror. At the last second, Comedian flew in, wearing a SEXY TEXAN T-shirt, drawing a few laughs when he pretended to trip over Dazzler's backpack. He bowed, and said, "My deepest apologies."

Ignoring Comedian, Beth began. "Everywhere in *Bleak House*," she said, "we see greed, cruelty, corruption, misery. Dickens is showing the decay of society on all levels."

"Why on all levels?" said Debater. "Life was great for the upper classes. Look at the way the Dedlocks live."

"But Lady Dedlock didn't start out on top," said Bubble Gum, so aroused she interrupted a bubble. "Her looks got her there."

"What do you mean?" said Debater.

"Dickens says so," said Bubble Gum, and to Beth's astonishment she opened *Bleak House* and started reading. "Right here it says, '—she had not even family,' but Sir Leicester had enough for both. And *then* it says, 'But she had *beauty*, pride, ambition, and sense enough to portion out a legion of fine ladies. Wealth and station added to these, soon floated her upward.' See? Her looks did it."

"It wasn't just her beauty that got her to the top," said Dazzler. "She had ambition. She had sense."

"Yeah, but without beauty," said Bubble Gum, "she never would have made it," and she blew a decisive bubble.

"How do you know she's so beautiful?" said Debater. "Dickens never says what she looks like."

"That's a stacked question," said Comedian, looking around, especially at Dazzler, for laughs.

"Yes he does," said Bubble Gum, who seemed to have made a study of Lady Dedlock's looks. "He says she has a fine face and an elegant figure, and somewhat—wait, I'll find it—" She turned pages furiously. "Here it is. That crazy cousin who talks funny says, 'She's beauty nough tsetup Shopof-women.' "

"But what color her hair? What color her eyes?" This from the bright Thai student.

"Her hair and eyes don't matter!" said Bubble Gum. "It's enough that she's beautiful."

"I think," said Dazzler, "that Dickens is really snide about making beauty seem bad. If you're beautiful, you're a loser. If you're ugly, you're a winner. Look at Esther. After she gets smallpox, she's ugly, but—"

"I don't *like* Esther," said Digresser. "She's such a goody-goody, always making tea, always nursing the sick, always jingling her stupid keys."

"Think about why Dickens has Esther jingling the house-keeping keys," said Future Rhodes Scholar, always somewhat intimidating.

I should get this back to social decay, Beth thought, and yet—someone had ventured a "Why?" to Rhodes Scholar.

"Because Dickens is *sexist*," she said. "That's why. The women he admires are housekeepers, homebodies. He *wants* women chained to the house."

"I *was* talking about Esther's ugliness," said Dazzler, "and—"

"Oh," said Digresser, "that's when she's the most sicken-ingly goody-goody—when she looks in the mirror and sees how ugly she's become. She goes, 'Heaven has been good to me'—or something like that. And she says good-bye to her beauty—I remember exactly—'quite thankfully.' Thankfully! Do you be-lieve it?"

"No, I don't. Who'd be thankful?" said Bubble Gum. "Dickens is clueless."

"But Esther, the ugly one, still wins out," said Dazzler. "In the end she gets Woodcourt—the guy she's always wanted. And Lady Ded—"

"Personally," said Bubble Gum, "I think Dickens was way off there."

"*If* you'll let me finish," said Dazzler.

"Yeah," said Comedian, "let the beautiful little lady finish."

Dazzler and Rhodes Scholar glared at him. Bubble Gum looked wistful. "I was *saying*," said Dazzler, "that Lady Dedlock's beauty destroys her. Tulkinghorn goes after her because she's beautiful—"

"Where? Where does it say that?" said Debater.

"She says herself she can't shake him off."

"Where?" said Debater.

"It doesn't matter—you know she can't shake him off. And listen to this"—Dazzler turned the pages—"it's here somewhere. Anyway, Dickens says something like Lady Dedlock's beauty makes Tulkinghorn want to pursue her all the more."

Oh, all right, Beth was thinking. I'll let her go on. She had wanted to talk about Lady Dedlock anyway, because she always connected her with Jill. "Then you believe," she said, "that Lady Dedlock's beauty is crucial?"

"It sure is," said Dazzler. "Her beauty gets her in trouble right from the start. If she hadn't been so beautiful, do you think whatshisname—you know—her first love—"

"Hawdon," said Beth.

"Stupid name for a great lover," said Comedian. "Sounds like Haw Haw—or Sawdust—or Sausage—"

"*Will* you let me finish?" said Dazzler. "If she hadn't been so beautiful, Hawdon wouldn't have wanted to have sex with her. And look where that got her. She had a baby—out of wedlock."

"Horrors!" said Comedian.

"Well, it was bad to do that then," said Bubble Gum.

"It's still bad. Look at those college kids who murdered their baby"—Digresser.

"That wasn't because of the disgrace—"

"Yes it was—"

"They didn't want the responsibility—"

Before Beth could come in, Dazzler got them back on her track. "I'm saying that Dickens makes Lady Dedlock *suffer* because she's beautiful. Underneath, she's miserable, frightened—"

"Scared shitless," said Comedian. "Oh, my goodness. I mean scared to death."

"Oh shut up." Dazzler was losing it. She looked ready to cry. "Lady Dedlock is *miserable*, always having to act snooty and bored to cover up her guilty sin. Because if society finds out about it, she'd be—she'd be—" The tears were starting.

"Good point," said Beth. "You mean she would be an outcast."

"Yes, an outcast." Dazzler had regained her composure. "And look where her beauty gets her. She ends down in the dirt in a filthy graveyard."

"In someone else's horrible clothes," said Digresser.

"Horrible clothes!" said Comedian. "Life was terrible then. No Gap. No malls."

"Oh, let's be sophomoric," said Future Rhodes Scholar.

"Sophomoric? What sophomoric? I junior," said the Thai student, unleashing peals of laughter.

"The point," said Rhodes Scholar, "is that everyone sets standards for how women should look, but no one sets standards for men. No wonder women are sex objects."

"That wasn't my point," said Dazzler. "I'm saying that Dickens makes chopped liver of beautiful women."

"All I know," said Bubble Gum, "is it's hell not to be beauti-ful."

But you are beautiful, Beth wanted to say. You just think you aren't. You have beautiful hair, beautiful eyes. Your skin will clear. . . .

"And I don't believe Esther did get Woodcourt," said Bubble Gum. "Not with all those pockmarks. Dickens got *that* wrong."

CHAPTER FORTY-SIX

Something about the class. Something that stirred the back of her brain. But what?

In the library, Beth unlocked her study carrel, slung her briefcase on the desk, and sat, head in hands, pondering.

The tension between Dazzler and Bubble Gum. It was there, whether Dazzler knew it or not. The same tension must have strained dreadfully between Jill and—and everyone—even if Jill was unaware.

Bubble Gum's glance at Dazzler. Then her peek in the mirror that proved to her she was vanquished. How often the same envious glances must have come Jill's way. And how often the Dall girls must have measured themselves against Jill.

Jill, running to take one of her millions of phone calls. Jill, stretching out her arms to slick and handsome Evil, pulling him up to dance. Jill dancing, her perfect white shoulders swaying with the music—Tony cutting in. Sexy, T-shirted Jill, bending, bending, over Tony. The kiss! How the girls must have gazed at her, captivated despite themselves, and how they, like Bubble Gum, must have felt all their efforts had been wasted. Against Jill, there could have been no winners. But who had most resented the crushing defeat?

Or was it, Beth wondered, the outcast point that had jogged her memory. *Outcast.* She scribbled the word over and over on a

legal pad. Then she wrote *Society* and *Lady Dedlock*, and drew
an arrow leading from *Society* to *Lady Dedlock*. For her sin,
society would make Lady Dedlock an outcast—just as society,
for the same reason, surely would have made Jill an outcast.

But it was not just society, condemning from without. There
were those who condemned from within, who made themselves
outcasts. *Bubble Gum*, she wrote. *Makes herself an outcast. Judges
herself inferior. Can never measure up to Dazzler.* Then she wrote:
Dall Hall. Losers. Had the girls who lost the race to Jill made
themselves feel like outcasts? Was there one among them who
felt so defeated that she had lost all hope?

Outcast, she wrote again, and suddenly thought of Cob Conner's column . . . Conner . . . Dewey. . . . Why hadn't
she heard from Abe? If Abe didn't call—shouting and whistling
from outside.

She stood and looked out the window. Passing beneath her
was a strange parade. Sonny and Cher. Mickey and Minnie. A
lamp shade. A Green Bay Packer. Madonna. Witches. Skeletons.
Who was that supposed to be in the gray sweatshirt and sunglasses? Of course—the Unabomber! She watched the Hal-
loweeners crossing the quadrangle, a heavily sheeted ghost
bringing up the rear.

She chuckled, thinking of the Ghost of Chesney Wold, that
harbinger of doom who cropped up in *Bleak House* whenever
Dickens wanted to shake his readers up. The essential Ghost, its
dreaded footsteps echoing on the terrace, its croaking voice issu-
ing periodic warnings. " 'Let the Dedlocks listen for my step!
Calamity is coming!' "—or something like that. Charles Dickens, I love you when you're melodramatic.

Getting late. Getting dark. Maybe Abe had been trying to
call. At that thought, Beth gathered her things and raced out of
her carrel.

In a hurry, she rushed out of the elevator when the doors were barely open and collided with a headless student—or so his load of books made it appear. He bumped her so hard she started to fall, managed to stay upright, but in saving herself gave her ankle a painful twist. Before she could vaporize him, the elevator doors closed and the student vanished.

Swearing to herself, she moved slowly across the lower level. "Yo, Beth," Circulation called, as she passed the desk. "One of your students was here, asking about you." One of her students? "Must have been—dressed for Halloween. Wanted to know your carrel number—as if I'd give that out. Wanted to know what time you leave the library—as if I know your—hey, why are you limping?"

She dragged herself up the steps, considered and rejected the Handicapped exit, painfully negotiated the swinging door—and found herself in the thick of the Halloween parade.

CHAPTER FORTY-SEVEN

Laughing and shouting "Trick or treat," the parade swept on, while Beth, slowed by her ankle, dropped behind, hardly noticing where she was walking. She kept seeing Dall Hall in her mind, the spiffed-up boys trailing in to give their names to the maid, the girls in their date dresses listening for the buzz that meant Gentleman Caller, Waiting Below. Boys downstairs, girls upstairs, always so apart—She heard a rustling sound, looked over her shoulder, and saw behind her the ghost she had seen from her carrel window.

There was something peculiar about this ghost who had separated from the parade. He was dressed like the usual Halloween ghost, draped in sheets from head to toe. The way he walked, she decided. An older walk—not aged—in fact, rather light and powerful—but he didn't move like a student. Not carefree or careless enough.

Her ankle throbbing, she went on, thinking she would soak it as soon as she got home. No. First she would check for a message from Abe. As she passed the dark Sciences building, she heard leaves crunching and turned. Odd. The ghost was still behind her. He should have passed her long ago. She walked on, picking up the pace a bit. Just ahead was Parker-Andrews Dorm, decorated—if it could be called that—P-A style, pulverized pumpkins, decaying haystacks, ribbons of toilet paper coiling over a sign—PARTY TONIGHT.

The parade was far in the distance now. They had passed Parker-Andrews and were swinging out of the quadrangle, probably heading for the Boulder, the not-so-ancient paint-coated rock that was the site of many a Midwestern celebration.

How quiet it was now that the shouts of the paraders had died down, and how lonely. Except for a couple of rollerbladers gliding in the direction of the parade, she was alone in the darkness. How easy it would be for someone to conceal himself behind the overgrown bushes along the walk—or to lurk just here in the shadowy alcoves of Journalism Hall. "Give us escorts, give us light"—she thought of the angry paraders of a few months ago. She heard a twig snap. Turning, she saw the ghost moving up on her determinedly, staring directly at her. Suddenly she remembered today's *Prairie Gust* article about the increase in rape on campus, a serious issue, campus police said, and the University had services to help. Wonderful. How could they help her here and now?

Raped by a ghost? Oh, come on. She had watched too many stupid *Return of the Taloned Nerd* Halloween movies. Still, instead of turning right, down her usual path toward home, she moved ahead toward Parker-Andrews.

Now, let's see. If he's following the parade, he'll turn. She glanced around. The ghost was crouched over, tying a shoe—or pretending? The rollerbladers were still in sight, and nearby a girl was walking along slowly, reading a book by flashlight. Is he stalling, waiting to get me alone? Is he following me at all? Well, there was one way to find out. The girl passed her, and for a moment, Beth thought of stopping her and asking to walk with her. Silly—she would find out for herself. She made for Parker-Andrews.

Entering P-A through a side door, she debated a second, then took the stairs down to the basement. Her eyes took in the narrow hall, scanned a wall of signs urging students to earn great money at nonsmoking child care, to prepare for LSAT's, to experience Jesus. Dashing past a cleaning cart loaded with rags and mops and Earth Save detergents, Beth almost had an eye gouged out by a broom handle.

NINETY PERCENT OF RAPISTS RAPE AGAIN! The poster leaped out at her as she passed the laundry room. Yes! She could take cover here. She looked inside. The room was in full swing, washers churning, dryers whirling, lights blazing down on discarded sweat socks and designer underwear—but their owners were missing. The place was empty. She hurried on, heard a door bang, and seconds later saw the ghost at the far end of the hall.

Now Beth really raced, or tried to. Ignoring the pain in her ankle, she rushed past storage rooms to the opposite end of the hall. Up the metal stairs she ran, dodging empty drink cans, her shoes sticking to the steps. She stumbled over a beer bottle, caught herself, reached the top, and opened the door. She hurried past mailboxes, study rooms—empty, of course. A bathroom! Here—I'll hide in here! She opened the door and almost yelled, "Man on the floor!"

The boy standing at a urinal looked at her inquiringly. "Oh," she said, "sorry." "Not a problem! Come on in." She fled—better rape than embarrassment—and saw the ghost heading her way, the sheets revealing his heavy shoes. He can't be a rapist, she decided. What rapist would take this chance, she thought as he moved closer. But he is following me. And he looks dangerous. Or have I gone completely bananas? What if he's merely heading for the party? All right. She would go to the party too. No matter what, she would be safe there. She ran toward the blast factory.

The scene that greeted her was out of a trashy movie about the dissolution of youth on campus. On a sofa turned bottom side up, a boy stood drinking from a wine bottle. On the crowded dance floor, a basketball player wearing a jockstrap over spandex shorts slow-danced with a vampire. A witch bounced to the beat with a ghost in mirrored sunglasses. At the heart of the uproar—music, rather—was the group in a corner whose drum proclaimed them the Vulgar Manners. "We like big butts," their singer screamed into the microphone. "*Yeah,* we like big butts," their fans roared as they swayed drunkenly to the music.

No sign of her ghost. What if he did come in? What would she do? Well, wait and see. "Hey! I'm going to marry Cindy Crawford!" "Well, I have a *humongous* lifeline." Beth moved past the fortune teller to a ravaged drinks table, where beer and wine spewed into potato chips and pretzels.

"What's your poison?" From behind a steaming witches' cauldron, a boy bartender emerged. She didn't know. "How about a Fuzzy Navel?" What was that—inadvertently looking in the direction of his belt. "Peach schnapps with OJ—here, try one." He handed her a drink.

She stood there holding her drink, listening to a mingle of "We like big butts" and blatant "macking"—Midwestern's word for putting the moves on someone. "You look familiar. Aren't you in my Econ.?" "Can I get you a beer?" "Can I see your room?" "Do you have a boyfriend? I'm praying, physically praying, you don't."

"Great costume." "Great costume," the voice repeated, and Beth realized the tall boy in a Midwestern Mudpuppies T-shirt was talking to her. "Oh, thanks."

"You're supposed to be a prof, right?" She nodded. "The briefcase is a great touch. What's in it?" Ungraded papers, she told him. "That's great—ungraded papers. Didn't I see you at the Chi Delt party last weekend?" Me, she said. No. "Well, I saw you somewhere. Want to dance?" She hesitated—then saw her ghost come in. No mistaking the walk. She drank her Fuzzy Navel to the bottom. Would the ghost join the party? No, he was just standing there—staring at her.

"Okay," she said, "let's dance," and in a few moments, she was limping to "Drop your drawers, Drop, drop your drawers." Good moves, her partner said. "Like it?" she said. "An old war injury. 'Nam." Seriously? "Okay, I'll tell you the truth—a student dropped some books on me."

"A student!"—he roared. "I love your quirky humor!"

"Drop your drawers, Drop, drop your drawers." A few guys followed directions and showed off plaid shorts. One—quite mad—stripped to his briefs as he jumped up and down. "Look at that fat guy doing the Roger Rabbit," said her date. "What a clown, still doing those eighties' moves."

"I think I'm being chased," she said. What? he said. "I think I'm being chased."

"I bet you are."

"I'm serious. I might be in danger."

"Who's chasing you?"

"A ghost."

He stopped dancing. "A ghost? Seriously?" She nodded. "Which one?"

Beth looked. The room was bursting with ghosts—dancing ghosts, drinking ghosts, ghosts getting their fortunes told—and she had no idea which was hers. "God, I'm not sure—I think he wants to get me alone."

"Then stay with me. I know—let's get out of here."

"Hey, Robbie." Beth's date turned. "Come on, you promised."

"Oh my God, I forgot," said Robbie, pulling on a turban and
dark glasses. "I promised to tell fortunes. Got to go. Wooooo!
Watch out for ghosts. Hey, I know. Wait for me. I'll polish off
the fortunes in a nanosecond. Then we'll go out to dinner and
bond. Wait! Don't forget—" He faded into the crowd.

The room was packed with ghosts now. Couldn't they be
more original? Was it the one at the bar? The one passed out on
the floor? Should I scream? What could I say? I'm not thinking
clearly—no more Fuzzy Navels. Now all the ghosts seemed to
be looking at her.

Okay, she told herself. Be logical. A: If I leave, and a ghost
leaves too, he is following me. B: Whichever ghost leaves is the
one who's been following me. C: If he does follow me, I'll call
911. She tore out of the room and took a corridor to the left.
Comic strips. Signs on doors. CHEM SUCKS. THE PIT. FEEL THE
LOVE OOZING OUT OF THIS ROOM. She was in student living
quarters.

The hall was empty, all the doors tightly closed. She turned,
saw the ghost coming her way—and panicked. Yelling, "Open
up!" she kept trying doors. No luck. She turned, her hand on a
doorknob. The ghost was just standing there. Suddenly she
thought, this is crazy. I've done this all wrong. I should have
just asked him what he wants. She started to move toward
him—a flash, a *pop*—the GO, MUDPUPPIES sign on the door
shattered to bits. He has a gun! She saw a sheeted arm go up,
and ran. Another flash and *pop*. A license plate flew off a door.

She wheeled around a corner, saw a sign. DO NOT DISTURB.
SICK MAN INSIDE. *Hypochondriac*, someone had scrawled underneath. Beth turned the knob—the door opened!

She ran inside and found herself in darkness, the only light from a computer, where a BULLS ROCK pattern moved endlessly across the screen. She turned the lock, leaned against the door, trying to catch her breath. "Is that you, Bunny?" said a voice from the darkness.

"No. Shh. It's not Bunny."

A light went on. The room looked like an overstocked discount outlet. Television. Toaster oven. Refrigerator. Cindy Crawford, Claudia Schiffer, Scottie Pippen posters. A basketball hoop fixed to one wall, and suspended from the ceiling swags of "Caution" tape crisscrossing the room. Seeing a familiar shape, she ran to it, discovered it was a chair, and shoved everything off. A metal coffeepot dropped on her foot and brought tears to her eyes. "Turn out that light!" she yelled, as she dragged the chair across the room and wedged it under the doorknob.

"Hey, who are you?"

In the center of a bed piled with cracker boxes, empty soda bottles, and a basketball, a boy—pale, fair hair in a buzz cut—leaned on an elbow watching her.

"Turn out that light!"

"Who are you?"

"I'm Professor Austin."

"Sure, and I'm Michael Jordan."

"Please! I'm being followed. *Will* you turn off that light!"

"Who's following you?"

"A gho—please, he's trying to kill me."

"Oh, sure. What are you drinking?" But he turned out the light.

A knock on the door. The light came on again. Beth had a second look at the boy. Stained gray T-shirt crawling up around a thin neck, an appealing face, greeny-pale now. And the darkest brown eyes she had ever seen, staring at her suspiciously. Another knock.

"Come on in, Bun," the boy called. "It's open."

"No, it's not"—a raspy voice.

"Damn." The boy pushed a recycling bin overflowing with cans and bottles out of the way and crawled out of bed.

Beth backed up against the refrigerator. "Don't open that door!"

"It's Bunny. I've got to."

"It's not Bunny. *Don't open it!*"

"I've got to." He weaved toward the door, mumbled, "What is this stuff?" and shoved the chair aside. He swung the door open, and Beth dived under the bed.

"Hey, you're not—where's Bunny?"

"I'm looking for—"

Under the bed, listening, Beth thought, whose voice is that? She had heard it before, she knew it. Whoever it was was disguising his voice. A man trying to sound like someone else? A woman trying to sound like a man? Who is it? Who's after me?

"Looking for who, exactly?" the boy said sternly.

"My date—we had a fight. Didn't I see her go in here?"

"There's no one here. Go away. Can't you see I'm sick? You'll catch bubonic plague." The door slammed shut, and Beth heard the boy bumping and swearing across the room. He jumped into bed, and the mattress sank down like a trash compactor, crushing her body into something wet and clammy. She didn't even want to think about what she was lying in.

"Hey, where are you?" he whispered.

"Under the bed," she whispered back.

"You can come out. I got rid of him. What's all the hoo-ha? It's just some jerk in a ghost costume. What happened? What were you fighting about?"

"I'm telling you, he's dangerous. Call the police."

"Oh, come on. They'll kill me if CP come to the dorm on a party night."

"And he'll kill me, if you don't call the police. Hurry up!" She shivered, feeling water trickle over her fingers. The rug was sodden now.

"Oh, all right. I'll call. Where the hell—" Bottles clinking. A heavy bump—the basketball bouncing to the floor? "Oh, here—" Clicking. Swearing. "Damn. I forgot Bun pulled the cord out when she got mad at me for not e-mailing her." At that moment Beth hated Bunny with a terrible hatred. "Anyway, you'll make it up with your guy. Uh—sorry I called him a jerk."

"Call him a jerk. He's *not* my guy."

"Whoever. He thinks you're gone."

"Not whoever. He has a gun."

"Just licorice. I've got one, too—I'll show you. It's here somewhere—oh, no . . . oh, God. . . ." Beth hoped he had found the recycling bin in time. "I feel like sh—groggy."

Sudden shouting outside. "What's going on?" Beth said.

"I don't . . . know. . . . Stay here. . . . You'll be safe," and almost instantly she heard regular breathing.

More shouting and pounding, so much racket she couldn't believe he was still asleep—and under the bed a stream of water.

Louder pounding. "Kelly! Kelly!"—a shrieking chorus. "Open up, Kelly!"

Whoever Kelly was, he wasn't interested.

"It's desperate, Kelly! You've got to come out!"

"Oh, for God's—what's the matter?" A girl's voice.

"There's a flood, Kelly."

"Go away, brats. I'm watching a Muppets movie."

"We're not kidding, Kelly. The bathroom's at high tide."

"Okay, okay. Let me get my shoes on."

"No shoes necessary, Kelly."

Drenched all down her front, Beth emerged from under the bed. In the dim light, she could see water seeping into the room. She looked at the boy, still sound asleep. She shook him gently, and his eyes opened. "Why'd you have to wake me up?"

"Who's Kelly?"

"The RA." He closed his eyes.

The hall was a river, jammed with students. Maybe the ghost was part of the mob squishing through the water, but she couldn't spot him. She followed the students downstream to a bathroom where a niagara was gushing into the hall. Inside, on the bathroom floor, a shattered urinal, and where the urinal had been, a pipe spouted jets of ice-cold water, tossing hair dryers and bottles off shelves, hurling toothbrushes into the air. The place reeked of fruit shampoo.

"What happened, Kelly?" someone said.

"Some incredible idiot thinks he's funny. We've got it under control." This from a girl in hitched-up pajamas, wearing plastic bags over bare feet. "Get those cans in here!" she shouted. "Go, go, go!"

A trash-can brigade started to form.

"Get more cans!" Kelly yelled. "Someone call Physical Plant! Get that bin over here, Bunny. Now, hold it over the pipe!"

"I can't hold it down," said a wiry girl sporting vampire teeth.

"Here, you"—Kelly looked at Beth—"you aren't doing any-thing. Help her hold it down."

"I can't," said Beth—seeing the ghost in the doorway. She ran into a shower stall.

"Stop! What are you doing?" Kelly screamed. "We're dump-ing water in there."

"Help!" Bunny yelled. "The bin's coming off!"

"You help her, Robbie."

Beth peered through a gap in the curtain, saw the ghost slipping and sliding toward her.

"Hey, you!" Kelly screamed at the ghost. "You're in the way. Get out or grab a can and start helping."

The ghost lifted an arm—flash! *pop!* Beth felt a rush of air pass her ear and an instant later a spray of tile chips.

Screams. Shrieks. "He's got a gun!"

Heavy feet. Two men in coveralls and boots splashing through the water.

"Get that ghost!" Kelly yelled. "Don't let him get away!"

The ghost was half out the door. One of the men threw a wrench at him. The ghost dodged and was off like a shot.

"Damn," said Kelly. "Bet he's the Beta who wrecked the urinal."

"What kind of pool party is this?" yelled Physical Plant. "What the hell have you been doing in here?"

"What have *we* been doing?" Kelly yelled back.

"Yeah," Bunny screamed. "Why blame us?"

Then the whole crowd was screaming. "You think we like it? My Nintendo is totaled." "My CD's are floating." "My hard drive is under water. I lost my whole paper—including the footnotes!"

Amid the uproar Beth slipped away, squishing rapidly down the hall.

"Wait! You said you'd wait!"

She turned. Robbie.

"What about dinner?"

"Another time, Robbie. My costume is soaked." She ran.

"But what's your name? I don't even know your name. What's your sorority?"

CHAPTER FORTY-EIGHT

TIDAL WAVE AT PARKER-ANDREWS;
FRACTURED URINAL INUNDATES DORM

Parker-Andrews, always lively, was even livelier in the wee hours of last night's Halloween party. A flood broke up the party after some jerk or jerks jerked a urinal off the wall of a first-floor bathroom.

"Basically my room was a monsoon. Water was spewing out of the wall like lava," said one student, whose computer was destroyed. "I lost my whole paper on the gender experience in today's society."

Residence Hall Head, Kelly McNulty, said she "responded immediately" to a knock on her door. "I promptly organized a trash-can bucket brigade, and a whole bunch of students worked together calmly to bail out the bathroom." When Physical Plant workers came to shut the water off, they were "amazed at how well we had it under control," said McNulty.

McNulty said that she "strongly suspects the culprits live nearby." Asked where, she would say only, "a certain fraternity."

Campus police are looking for two students, one costumed as a professor. The other, wearing a ghost costume, allegedly fired a BB gun into the shower. Campus police conjecture that he was intoxicated.

One student reports that he danced with the student
in the professor costume. "She was very evasive," he
said.

Anyone who knows anything about this incident is
asked to contact campus police.

Evasive, Beth thought, reading the *Prairie Gust* article over a
late breakfast. Robbie doesn't know how evasive I want to be.
So campus police—those Sherlocks—are looking for me and the
ghost. Great. They think we're in cahoots—just two fun-loving
partygoers fracturing a urinal together.

But the BB gun—that was really strange. It wouldn't be the
first time the *Gust* had it wrong. Could the error be deliberate—
CP playing it cagey? Or did they really believe the ghost was
shooting BB's?

She knew better. Someone *was* after her—face it, trying to
kill her. I'm stirring up something that someone wants to keep
buried. But who? Someone older—someone I could have easily
outrun, if it hadn't been for my ankle. Someone I'd recognize, or
why the disguise? The murderer thinks I know something. I
don't. Or do I?

Dewey must have known who the murderer was. . . .
Dewey, Dewey, everything comes back to you. If only I knew
more about you. If only Abe- -why hadn't she heard from Abe?
No message when she came in, and even if she hadn't been so
drenched and exhausted, it had been too late to call. She added
warm water to the tub where she was soaking her ankle, then
picked up the phone.

"I was just going to call you," said Abe, again startling Beth
because his voice was so like Link's. "How did you say you got
interested in Dewey Conner?"

"I didn't. But did you learn anything?"

"I'll say I did. But first—if I go to jail, tell Laurie I expect her to bail me out." The charming chuckle.

"I'm sure she'll be happy to. Did you commit a felony?"

"Not quite. But I did have to phony up a research idea. Then I had to play nice with the director of medical records—and she's tough. Jessie, I said, I'm doing a retrospective research project. I need all the charts on sudden deaths in the ICU over a five-year period. I can't do it, says Jessie—other doctors' records, approval from the research committee—on and on. Come on, Jessie, I said. You've known me for years. That's what I mean, she said. Oh, come on, I'm not going to publish, I said. I sweet-talked her, and she finally agreed—and then she said since she's being so nice, I have to take her to dinner. So now I'm in for it—candy, flowers, dinner—the whole shmear— all because of you. And Laurie, too, since you're her daughter." Again, the low chuckle.

"I take complete responsibility," Beth said. "Send me the tab for a big evening"—and get to the point!

"When she finally had the charts pulled, there was quite a stack. Hey! Maybe I do have a research project!" Egotist! Stick to the subject. "I made a big deal about looking through a lot of charts, taking notes, before I concentrated on your friend Dewey." Wasn't she *your* friend, Abe? You must have known her. "And then—" said Abe.

"And then?" keeping her voice calm.

"I have to say you may be onto something. Your friend had pneumonia with high fever and sepsis, which, as you know, is a bloodstream infection. They were giving her IV antibiotics for the infection. They were giving her dobutamine to raise the blood pressure to a reasonable level. Then she defervesced."

"What's that?"

"And you a doctor's daughter. Her temperature came down

to normal. The blood pressure was maintained. She became more alert and responsive. Then all of a sudden she has an arrest."

"A cardiac arrest."

"Right. Her heart stopped beating. So they bagged her, started pumping oxygen in. They threw an electric shock into the heart. She had a few contractions, but failed to respond. She remained in cardiac arrest. The end."

"But what makes you suspicious? You *are* suspicious?"

"Indeed I am. My dear Beth, it's bizarre. The post showed no cardiac abnormality. The EKG was normal. She had no history of rhythm disturbances. Then she dies suddenly of a cardiac standstill. *Very* suspicious. Her heart shouldn't have stopped. Not only that, the heart died in diastole instead of systole—which proves the heart failed to contract. It doesn't make sense."

It didn't to Beth, either.

"The only thing that does make sense," Abe said, "is hyperkalemia. The arrest looks like hyperkalemia," he said, his voice—Link's voice—weighted with meaning.

"Hyperkalemia?"

"An excess of potassium in the blood. I suspect someone gave your friend a huge squirt of potassium. And potassium, as you, a doctor's daughter, know, is one of the blood salts that helps maintain a lot of normal functions."

"Like what?"

"Breathing. Moving the body. *The heart beating*. Don't you know the body is composed of lots of different parts, all of which have to work?"

Skip the condescension, Abe. "So how does someone slip in the potassium?"

"Easy—a needle into the tubing. Just squirt it—a *big*

squirt—into the IV, and the potassium charges into the blood-stream."

"Wouldn't the person with the needle be seen?"

"Have you ever been in an ICU? There's so much going on. And even if it's a quiet night, walk into any hospital wearing a lab coat, and they'll let you transplant a kidney—on the unlikely assumption it's okay with the patient's HMO."

"What would the potassium do?"

"Paralyze the heart muscle so it can't contract. That would explain why the heart died in diastole instead of systole. She must have been poisoned."

"But why wasn't her doctor suspicious?"

"Ah, her doctor. Let's just say some high-priced docs aren't as good as their reputations."

"But still—why didn't it show up on the post?"

"They don't always routinely check electrolytes. Now listen. I can't prove any of this. I just have a strong suspicion. It's up to you to prove it—and to find out whoever did it. What are you after anyway?"

Is he playing dumb? He must have known Dewey. "I've got my own retrospective research project," she said.

"Oh, yeah? Do you need some charts?"

"This is research into a campus murder from long ago."

"A campus murder? You don't mean Jill Jansen? I thought that was put to rest years ago."

Why did Abe sound so uncomfortable, so—guilty? Then she remembered. The Open House. Laurie in her room, waiting for Abe. Laurie leaving her room, running down the hall—she stops. In the ironing room, Jill and *Abe*, kissing passionately.

"Beth?" Abe's voice brought her back. "I asked you, does Laurie—"

"Does Laurie what?"

"You didn't hear my question?"

"No, what was it?"

"Nothing—be sure to give her my love."

"I will—and thanks." The conversation ended. She knew she had sounded cold, but she couldn't help it. That's the man my mother almost married—oh, don't think about it now.

Dewey. Poor Dewey. Dewey in the ICU. It's night. She's lying in bed, asleep. No, she's awake, thinking how much better she feels, that she's pulled through. Someone comes in, stands at her bed. Was Dewey terrified? No, she must have recognized the person. She's surprised—not terrified. Not at first . . .

So someone murdered Dewey. The thief!

She called Link. "You had the right idea about Dewey."

"What idea?"

"Don't you remember? Conner's 'Her Naziness' column. You thought Dewey told her father not to publish—"

"Oh, yeah," said Link. "Because Dewey was afraid if the thief found out what Dewey knew. But the thief—I was thinking of a weird teenager a long time ago."

"Well, your teenager grew up."

"What are you talking about?"

"Your father thinks—"

"My father! You talked to him?"

"Yes, I talked to him." She told him about the conversation.

"He thinks Dewey was murdered?" said Link. "But who—"

"Just what you said—the thief covering up."

"But the thief's an adult now. What's the motive?"

"The motive's the same—and more."

"The same? My theory doesn't make sense now. Why would an adult worry about a few teenage peccadilloes from a long time ago?"

"Because the adult realizes Dewey knew that the thief killed Jill!"

"I don't know about that, Beth. Anyway, you said Dad wasn't positive."

"But he's *very* suspicious."

"You said he couldn't prove it."

That, Beth thought, was the problem.

"Well, one good thing," Link said. "This lets my father off the hook."

"Why?"

"Why would he go to the trouble to prove Dewey might have been murdered? And by the way, it was damn decent of him."

"He still could have done it," said Beth, thinking Abe was clever. He thought of phonying up the research. "He was in New York at the time, wasn't he?"

"I don't know. I suppose so. Then what's his motive?"

She was stumped.

"What about your mother? Was she in New York?"

"She might have been," Beth admitted. "What's *her* motive?"

"Maybe she was—"

He didn't finish the sentence, but she knew what he was thinking. Her mother a thief—a murderer! This was too much.

"My mother," she said, "did *not* go around necking with every boy who crossed her path."

"What the hell are you talking about, Beth?"

She put down the phone.

The nerve. Accusing her mother, when his father—To think that Abe, that two-timer, could have been *her* father. What was it Abe was going to ask—does Laurie *what*? Probably, does Laurie forgive me? She hoped that Laurie did not. Beth certainly didn't.

CHAPTER FORTY-NINE

On a rainy November afternoon, Bubble Gum arrived at Beth's office. The girl looked rather seedy, an unfortunate outbreak on her forehead, her frizzy hair tied back in a midterms ponytail. "I wanted to talk to you about my paper."

"Not much here yet," said Beth, looking over the few wrinkled pages. " 'Feelings of guilt,' 'shame,' 'boredom,' 'despair.' You're writing about Lady Dedlock?"

"Yes, but I don't know what I want to say."

"You mention her boredom—her fashionable boredom. Is that what interests you?"

Bubble Gum shook her head.

"Well then, her disgrace—an out-of-wedlock baby. What do you think of the difference between then and now?"

"Oh, I don't care about that."

Beth refrained from saying, What *do* you care about? "What," she asked, "do you think of Lady Dedlock, herself?"

"What do I think of her?" Bubble Gum sat up straight. "I wish *I* were Lady Dedlock!"

"But why?" said Beth, though she could guess and dreaded the answer. "She's so unhappy."

"Not *be* her exactly. I mean look like her. Not her clothes and all that. What I mean—well, I wish I were so beautiful that I could stun everyone like she does."

"Surely not everyone," said Beth, playing for time. "What about Inspector Bucket?"

"Well, almost everyone—Sir Leicester, Sir Leicester's funny cousin, Guppy—even that mean old guy Tulkinghorn. They're all obsessed with her because she's so gorgeous. And if I had her looks, I could—could—" She stared dolefully at the ceiling.

"Could what?" said Beth.

"Have someone obsessed with *me*," she said, chewing her gum as furiously as Michael Jordan in a close game.

Beth started to ask if she had someone special in mind, then thought better of it.

But Bubble Gum persisted. "I don't want to say who exactly—but it's someone you've seen." She giggled. "He wears these crazy T-shirts—and he's *so* funny."

Oh, my God. She has a crush on Comedian. Go figure.

"If only he was interested in me—even a little," said Bubble Gum. "I know he *was* interested—once."

"Well, that was nice," said Beth. "About your paper—"

"He walked to the elevator with me after class," said Bubble Gum, "and we had this amazing conversation about the Mudpuppies' chances for the Rose Bowl. I don't really care about football, but it was so wonderful just talking to him—and then *she* had to come along."

Beth said nothing. *She*, of course, was Dazzler.

"I've given him all sorts of chances," said Bubble Gum. "I've walked and walked past his fraternity house. I stood right next to him at the Dance Marathon. I sent him an e-mail."

"Did he answer?"

"No—it's hopeless. He doesn't care about me anymore. He likes *her*."

"Your paper—"

"I can't even think about my paper! All I think about is him!"

Beth pushed the Kleenex over, thinking, what can I say? Tell her she *is* beautiful? No. That is not what Bubble Gum needed to hear just now—she wouldn't believe it anyway. "Bubb—I mean, Florence," she said, and why, she thought, did your parents saddle you with Florence? "I want to make you a promise."

"What?"—reaching for Kleenex.

"Someday you will be on the top floor of your dorm, and someone will tell you that this person—whoever he is—is just outside, walking down the sidewalk. And you won't care enough to look out the window. I promise."

"That could never happen"—almost smiling.

"Wait and see," said Beth. "Give it some time."

They spent the next half hour discussing her paper, and when Bubble Gum left, she blew a large pink bubble.

Beth brushed the sodden pile of Kleenex into the wastebasket. Poor Bubble Gum. And not just Bubble Gum—all the wretched girls who become as obsessed with a man as—as a Trollope heroine. Ready to give up their interests, their opinions, their time—to devote themselves to one undeserving male.

Crushes. How easily they formed. One casual conversation, one meaningless gesture, and the already smitten girl—or boy—recklessly assumed that true love was returned. She sat thinking . . .

"What's your hurry?" yelled Dot, the department secretary, as Beth ran out of the English office. "Chasing criminals again?"

"Sort of."

A short time later she was home, skimming her notes. The early days at Dall . . . The bridge games . . . The scent of Tabu . . . The gang in Laurie's room, talking about "doing it" . . . Mrs. Primwell's cultural evening—Dewey serving coffee . . . The Gang in Louise and Jill's room, transforming Louise into a glamour pants for Tony . . . Date night—and shattered hopes. She understood now.

Then another idea suggested itself. She flipped the pages to the Open House. . . . Laurie running down the hall . . . Jill and Abe kissing . . . Yes! She played with the idea for a few minutes, then went to her desk and tore through a pile of papers.

> Dewey Cobwell Conner, daughter of the late Charles "Cob" Conner, noted columnist, died yesterday in Manhattan Hospital. She died suddenly after a brief illness, said Ms. Evelyn New, her companion. Ms. Conner, who served for years as her father's assistant, was known for her support of feminist causes and worked with the National Organization for Women on behalf of the Equal Rights Amendment. For the past year, said Ms. New, she had been writing a memoir of her childhood. There were no survivors.

Beth tossed the papers aside and headed for the library.

In Microfiche, she scanned *The New York Times* for the days following the obituary. Day one. Nothing. Day two. Nothing. Was she wrong? Day three—here it was—what had taken them so long?

But why did the name ring a bell? She stared at the page, absorbed in thought. Then she leaped up and went to a computer. She punched A for Author, punched in a name, pressed ENTER—

"Thinking of giving a play reading?" said Arthur Hewmann, looking over her shoulder at the titles on the screen.

"No," she said, "but I am thinking of becoming a producer."

CHAPTER FIFTY

Mid-November

The class had been discussing the grotesques, the devilish monstrous characters in *Bleak House*—the Smallweeds, Crook, Madame Hortense. When Hortense came up, the topic shifted to Tulkinghorn's murder.

"I love Inspector Bucket," said Comedian. "Him and his fat forefinger. I love how he puts it to his lips so he'll remember to hide what he knows, and the way he rubs it over his nose to sharpen his scent."

"Yeah," said Dazzler, "and the way he shakes his finger at someone who's guilty. I love him, too," flashing a smile at Comedian.

"I don't see why you love him," Bubble Gum said suddenly, the first time she had spoken.

Bubble Gum was looking positively pretty, Beth thought, her skin clear, her brown hair flowing over a velvet headband.

"I don't mean love him exactly," said Dazzler, sounding annoyed. "I admire him."

"But—but why?" said Bubble Gum. "Why would you admire someone like Bucket?"

"Obviously, I admire him as a detective," Dazzler said icily.

"He's so good at what he does. Isn't that what *you* meant?" turning to Comedian.

"Sort of," said Comedian. "I like his subtlety."

"What do you mean, subtlety?" said Bubble Gum.

Go for it, Bubble Gum, Beth thought. Make them explain.

"I mean," said Comedian, "like when he talks to the footman. Instead of asking, was Lady Dedlock out on the night of the murder, Bucket's subtle. He says Lady Dedlock doesn't look healthy—and gives the footman an opening. Then, when the footman says she gets headaches, Bucket says walking is good for headaches. He gets the footman to say she does go walking—" Comedian stared at Bubble Gum, who was shaking her head.

"—and the footman says she even goes for walks at night," Comedian continued. "Bucket's subtle. He doesn't say, what nights? He gets the footman to say that Lady Dedlock was out walking the night of the murder, and—" He stopped, looking puzzled. Bubble Gum was shaking her head vigorously.

Dazzler stepped in. "Oh, yeah, that was good," she said, "and he uses the same technique to get the footman to say she was wearing that fringed black mantle. So subtle," another smile at Comedian. "I love"—she caught herself—"I admire Bucket."

"I don't admire him!" said Bubble Gum. "I hate him!"

"What's to hate?" said Comedian, looking at Bubble Gum, interested.

"I hate him for setting Lady Dedlock up!" said Bubble Gum.

"How do you mean, set her up?" said Comedian, elbows on the table, gazing at Bubble Gum.

"He sets her up to look guilty! Bucket knows Hortense hates Lady Dedlock. He knows Hortense wrote the letters accusing Lady Dedlock. And he knows the letters are trash—because he already knows that Hortense murdered Tulkinghorn! But he has to go and tell Sir Leicester that the murderer is a woman, that strange things happen in high families—Bucket does everything he can to make Sir Leicester believe Lady Dedlock did it. He's *cruel*!"

"He's fooling the reader," said Dazzler. "Like in a mystery—he's throwing in false clues, like the fringed mantle. That's part of telling a story," she said, giving Bubble Gum a condescending look.

Come on, Bubble Gum, Beth thought. Don't let Dazzler get the upper hand.

Bubble Gum didn't hesitate. "He could have fooled the reader with another character. He didn't have to be so hard on Lady Dedlock."

Future Rhodes Scholar spoke up. "Maybe he's hard on her because she's beautiful. I've been reading the critics, and Angus Wilson says Lady Dedlock's sin is that she's a beautiful woman."

"What's that supposed to mean?" said Dazzler.

"I'm not sure," Rhodes Scholar admitted.

"It means," said Bubble Gum, "that Dickens treats Lady Dedlock like dirt. And he does it because he *hates* her for being beautiful. And that's why Dickens has Bucket act so cruel. It's not enough that Bucket makes Lady Dedlock look like the murderer—when he knows she isn't. He has to go and make Sir Leicester suffer, telling him about Lady Dedlock's sinful past. What does that have to do with the murder? Bucket's trying to break up their marriage. He's a creep!" said Bubble Gum, her face pink with anger, which, Beth thought, made her look even prettier.

"Like I said, it's a story," said Dazzler. "Dickens has to find a place somewhere to reveal Lady Dedlock's past to Sir Leicester."

"Then he should have found a better place!" said Bubble Gum.

"Why are you so worried about Sir Leicester?" said Dazzler. "I find your approach somewhat shallow." She looked at Comedian, as if expecting his support.

But Comedian was gazing at Bubble Gum. "Because Sir Leicester's a decent human being," she said. "He backs Lady Dedlock to the end—when it's too late. Too late," she repeated. "And it's all Bucket's fault."

"Why too late?" said Future Rhodes Scholar.

"Because Dickens never gives Lady Dedlock a chance to speak to Sir Leicester for herself!"

"Why don't you speak for yourself, Lady Dedlock?" said Comedian in a high voice. But he smiled at Bubble Gum when he said it.

As the class was leaving, Beth watched Comedian, astounded. "Wait!" he called to Bubble Gum, who turned and said something about being late for a class. "I just want to tell you," said Comedian, "I like the way you went to bat for Lady Dedlock."

"I wish *Dickens* had gone to bat for her," said Bubble Gum, and ran out the door, Comedian running after her, yelling at her to wait.

CHAPTER FIFTY-ONE

"Dickens *hates* her for being beautiful. And that's why Dickens has Bucket act so cruel." Beth was stretched out on the sofa, thinking, thinking about Bubble Gum's analysis. *Is* it her beauty that destines Lady Dedlock for the graveyard? Bucket does make Lady Dedlock look guilty, almost as if he *is* framing her. . . . Dewey. Who wanted to frame Dewey? For of course she was framed. . . .

Next to her on the table was the collection of Cob Conner's columns. Beth picked up the book and turned to "Chronicle of a Coed."

So all the girls loved her? Who ya kiddin'?

They were jealous. They were mean. They called her the Rich B---h Who Walks by Night. . . .

And then these b---hes accused this kind beautiful *rich* girl of stealing gewgaws. . . .

But all along Miss Gorgeous knew who the real thief was! Late at night Miss G. had seen her filching fripperies. . . . Get the picture?

Dewey knew the thief. And the thief's hiding place. She must have known she was framed.

Did Miss Gorgeous tell? Nosiree.

Why not? She was nobody's snitch. Anyway, she couldn't imagine any more ecstatic escapeapade than breaking out of . . .

Why, Dewey? Why didn't you tell? What was the real reason? Beth turned the pages and reviewed "Madcap Moms."

In my script, Miss Coed makes a date to meet her boyfriend. . . . "You're going to be a proud papa." . . . she revives Mr. Muscles . . . "I'm going to have your baby," she says. . . .

"Me, bottles? He howls. "Me, diapers?" He beats his chest. . . .

Nothing there.

She started to put the book down, then looked at the table of contents. Anything else? Anything at all? Dewey's biographical note caught her eye. Beth began skimming.

> *My father began as a journalist . . . stumbled into being a columnist . . . asked to fill in when . . . The rest, as they say, is history. . . . Every day millions of readers turned to his column first . . . his unique take on world events . . . latest gossip . . . known for his vivid prose, for coining words. Recently-married couples were the "newly yoked." The divorced, in Conner language, were "the unyoked" or "scrambled eggs." Get it? as Daddy would say. My father and mother were "scrambled eggs," but their divorce was kept secret for years . . . conservative publisher . . . World War II wrote propaganda for the government . . . supported Roosevelt . . . played the market . . . made a killing on Coca-Cola . . .*

Beth started to put the book aside, then struck by a sudden thought, reread closely and rushed to her notes. She flipped through the pages and stopped. Yes! Of course that was why Dewey didn't tell.

But now she was left with another, more crucial question. She stretched out again, absorbed in thought. . . . Jill . . . Was it her beauty that put Jill in her grave? . . .

"How do I look?" . . . "Knockout. Wait! Smile! Lipstick on your teeth" . . . "I'm so upset. I've got a run." . . . Beth was in Dall Hall. Preparations for the Open House were in noisy swing, high-pitched voices and low-pitched Sinatra resounding from every room.

"God that dress is gorgeous!" . . . "I smell Tabu." . . . "It's a Ceil Chapman." . . . "Hey! My turn at the iron!" . . . "Anybody got any food?" . . . "Whose buzz was that?" . . . "Anybody got any stockings?" . . . "I'm starving!" . . . "Someone's gotta be kissed." . . . "Me, Frankie! Kiss me!" . . . Intoxicated with the energy, the vivacity, the joyful activity, and the indefinable essence of dormitory, Beth rushes down the hall.

Sunlight streams into Laurie's room, lighting up the neatly made bunks, the shelves filled with Modern Library books, the Brahms and Bach records that Laurie is stacking so carefully. Beth sits on the lower bunk, watching Laurie, who looks thoughtfully at a Sinatra album. She hesitates. Don't, Beth thinks. You don't need to impress Abe. Laurie pitches Sinatra into a drawer. At the dresser now, Laurie opens *Aristotle* to "Intellectual Virtue," places the book next to the Tabu, and stands back to admire the effect. Satisfied, she runs out the door and down the hall, Beth following.

"Gorgeous. Perfect," Laurie says from the doorway. Carol asks if she really likes it. Beth thinks the room is perhaps too

perfect—almost sterile—but Laurie is ecstatic. "It's so unbelievably neat, so—so—" So un-Dewey? Beth thinks, and thinks of
the later Carol of the uncluttered house, the Carol who perhaps
drinks too much. Laurie is pointing at a bra that dangles from
the doorknob. Laughing, Carol throws the bra into the closet
and jams the door shut. "The boys are coming!" she yells.
"Let's go!" They look so excited, both of them, so happy. They
think the whole day will be perfect. They're way down the hall
now. Beth runs to catch up.

Beth watches with them while Em removes the underpants
from the radiator and tacks them to the back of the dresser. Em
points to the *Dark Victory* poster: DO YOU WANT HIM FOR
YOUR DOCTOR WHEN YOU COULD HAVE— In this Em, the Em
who has ruthlessly ousted George Brent in favor of herself, Beth
sees the same kernel of toughness that will make the later Em an
aggressively successful lawyer. Wonderful, Laurie and Carol are
saying. Em will draw a crowd. A crowd, Beth thinks, but not for
Em. Jill will draw the crowd. "Come on," says Carol. "I want
to check out the competition."

Beth tags along, almost tripping over someone's chic travel
case in the hall. She watches from the doorway, while the others
crowd in to watch Lana, who is frantically snipping the orange
out of Rebecca's hair. "She peroxided her bangs, so she could be
blond, like—" Rebecca gives her a look and Lana shuts up. In
that look, Beth sees the later Rebecca who dominates Richie.
Richie, who once deserted her—briefly—for Jill's charms, who
would desert her again if Jill beckons. Beth wants to linger to see
if the shorn Rebecca will show any trace of Rebecca the gray-
haired matriarch, who defended Dewey so vigorously. But Laurie yells, "Onward," and down they go to the other end of the
hall.

Now the whole gang is in Jill and Louise's room, staring at

the painted figures on the walls. Beth stares at Louise, so giggly and gangly, miles apart from the poised and capable Dr. Louise Hallman who has Tony well in hand. "She talked me into it," Louise is saying. *She* being Jill, who is just now slipping on a divine pink angora. Cute, Beth thinks, is not the word. Jill is beautiful, more beautiful, surely, than Lady Dedlock, because hers is a more lavish beauty, golden hair, golden skin, and under the angora a golden voluptuous body. Unlike Lady Dedlock, Jill has collected a beauty's trophies—the dance cards, the fraternity pins. All that's missing, Beth thinks, is a string of scalps—oh, God! Lana's coming in!

Lana stares at Louise's caricature of Jill. Her hips start to sway. *Don't—don't, Lana. Just borrow the damn headband and leave.* Hips swaying, Lana chants, "Ashes to ashes, dust to dust . . ." Why, Beth thinks, why did she have to come up with that particular old saw?

Now the Gang is downstairs, Beth running to keep up as they race through Great Neck and Little Neck. "Look at the food!" says Jill, and filches a potato chip. They tear into Oyster Bay. "Look at the flowers!"

Beth sits on the window seat next to Laurie, who is watching Louise drag the ottoman over. In the doorway, Rebecca is watching, too. Jill smiles as Louise reaches toward the portrait. Jill doesn't even bother to look at Em, who's telling her about this guy who knows this doctor. Doesn't even seem to care. But Louise cares. "Are you sure it's safe?" she says. Em swears it is. So Louise turns back to the portrait.

"Here come the boys! There's Mrs. P.!"

Louise jumps—and Beth was back in her living room. She had it now. She had it wrong before, but now she knew. She knew, and it was very terrible.

* * *

She phoned her mother. "I'm giving a party." What kind of party, her mother wanted to know. "A reunion party," said Beth.

"A reunion? Whose reunion?"

"The Dall girls."

"I don't think that's a good idea. We never see each other."

"I think it's a great idea—be there or be square."

Beth thought awhile, then made another call.

"Let me think about it," said Carol, startling Beth because she sounded so different from the young and laughing Carol of Open House day. "Oh, why think about it," Carol said. "I'll do it. It'll be fun. Like doing a stage set."

CHAPTER FIFTY-TWO

December

1.

They were all there—oohing and ahing.

"The grandfather clock! I'd forgotten. Does it still work?"

"Floor ashtrays. Do you believe it?"

"And there's Letitia—over the mantel! How did you get hold of Letitia? I thought they put her in storage after—"

"After what?"

"Doesn't matter—they were redecorating or something."

"But it's Oyster Bay, exactly. How did you do it, Beth?"

And when Beth said Carol had done it, wasn't she wonderful, a chorus of agreement, Carol looking pleased.

"Where on earth did you find the furniture?"

Carol explained that Beth had persuaded the people in a place called the Blond Office to let her raid the storage rooms. "I couldn't believe it. Everything was there—lamps, piano, chairs, sofa—tattered, but I have a store of forties' chintzes. Laurie did the food," she added, unaware of the pressure Beth had brought to bear on her mother.

"Oh, look—pigs in blankets! Deviled ham! Cream cheese spread! All the old snacks!"

"And punch!"

"Is it spiked?"

"What *is* that?" someone said. "What is that scent?"

"The flowers?"

"No, something else—I know that scent. I know it so well."

"Tabu!"

"That's it—Tabu!"

They were all there. All the old girls and boys. At one end of the enormous sofa, Louise, in a black dress whose simple lines shouted money. At the other end, Tony, his tan—just back from Boca?—flattering his dreamy blue eyes. Between them, Carol, chic in a black pants suit. Rebecca, in an unforgiving floral tunic, sat solidly in the big chair. Beneath her on the ottoman, Richie, in jeans. Rebecca mumbled something about the invitation saying casual and glared at Tony in his Armani suit. Em, in one of her television-anchor suits, black—why so much black?—at the piano, lightly picking out the tune of "A Man Without a Woman." Laurie, on the window seat, looking radiant. Was it, Beth wondered, because Abe sat next to her? Abe interested Beth the most. Trim and, she had to admit, handsome, in a flamboyant, styled-haircut way.

They were all there, but after the initial cries of surprise and admiration—nothing. These women, who had not seen each other for years, had talked at each other about the room, never to each other. No big hellos. No do you remember's. No whatever happened to's. It was as if they were separated by self-created iron curtains—a forties' image, Beth thought, if ever there was one.

What were they thinking? She wanted them to be on edge, off guard, ready to blurt out their secrets. But except for Rebecca, who appeared to be feeling socially incorrect rather than apprehensive, everyone seemed calm. Tony was glassy-eyed, and so was Carol, the result of drinks, probably, rather than stress. Perhaps a touch of tension in Louise, sitting so upright, and Em, at the piano—deliberately setting herself apart? Hard to tell about Abe and Laurie. They stared straight ahead, as if posing for the camera, he smiling, she serious. When to start? That was the question. This seemed the wrong time to break the silence.

"Well, here we all are again," Rebecca said. "I don't know who *he* is," looking at Link, who stood with Beth in front of the fireplace. Beth introduced him, and Abe complacently received congratulations on his famous son.

"Link's going to help with the lighting," said Beth.

"What lighting?" said Em.

"Nothing fancy," said Link. "Just dimmers—for dramatic effect. A last-minute thought—the electricians fixed it up."

"That reminds me," said Beth. "We might hear noise from downstairs—the electricians are doing some repairs."

"Dimmers? Dramatic effect? What's going on here?" said Rebecca. "What's all this for, Carol?"

"I'm not sure."

"It's the Open House, isn't it?" said Em, her fingers still on the piano keys. "The flowers. The snacks. The punch bowl. You've recreated the day of the Open House."

"Perhaps we're going to play mind games," said Louise. "Like an Agatha Christie. Doesn't Poirot entertain all the suspects at final gatherings—ostensibly to trap the murderer. His real purpose, of course, is to display his cleverness."

And that, Beth thought, is exactly what I do not want. How soon would there be jokes about "*Mon ami*, he overlooked my little gray cells"? How soon would someone pull an Alice, say

"You're nothing but a pack of cards," and walk out on the whole proceeding? Better get on with it. Glancing at Link, who nodded his readiness, she started to speak—to be interrupted by four chimes. They listened as the Rockefeller bells sounded the sweet notes of the half hour, the three-quarter hour, the hour. *Bong. Bong. Bong. Bong. Bong. Bong. Bong. Bong.*

"Eight o'clock," said Abe, "and all is not well. I feel a show coming on."

"Not a show," Beth said hastily, "or even charades. More a fact-finding session—as if we're in a think tank. This seems the time—and place—for us to get at the truth of the murder so long ago."

"The tank that sank—thought this was a party." Tony.

"I'd rather play charades." Carol.

"A trap." Richie.

"Crap," said Rebecca.

"Come, come, children," said Abe. "It's a blast! Jurassic Hyde Park. Part Two. Go for it, Beth!"

"I will," she said. A deliberate pause, a signal to Link. The lights dimmed. "Imagine," she said, "the afternoon of the Open House. You are here in Oyster Bay. . . ." Through Beth's guidance, they smelled the flowers . . . the Tabu . . . saw the dressed-up crowd of girls and boys, jamming every inch of the floor, packing the furniture, three to a chair, six to the sofa . . . heard the piano . . . the singing. . . .

"Oh, you can't get to heaven,
   OH, YOU CAN'T GET TO HEAVEN,
At Dall Hostel,
   AT DALL HOSTEL,
Cause the Lord don't like
   CAUSE THE LORD DON'T LIKE

No Aristotle. (laughter)

   NO ARISTOTLE.

OH, YOU CAN'T GET TO HEAVEN, (the whole room sang out the chorus)

   AT DALL HOSTEL . . ."

   On the floor, surrounded by adoring girls, Tony started to get up.

   "Don't go, Tony."

   "I have to—"

   "Whyyy do you have to?"

   "I have to see a man about a dog."

   Giggles. "Hurry back."

   Tony smiled, threw kisses. But instead of heading for the bathroom, he ran up the stairs to the fourth floor, knocked on a door.

   "Just a minute," said Jill. Then a few seconds later—"Okay, you can come in."

   "What were you doing?"

   "Finishing getting dressed."

   "Dressed? Oh, I'm so upset! But as long as you did, how about let's go down? Unless . . . you'd rather wait—" His hand caressed the length of her sweater.

   "Tony"—slowly moving his hand away—"there's something I want to tell you." A swift glance at the closet. "I'm PG."

   "PG. What's that?"

   "Pregnant, you dolt—"

   A pause. As she described what had happened, the scene had become so real to Beth that she had almost lost herself. The lights were bright now. She studied their faces, wishing their expressions weren't so hard to read. Bewilderment? Surprise?

Tony was sitting on the edge of the sofa, an arm around Louise. She leaned into him gratefully, her face pressed into his jacket.

"Do I have it right, Tony?" Beth said.

He looked up. "How did you know what Jill said? . . . Yes, it was something like that," he went on without waiting for an answer. "Except you left out the end. I asked Jill to marry me, and she said she couldn't or maybe it was she wouldn't—I'm not sure. I was in a daze. Anyway, she sent me packing and"— he rubbed his bald spot— "I have to say I was glad to go."

The lights dimmed, and Beth said, "You're in Jill's room again. . . ."

The door opened, and a boy emerged from the closet. "Whew! Hot in there!" He removed his leather jacket.

"Hot in here, too," said Jill.

He went to the bed and stood in front of her. "Why did you tell him that, Jill?"

"I wanted to get rid of him." Laughing, she held out her arms.

The boy leaped on the bed, embraced Jill passionately. When the door opened, the two on the bed heard nothing.

"So there they were," said Beth, "engaged in some heavy neck-ing—or more." As she talked, she peered into the shadows. Was he here yet? He'd promised. She plunged on anyway. "Then someone came in, someone who had visited Mrs. Primwell that day, someone who hated Jill, someone madly in love with the boy you knew as Evil. . . ."

Dewey Conner stood staring at the boy and girl on the bed. From her handbag she took the gun she had stolen from Mrs. Primwell's rooms. She watched as long as she could bear it. Then she pulled the trigger.

THE CHARLES DICKENS MURDERS   267

"Jill died instantly. She never saw who shot her. Evil, on the bed, splashed with Jill's blood, saw everything. . . ."

Lights full on, and the silence broke in a burst of colliding voices.

"Dewey!"

"I never saw her!"

"I never thought—"

"But she left months before—"

"The train case in the hall!"

"The case." A deep voice, touched with an Eastern accent. "She wanted to put the gun inside it."

Everyone stared at the tuxedo-clad man in the doorway. Tall. Thin. Painfully thin.

"But that *was* how it happened?" said Beth. His face—scholarly, Auden-like, seamed with wrinkles. Not at all how she had imagined him.

"Not exactly," he said. "Dewey might have seen us in bed. What am I saying? Certainly she saw us, but when Dewey banged into the room, I was in the tree outside Jill's window. I saw the whole thing—and I helped Dewey get away. I told her to climb down with me. She wanted to put the gun in her train case. 'Leave it,' I said. 'Wipe it off with your scarf, and leave it.' She looked—she was sobbing. I never saw anyone so pathetic. She—" A crash and loud voices from below.

"The electricians—" Beth started.

"To hell with them!" Rebecca shouted. "Who the hell *is* this?"

2.

". . . Mr. Evelyn New," said Beth. "You knew him as Evil."

"Evil!" said Rebecca. "I remember you in your leather jacket."

"So do I," said Em. "I thought you were so exciting." He flinched as if he'd been stabbed.

"I saw you," said Laurie. "I saw you in the hall that day." Yes you did, Beth thought, and I almost forgot. And Tony must have seen him, too—the inspiration for Tony's tale.

"You were watching. You saw—what Dewey did," Carol said. "Why did you help her get away?" Evil shot her a look of intense dislike.

"Did you know she was in love with you?" said Em.

"I never knew how Dewey felt about me—not then."

"Then why?"

"If you insist on knowing—I hated Jill. It's hard even for me to believe how much I hated her that day."

"I always thought you were mad for her," Louise said, "and then you disappeared."

"With Jill"—a moment's pause—"it was always on and off."

Someone asked what he meant, *on and off*.

"I mean," he said angrily, "for Jill I was always the boy on tap. Sometimes I'd call, and she'd say she didn't want to see me. Then a week later, she'd call and ask me to come over—and of course I did. On and off. On and off. Then one night—I thought it had been a perfect night—she said she didn't want to see me anymore. 'Don't call. Don't come over. Thanks, it's been divine.' Just like that. Once I came to the dorm, and the maid called her, the damn maid, coming back with a smug smile on her face. 'Miss Jansen is out.' I knew better. I climbed the tree and saw her through the window. You were there, too, Louise," turning to face her. "The two of you were giggling—about me, no doubt."

Startled, Louise said, "I'm sure you're wrong. I don't remember."

"I quit then. I resigned myself to never seeing her again."

"Then why were you at the Open House?" Tony asked.

"Because she called—and I came running. I think you can understand that," he said. He looked so infinitely weary that Beth asked if he wanted to sit down. "No, thanks," he said. "I'd rather stand."

"That day," Abe said lazily. "You said you hated her then. What was so earthshaking about that day—before the murder, of course?"

"That was when I understood. Partly, it was seeing her with you, Tony, hearing what she said." He looked at Tony, who was at the punch bowl pouring himself a drink. "I saw her put her arms around you. I heard her say, 'Don't forget tonight—we'll go out on the Midway.' . . . And partly it was, when I came out of the closet—that drawing of Jill—it jumped out at me. Her belt."

"I drew that belt," said Louise.

"All the trophies dangling from it—her spoils, I thought."

"Her string of scalps," Laurie whispered.

"Yes, her scalps—and I was another, right from the start, someone novel, someone new to conquer. That's what she thought when I met her on the Midway. I was horsing around with some guys from school—Tech High. All of us played around with her. But for some reason, some damnable reason, she singled me out. I think I knew even then, but I didn't want to admit it—she loved the thrill of romance with the lower orders."

"Lady Chatterly," said Abe.

"Hardly. Lady Chatterly was never elitist."

"Oh, stuff," said Rebecca. "If you hated her, why did you stay and neck—or whatever?"

He smiled. "Who could resist when Jill held out her arms? . . . Then we heard the knock on the door. Jill wanted me to hide in the closet again, but I'd had enough. Another knock—I went out the window, stood in the tree, never expecting to see Dewey. I thought I'd see another casualty of Jill's charms," Evil said. He went to the big window and seated himself, well away from Laurie and Abe.

For some time the room was quiet. Then Carol said tentatively, "I never thought of Jill that way."

"I did," said Rebecca. "She was nothing but a temptress—a vampire."

"Typical," said Em. "Blame the woman. Must you indulge in stereotypes?"

"Remember how beautiful Jill was?" Laurie said. "Remember how she—sparkled? It's horrible." She clenched her hands. "Dewey! I never thought of Dewey—"

"If Dewey had only told someone she had a thing for Ev—"

"Who could she have told?"

"We weren't very nice to her."

"That's no reason."

"Maybe if she had told Jill."

"I doubt that would have helped," said Louise. "Jill knew how I felt about—" She caught herself. "Dewey," she said. "It's inconceivable."

"Not to me," said Carol, "at least now that I've had a chance to think about it. Dewey was always so—tenacious."

"You're still thinking about your room," said Em, "after all these years."

Another silence. Were they picturing the dark room, the drawn shades?

"We should have been—nicer," said Laurie.

"Yes, *you* should have," said Rebecca, "all of you."

"Forget the guilt trip," said Carol. "Dewey was obviously demented. Me—I'm mad."

Mad, they said, and asked her why.

"For one thing, if I'd known it was Dewey, I would have called you, Em."

"I don't understand," said Em. "Why have we avoided each other? Carol, why *didn't* you call me?"

"I thought you did it," she said.

"Me! But why?"

"Remember when Jill wouldn't let you borrow her diamond drop earrings—said she was tired of farming them out."

"They were rhinestones—anyway, that was nothing."

"I know. I see that now. But I thought you were really hurt."

"Hurt? Maybe a little, but not enough to—I thought it was you, Carol. Remember when Jill spilled the shrimp sauce?"

"On my white cashmere. She paid to have it cleaned—it never came out, but so what? You thought I'd kill for a ruined sweater?"

"Richard, I thought you did it," Rebecca said.

"Damn it, Rebecca—can't you let it rest? You thought I killed her out of jealousy? How many times have I told you it was an interlude!"

"Laurie," said Abe, "who did you think?" She didn't answer. Beth would always wonder.

"This is silly," said Louise. "This dredging up of stupid trivial slights—sweaters, earrings. Can't we remember anything better?"

"Like the night they gave us heart for dinner?" said Em, and there was an explosion of laughter.

"That was so yucky."

"How about when Mrs. P.—that bitch—put the whole dorm on suspension? In by ten P.M. for a week, and I can't even remember why. Does anyone remember?"

No one did.

"Maybe because we wouldn't eat the heart!"

More laughter.

"Remember the cocoa on sing nights?"

"Remember the buzzes?"

"I still know mine. One short—two longs."

Memories flowed—memories they had dammed up for years. It was as if they had been released from a terrible burden, Beth thought, and she wished that their joy in each other never had to end.

Everyone was milling around, Carol and Tony at the punch bowl, the others nibbling on the food, all of them talking as if they would never stop.

"Love the snacks" . . . "Remember Tiffin Room milk-shakes?—so *thick*" . . . "And their hamburgers—*dripping*" . . . "Triple features on Sixty-third Street" . . . "Necking on the Midway" . . . "Wash Prom" . . . "Oh, I want to go back." . . . "Are you sure? Remember comps?" . . . "I don't care. I want to go back. . . ."

The talk went on, Beth, Link, and Evil on the sidelines listening, as if, Beth thought, we are a jury.

"Remember Phy. Sci. with Fermi?" . . . "Remember Nat. Sci.—counting fruit flies?" . . . "Hey, Tony, remember when you ate the banana you were supposed to feed the fruit flies and gave them the peel?" . . . "Never could figure out why mine didn't multiply." . . . "Remember lounge lizards—that's what you were, Tony." . . . "You, too, Abe." . . . "Remember

Quiet Hours?" . . . "Oh, yeah. Everyone screaming 'Quiet Hours' " . . . More laughter.

This would be the right time, Beth thought, but she could not bring herself to interrupt.

The others were still reminiscing when Em walked over to Evil and gave him a teasing look. "Why did you keep on protecting Dewey?" she asked, almost flirtatiously. "You were aiding and abetting a murderer—that makes you guilty as a principal—and the statute of limitations never runs out on murder. . . . So why did you?"

"Protect Dewey? Because I cared about her," he said, "unlike the rest of you," his voice so harsh that Em backed away.

"*I* cared about Dewey," said Rebecca. "I was always nice to her."

"You," he said. "You were obsequious. It was her money you loved, and she knew it. You loved what her money bought you. The taxicabs. The dinners out. The presents. And the rest of you." He looked around the room, his eyes accusing them. "You were unspeakably cruel. You made her an outcast—you made her life a tragedy."

Now is the time, Beth thought, for Evil's outburst had reduced them to silence. *But why, why do I have to? I hate this.* She stood. "There's another murder we need to discuss."

They looked at her like children suddenly robbed of their treats.

"Another murder? Who?"

"I know. Someone killed Herman. Remember It's Only Herman?"

"Plenty of times I wanted to kill him."

"You're joking, right?" said Carol, looking from Beth to Evil to Link.

"Not a joke?" said Tony.

"Who was murdered?" said Em.

"Dewey Conner was murdered," Beth said, and with that sentence she knew she had killed the laughter forever.

3.

"Years went by," said Beth. "Dewey created another life for herself, a life that included Evil—sorry—Evelyn New. Mr. New, will you take over?"

They turned to Evil, giving him all their attention. He remained on the window seat. "A few weeks later," he said, "I graduated from Tech High and left Chicago for New York. I moved in with Dewey. She had her own apartment by that time, and—"

"Why did she let you move in?" Rebecca broke in, her voice a screech. "You must have been blackmailing her!"

"You would think that," said Evil. "It wasn't *let* me move in. She begged me. After Chicago, she didn't think she could make it alone. She was desolate about the murder—wanted to turn herself in. I discouraged her. What good would it have done?"

Rebecca muttered that it wouldn't have done him any good either.

Evil ignored her. "And her parents were getting divorced. I tell you, she was despondent. I thought I'd stay for a few weeks, but the years stretched out. Dewey was going to CCNY, taking one course at a time. If I moved out, she told me, she'd give up on the whole thing. And I was trying to—Dewey helped me get my start."

"Start at what?" someone asked.

"My start as a playwright."

"You write plays? About what?"

"About class hatred—some of them get produced. That's not important now. At any rate, I did my work. Dewey did hers. She never did finish at CCNY, but she found other things to do. Politics. Committees. The arts. She dabbled in painting, writing—I'd like to read from Dewey's memoir," he said abruptly. From an inside tuxedo pocket, he brought out some typed pages and began to read.

> *Looking back at my brief time at Chicago, I see that the University taught me more than I realized. I learned that everything is relative. I learned that a shout of "Define your terms!" was an effective comeback in any argument. I learned to play bridge. I learned to shave my legs. And I learned that Aristotle was right—*

Here Evil paused and looked around the room. Then he continued.

"Without friends no one would choose to live, though he had all other goods."

"There's more," said Evil. "I won't bother you with it."
Someone asked if Dewey had finished her memoir.
"She couldn't—she became ill. A pneumonia, very serious, but she was responding well to treatment. They were going to move her out of the ICU . . . in a few days. . . . She was so much better—" His voice, was he crying? "Beth, will you—"
They looked at Beth, their faces eager, fearful.
"It's the time of Dewey's illness that concerns us now," she said. "Dewey is in Manhattan Hospital, a patient in the ICU. Someone needs to get in to see her. Someone who is not on the staff."

"No problem," said Abe. "Don a lab coat, and you're order-
ing nurses around—if you can find a nurse." Weak laughter.

"Right," said Beth. "You're wearing a lab coat, so it's easy
to find out that Dewey is in the ICU. You go there, to Dewey's
room. Perhaps she recognizes you. . . ."

*Could this really be Dewey? She looked so frail, so old. Her hair
had gone completely white. She lay in the bed. Slowly, her eyes
opened. . . .*

"You! God! I haven't seen you in years."

"It has been a long time."

"What have you been doing?"

"This and that. Your IV. It's infiltrated. Let me fix it."

"Oh—you're on the staff?"

"Well, of course."

"Confused—didn't know."

*A syringe was taken out of the lab coat. Dewey watched as the
syringe was injected into the intravenous. Seconds later Dewey
gasped and her head lolled back. Her heart had stopped beating.*

"The syringe," Beth said, when the lights were full on, "held
a lethal injection of serum potassium. They called a Code Blue."

"They shocked her," said Evil. "They defibrillated her.
They did all the things doctors do—they could not start her
heart again."

"A sudden rise of serum potassium," Beth said, "causes a
cardiac arrest."

"How do you know?" someone asked.

"Yes, how do you know she was injected with the serum—
whatever?"

"The body was exhumed," Beth lied. "They did a second

autopsy to make sure nothing was missed on the first. That was
when they discovered an incredibly high level of potassium."

"It was you, Evil," Rebecca said. "You injected the—I bet
you inherited a bundle."

"I did. I'm rather wealthy."

"There's your answer," said Rebecca.

"I doubt it," said Beth, and lied again. "Mr. New gave permission to have the body exhumed."

"Are you saying it was one of us?"

"It can't be us."

"That's right—it can't be. It happened in New York."

"Oddly enough, you were all in New York that day," Beth
said. "I've checked it out."

Cries of disbelief. A nervous giggle.

"Tony and Louise," she said, "you were in New York."

"Celebrating our anniversary," said Louise.

"Theater, concerts," Tony mumbled, "dinner, galleries . . ."

"You were there, too, Mother."

"Business," said Laurie.

"And Carol, you—"

"The Phipps-Hay Decorators' Show. I always go. So what?"

Then Em said it must have been when she was giving a talk
on dealing with insurance companies.

Rebecca followed up indignantly. She and Richard were at-
tending a symposium on modern grandparenting.

"In case you're thinking of me"—Abe threw up his hands—
"I'm always there."

"You're right, all of you. New York is no help."

"Then forget it."

"Yeah—forget it!"

"This is absurd!"

"However," said Beth, "there is another way to find out who murdered Dewey."

Silence. Suddenly the piano tinkled a four-note fanfare in a minor key. Em looked up and grinned.

CHAPTER FIFTY-THREE

No laughter now. They were tense, their eyes riveted on Beth.

"It's evening," she said, "much earlier in the quarter. Up on Four is a gloomy room, where the shades are always drawn, a messy room—a shambles."

"She means Carol and Dewey's room!"

"Dewey is out," said Beth, "but someone else is there."

She locked the door, then went to the desk, opened her wallet, and dumped out the change. Separating the pennies, she dropped them one by one in the wastebasket. Using the key the luggage shop had made for her, she opened Dewey's trunk. On top was an envelope. She took out the letter and read it. Then she put her wallet deep in the trunk and locked it. A few minutes later, she ran down the hall to Laurie's room, shouting, "Have I got news for you!"

"Exactly nine pennies," she told Laurie and Em, "and they had to be from my wallet! I know I had nine because I almost had enough to buy fudge, but I had to use a dime instead. And Dewey! She's lying in bed as if nothing happened. She doesn't know she just hung herself with those pennies!" She hopped around the room, doing a crazy war dance, chanting, "I've got the proof! I've got the proof!"

"But everyone knows Dewey treats pennies like rubbish," said Em. "Why would she be so obvious?"

"Christ on a crutch! How should I know? Because she's off her rocker, dippy—just plain nuts! I always knew it was Dewey—and now I've got proof!" Carol grabbed Em's milkshake and took a big swallow. "First thing tomorrow I'm going right to Mrs. P. This time she won't dare give me the gate!"

"I never! I didn't!" Carol shouted, her face a bright red.

"You had the motive, Carol—the hideousness of rooming with Dewey. You had the credo—you believed with Machiavelli that the end justifies the means. In retrospect—"

"That's not proof!"

"In retrospect," Beth repeated, "Dewey's response was strange. Wrongly accused, summarily expelled, completely and unjustly humiliated—knowing, always knowing, she was not the thief. She must have been furious. She should have been! Yet she was willing—eager—to leave. Why?" said Beth, looking at Evil.

He was glowering at Carol. "Because she *wanted* to get home," he said, "and fast. She had received a letter telling her her parents were getting a divorce. She told me later she thought the divorce was her fault—which was nonsense. But she thought it was up to her to patch things up and bring her parents back together. A lost cause. Still, she tried—Dewey always tried—and of course she failed."

"The divorce was kept secret for years," said Beth. "That's made clear in Dewey's biographical note to the Conner collection. Yet, Carol, you knew about the divorce at the time—you told me you knew. You found the letter in the trunk—and you read it."

"I put it back! I put the letter back!" Head down, Carol hugged herself and sobbed.

Laurie went over to her. "Stop, Carol," she said gently. "I understand. I wish—"

"Wish what?"—through sobs.

"Just that I wish you could have held out."

"So do I," said Louise, kneeling next to Carol. "But I understand. She made your life miserable. We should have helped."

"It's not as if you committed a felony," said Em, an arm around Carol, patting her. "It's over—forget it."

The Gang together again, Beth thought, while Evil stares as if they're distasteful specimens, and Rebecca—

"Out of my way, Richard." He slid the ottoman over. Rebecca marched over to Carol. "You let everyone think it was Dewey—when you were the thief. You—you're despicable!"

"I'm not the thief! I'm not!" She lifted her head. "All right—I admit I put my wallet in the trunk. But I'm not the thief! It *was* Dewey. It had to be!"

"No, Carol, you weren't," said Beth, "and neither was Dewey."

No one spoke. Then from below, breaking the silence, came strains of country music from a radio. The workmen, Beth thought.

"Then who?" someone asked.

"Yes, if it wasn't Carol or Dewey—then who?"

"That's what I'm about to explain," said Beth. "First—"

"*Watch it!*" Shouts from the basement, followed by rowdy laughter. "Touch that, and you'll fry your—" Beth got up and closed the double doors.

"First," she said, "we need to understand that Dewey had spotted the thief."

"Dewey?"

"She knew?"

"How do you know she knew?"

"Her memoir," Beth said.

"What kind of a scam are you pulling?" Rebecca screamed. "She didn't finish it."

"That's right." Laurie spoke up. "Evil, you said she never finished."

"She didn't," he said. "But"—he paused—"she had completed a considerable body of work." They gazed at him, fascinated, as he drew some pages from his pocket. "Work," he said, "from which I would like to read, if you would end the senseless cackling and—" Suddenly the room was thrown into darkness.

A scream. Em? Louise? A thud. Someone dropping a glass? Tony? Carol? A chuckle. "Let there be light, goddammit." Abe, definitely Abe.

Sounds of feet clumping up the stairs. The door opened, admitting a shaft of light from the hall. A stocky man ambled in. He was covered with sweat, sweaty T-shirt embracing his pot, sweaty hair tied back with a bandanna. Beth started to laugh— she couldn't help it. He looked so exactly like Eliza Doolittle's father that she almost expected him to drop his aitches—which he did not. "Sorry," he said. "We're working on the breakers. Afraid you'll be in the dark a while." How long? someone asked. "A while," he said, and disappeared.

"I don't like this."

"Neither do I."

"It's spooky."

It was spooky. Beth found it impossible to see anyone clearly or to identify voices with certainty.

"There's enough light for me to read," said Evil. Beth could just make him out on the window seat.

"Can't we wait?"

"At least until we have lights."

"We should leave."

"Yes, we could be in danger."

" 'A smell of burning fills the air, The Electrician is no longer there.' "

"Not funny, Abe." That was Laurie's voice.

"But it is funny. We're in no danger. We've come this far— let's go for the whole enchilada. Proceed Ev—uh—New."

"I will," he said, and went to the doorway. Holding the pages out to catch the light, he began to read.

> It is night, and I walk down the hall, feeling as I always do, the thrill of power at being the only one awake. While the others sleep, I'm in charge. Can I sneak past the night entrance? Easy. Go to a movie? Suddenly I see some-one in front of me—light glints on something she holds in her hand. I watch her run down the stairs. I follow slowly. She looks around. I step back. She's downstairs now. I wait a moment, then follow. It's pitch dark when I hit bottom and bang into the maids' table. Wow, my elbow hurts! Where is she? A light in Oyster Bay! I run down the hall. There she is, standing on a chair. She's taking the portrait down! Why? She turns. I see her face!

Evil paused. From the darkness came a whisper. "She saw! She saw who it was!"

> She's got the portrait on the floor. She's turning it over. What is she doing? I wait and watch until she rehangs the portrait. I step back into the shadows and stay there, oh, so still, until I hear her padding up the stairs. Then I take the portrait down and look over the loot.
> I saw her, yes, I saw her, opening my gold bag, stroking Jill's bracelet, trying it on. Oh, this is so terrific! I want to tell someone! I will! . . .

Evil stopped.

"Go on. Go on." A choked voice. Whose? Beth couldn't be sure.

"Please go on. Who did she see?"

"Who did she tell?"

"She ended there," said Evil. "I don't know why. She probably meant to come back to it. The next passage takes up her parents' divorce."

"Smoke and mirrors." Unmistakably Rebecca. "We didn't learn a thing. Richard, let's get out of here."

"Quiet, Rebecca! Sit down!"

"We did learn something," said Beth. "We have confirmation that Dewey discovered the thief and that she told someone."

"She intended to tell someone—we aren't certain she did." Whose voice was that?

"But it is certain," said Beth, walking to the doorway. "I know who she told—and so do all of you."

From the darkness. "Us?" "We know?" "But how?"

"Think back," said Beth, "to the day of the Open House. The whole Gang—Laurie, Louise, Jill, Carol, Em—is downstairs in Oyster Bay. Rebecca stands in the doorway, watching."

"Now," said Louise, "for my look at Letitia. Oh, dear. She's crooked."

"Come on, Louise. Straighten the poor lady," said Jill. Smiling, she watched as Louise dragged the ottoman over and reached up to straighten the portrait.

"Jill," said Em. "I talked to him."

"Who?" she said, her eyes on Louise.

"You know—this guy who knows this doctor."

Louise turned. "You're sure it's safe?"

"I swear it is."

"See—it's safe." Jill grinned. "Now, hurry up," she said, "and straighten Letitia."

Louise gave Em a stern look and turned back to the portrait. She stood on her toes, reached, reached higher—

"Here come the boys! There's Mrs. P.!"

Louise jumped off the ottoman.

"So there," said Beth, "we have our answer."

"What answer?"

"Why was Jill smiling?" Beth asked.

"Em had found her a doctor?"

"That can't be why." Laurie's voice. "Jill seemed so indifferent. I'm not sure she wanted an abortion."

"Think," said Beth. "We know the thief had hidden her loot behind the portrait. Someone else knew what was hidden there. Who?"

"The one—that Dewey told?" A woman's voice.

"Right," said Beth. "Who was it who kept urging Louise on? Who was it who kept after Louise to straighten the portrait?"

A long silence.

"Jill?" Louise's voice, Beth was certain.

"Of course. Jill—so intent on watching Louise she couldn't be bothered to hear about doctor. Jill—smiling as she watched Louise. Jill—telling Louise to hurry. Because Jill knew—"

"—that when Louise straightened the portrait—"

"—everything would fall out."

"Or so Jill hoped," said Beth.

"It was Jill who Dewey told."

"And I bet I know when. The night Dewey left—remember? Jill was at the window, waving to Dewey."

"So Jill knew all the time."

Wondering if this would work, wondering if she could spur them to bring their betrayer out of hiding, Beth said, "So did someone else."

Who? they asked.

"Obviously, the thief." That was Richie.

"The thief had to do something, anything, to stop her." Beth paused. "Who was it?" she said. "Who was it who suddenly shouted, 'Here come the boys! There's Mrs. P.!' "—the lights came on. Beth saw them staring. Laurie, Carol, Rebecca, Louise, they were all staring—staring at Em.

Em sat on the piano bench, staring back. Her eyes. God, they were cruel. "Rich bitch!" Her voice, so deep, like the voice of Beth's pursuer. "She deserved to die!"

What happened next registered on Beth's mind in a series of freeze frames. Evil lunging, his hands around Em's throat. Link pulling Evil off. Link and Evil grappling. Em bolting into the hall. Evil wrenching himself free, tearing after her. Richie tackling Evil, pinning him down. Evil yelling, kicking.

Em in the hall looking around wildly. Em heading for the outside door. Em turning—why? Why hadn't she run outside? Did she think she could hide below? Evil hurtling into the hall, Richie, his head bloody, chasing him. Em plunging down the stairs, Evil stampeding after her.

At the top of the stairs, a terrified crowd. Below, workmen sprawled on the floor, drinking beer. A pager spouting, "Jake, call home already!" A huge whirling fan. Next to it the power cage—its door wide open. Inside the cage, dangling from a cabinet, a gold bar like a loose trapeze.

Em running, reaching bottom. Workmen up and yelling. "Jesus! Watch out!" "High voltage!" Beer eddying over the floor.

Beth starting down the stairs. Link catching her wrist, holding her. Beth fighting him, her eyes fixed on Em.

Em skidding in the beer, lurching into the fan. Evil grabbing her, dragging her. Em yelling, "Let go!" Evil, one hand grasping Em, the other reaching, reaching—up to the gold bar.

Screams. Sizzling. Smoke. Stench. Two frenzied bodies. Would their spasms never end?

"Out of the way!"

"Throw that switch!"

It was over.

CHAPTER FIFTY-FOUR

There were questions, of course.

During the next few days, Beth was asked how she had known that Evelyn New was a man. A hunch—confirmed when she checked *The New York Times* "Corrections" for the days following Dewey's obituary and saw that her companion had been amended from Ms. to Mr. Evelyn New. She had followed up with a phone call to Evil. After she had told him her suspicions about Dewey's death, he had been quick to cooperate, almost desperate to tell her what he knew, beginning with Dewey's accepting Mrs. Primwell's invitation to visit. Mrs. P. never did believe the daughter of a celebrity could be a thief.

Beth was asked how she knew that Em murdered Dewey. Because Em had the knowledge—a former medical student. Iffy, she was told, since the information about potassium was readily available. Anyway, everything depended on Em's being the thief, and how did Beth know that until she confessed? Em, she answered, had a pattern of concealment. In college, Em tacked her underpants behind the dresser. In her office, she hid a document behind a painting.

More, Em had a powerful motive—protecting her reputation. Dewey, as Conner's column made clear, knew Em was the thief. Would Dewey, a tormented Em must have wondered, still keep silent? Or was Dewey, still seething at being kicked out of college for the crime Em had committed, ready to reveal the truth? Em couldn't afford to take the chance.

Obsessed with building a professional career, profoundly disappointed that she had not made it as a doctor, Em had reached the top as a lawyer. If word leaked out that she had committed a crime—a minor crime, admittedly, but she had allowed someone else to be expelled from college for it—the disclosure surely would have cost her clients. Revelation of a crime is not superb advertising for any lawyer, especially a highly successful lawyer like Em. Worse, perhaps, discovery would have shattered her reputation at her firm, where, Beth learned, she had won the liking, respect, and admiration of her colleagues.

Em? Popular with everyone, Beth was told. Not too proud on occasion to do the work of a lowly associate. Why, just recently she had made several trips to Midwestern to do research on a case. Em? Known throughout the legal community. A star at the annual Bar Revue, where she was famous for taking male roles. "You should have seen her playing Dennis Rodman! Hilarious!" Hilarious? Beth thought. You should have seen her playing a ghost.

Connected with the theft was another question. Why the brief Dall Hall rift between Louise and Jill? Jill had assumed Louise was the thief—she had told only Louise where she had hidden the bracelet. Jill could not have known how easy it must have been for Em, so skilled at concealment, to discover another hiding place. A tennis-racket cover? A sweater sleeve? When Jill learned who the real thief was, her coolness to Louise ended. Furious at Em for causing the rift, Jill made up her mind to get even. When the chance came, she did, and she set Louise up to help her.

About other questions, questions Beth asked herself, she could only speculate.

Why was Dewey so enamored of Evil? Her powerful crush must have been born of two slight occurrences—a couple of casual whirls around the dance floor.

Why did Jill stay behind to say good-bye to Dewey? Perhaps because Jill saw in Dewey a fellow outcast. Jill saw herself as an outcast because she was pregnant, at a time when unmarried pregnancy still meant scandal and humiliation. She saw Dewey as an outcast because she was stigmatized. Long before Carol set her up, Dewey was labeled a thief by most of Dall. Jill, of course, rejected that label and must have told Dewey that she did.

But why, if they had established not friendship, but a brief rapport, did Dewey murder Jill? When Beth thought about this question, Jill and Lady Dedlock merged in her mind. Tulkinghorn pursued Lady Dedlock because he wanted to punish her for her beauty. Surely Dewey's motive was the same. Dewey perceived herself as lacking beauty. Her haggard waif look was at odds with the lush Rita Hayworth allure of that time. If Dewey had possessed the right kind of beauty, or so she might have thought, she could have attracted Evil. As it was, Jill kept him roped in, and her fling with Evil dealt a death blow to any budding friendship. Or—was Dewey's motive more intense than jealousy? Perhaps she murdered Jill because she saw her as a temptress who had profaned her beauty.

Who won in the end? Not Jill and Lady Dedlock, victims of their beauty, but Dewey, who had made a life with Evil.

The Fourth Floor Gang was gone—never to return. Carol went her own way, becoming ever more noted in decorating circles, famous for the purity of her interiors. Earlier, she had made some overtures to Laurie and Louise, invited them to a show-home opening. But neither had any desire to see her.

"For the chemistry to work," Laurie told Beth much later, "we needed the whole Gang—together. Losing Em was shattering, but the chemistry was lost long before—when we lost Jill."

"But why?" Beth asked Laurie. "Why couldn't you have gone on, even without Jill?"

"Because we each had something the others needed. We needed Carol to be playful. We needed Em to be serious, especially about feminism. We needed Louise's ingenuousness as much as we needed Jill's riotous interest in sex. And me—what did I have? I don't know."

"You had enthusiasm—you appreciated everyone. I think you were a unifying force."

"Maybe so. All I know is, it was wonderful when we were together."

"Why? What did you do together that was so wonderful?"

"Everything! Reading Cellini's autobiography, asking each other, 'Did you get to the part where he upchucks the worm?' Borrowing each other's clothes. Fixing each other up. Trooping to exams—hiding our smiles when the maid said, 'Good luck on your testes, girls.' Talking all night—about sex, about *Anna Karenina*, about mistakes our parents made. Always someone to talk to, to listen to. Losing the Gang was like losing a family—lost, all lost with Jill."

And Laurie and Abe? Their latter-day meeting rekindled no flames—though it might have. Abe stayed on a few days at the Ritz—medical meetings he said, but he begged Laurie to meet him for dinner. She spent a day getting ready. Hair. Nails. Three-hour Tabu-scented bath. An age getting her makeup right. An eternity deciding what to wear. "Your father," she told Beth. "I suspect he knew what I was thinking."

"What were you thinking?" Beth asked. They were in Laurie's comfortable study, their coffee cups atop stacks of books.

"Oh, I don't know. Would he? Would I?"

"Lots of 'woulds'—would what?"

"Would there be an attraction? That night, at least early in the evening, when you recreated Dall—I know I felt something—all right, a sexy something. Would I still feel it? Would he? Would he ask me to go to his room? Would I go?"

"How interesting. Where did Daddy fit into your picture?"

"Called away on an emergency at the last minute—or so he said."

"So you were alone? Tell!"

"The place was perfect. You know how the Ritz Dining Room reeks of romance."

"And so convenient to Abe's room."

"We drank champagne. We toasted each other—frequently. I'd forgotten how witty Abe can be. He ordered for both of us. I couldn't touch my dinner."

"Because he ordered for you?"

"No. So much—uh—romantic tension I couldn't eat. I'd forgotten how that feels. . . . He drank a toast to my face— told me I'm beautiful."

"You are."

"If you like." She shrugged. "Anyway, it didn't work."

"It didn't?" Beth heaved a mental sigh of relief. "Why not?"

"Maybe because he reminisced. 'After all,' he said, 'I spent the happiest days of my life at college.' And then he talked about the time he saw Jill in a wet T-shirt. Or—maybe his mannerisms turned me off. He still sings under his breath when there's a gap in the conversation."

"I didn't think there were any gaps."

"Oh, stop. Maybe—no, definitely—what really turned me

off was his constantly asking me what I do. When I finally told him—well, now I know. Jaws do drop. 'You,' he said. 'I can't believe it. You were never that—'

" 'That what?' I said. I know he wanted to say 'that brainy,' or 'that intellectual.'

" 'I mean,' he said, 'I never thought you had a flair for—No, I mean that you were so serious about—No, that's not what I mean. Sorry,' he said, and I give him points for this, 'I think I was somewhat obnoxious in college—and I suspect I still am.'

" 'Nonsense,' I said, 'you're a brilliant doctor.' "

"And then what happened?"

"We spent the rest of the evening talking about his wife."

"Oh? What about her?"

"She has a Ph.D. from Oxford, and she specializes in the portrayal of women in Restoration drama. I heard perhaps more than I wanted about the connection between William Wycherley and Molière. Maybe that accounts for Link's literary—darling, what about you and Link?"

Both their parents exonerated of murder, Beth and Link resolved their conflicts, which now seemed trivial. The following day Beth had driven Link to O'Hare, and they had talked about seeing each other. He would come to Chicago. Or she would go to New York—but she knew she would not. What was it? she asked herself. Had she seen too much of his father in Link? Not at all. Link had no irritating mannerisms. He believed in her and in her work. He was her good friend and she was his—but friendship was all she felt. For whatever reason, the spark was no longer there. And without the spark, life seemed flat and monotonous—no fizz. Surely there was more to existence than tracking image patterns in *Jude the Obscure* or deconstructing *The Pickwick Papers*.

* * *

Still lingering was the question: Who was the father of Jill's baby? The answer came during Winter Break, when Louise and Tony invited Beth to dinner. "Just a small party," said Louise. "Call it a thank you."

"For what?"

"Just thank you."

Thank you, Beth decided when she saw Tony and Louise, for freeing them to love without an underlying suspicion of murder. Joking and teasing, feeding each other toasted marshmallows, kissing under the mistletoe—how blissful they were. Unlike Rebecca and Richie.

"I heard they're getting a divorce," said Louise.

"Rebecca wants out?"

"No—Richie. He's dating a plumber." She paused, as the waiter offered Beth a tray of hors d'oeuvres. "A female plumber. Blond—like Jill."

"Jill," said Beth. "I'll always wonder. Who was the father of her baby?"

"I thought you knew," said Louise. "Her old boyfriend, the football star. It happened one weekend when Jill went home. She swore me to secrecy."

Suddenly Beth remembered Mr. Muscles, the letter man of Cob Conner's column. "She must have told Dewey, too," she blurted out. Louise asked why she thought that. "Just a guess," she said. Let it rest.

"Jill planned to leave at the end of the quarter and get married—there's the bell, Tony. Will you get it, darling?" Louise turned to Beth again. "Jill hated leaving. I think that's why she went completely crazy, snagging every boy in sight—here you are at last!"

Behind Tony, coming toward Beth, a lanky man. The urbane

features, the faintly amused expression—like Laurence Olivier in *Rebecca*. Where, where had she seen him? He was giving her a playful glance.

"Beth, I want you to meet Tony's nephew, Victor Valentine—Dr. Valentine. Vic—Beth Austin. Professor Austin."

"We've met," he said, while Beth tried to remember.

"I didn't think you knew each other," said Louise.

"We've never been introduced—we met by accident. But I hope"—he gave Beth a conspiratorial grin—"we'll meet again. Perhaps we can go for a drive?"

"Stop being so mysterious, Vic. Where did you meet?"

"The hospital parking lot." He looked at Beth. "Remember?"

Slowly, Beth nodded. Of course—the parking lot, when she had been scared out of her mind. The man in the red Bentley—he had offered to help her find her car. And he was Tony's nephew! What an outrageous coincidence.

Well, why not? Dickens loved coincidence.

ACKNOWLEDGMENTS

The following works have been particularly helpful in providing background information: *Annals of the Chicago Woman's Club for the First Forty Years of Its Organization*, compiled by Henriette Greenbaum Frank and Amalie Hofer Jerome, Chicago Woman's Club, 1916; Thomas Wakefield Goodspeed's *A History of the University of Chicago*, University of Chicago Press, 1916; Frank Hurburt O'Hara's *The University of Chicago, An Official Guide*, University of Chicago Press, 1928.